An offer she couldn't resist . . .

"So, how about dinner around seven and then back to your place?"

"Dinner? I told you this wasn't a date, Gray. You're getting lucky tonight; there's no need to wine and dine me," Suzy replied drily.

Chuckling, Gray said, "We both have to eat. I'll meet you in the lobby around six if that's okay with you?"

Suzy knew it would do no good arguing and she was desperate to have him out of her personal space. "Yeah, yeah, whatever. I guess I can do that. Now, don't you have a job or something to do here?"

After another leisurely inspection of her, Gray smiled and blew her a kiss. "You will be on my mind all day, Suzanna." With that, he turned and left.

Suzy's knees were in serious danger of giving out so she slid into her seat and tried to slow her breathing. How could something as simple as an air kiss make her melt? She would not get attached to this man, and she sure as hell wasn't going to fall in love with him. . . .

NOT PLANNING ON YOU

A DANVERS NOVEL

SYDNEY LANDON

A SIGNET BOOK

SIGNET
Published by New American Library, a division of
Penguin Group (USA) Inc., 375 Hudson Street,
New York, New York 10014, USA
Penguin Group (Canada), 90 Eglinton Avenue East, Suite 700, Toronto,
Ontario M4P 2Y3, Canada (a division of Pearson Penguin Canada Inc.)
Penguin Books Ltd., 80 Strand, London WC2R 0RL, England
Penguin Ireland, 25 St. Stephen's Green, Dublin 2,
Ireland (a division of Penguin Books Ltd)
Penguin Group (Australia), 707 Collins Street, Melbourne, Victoria 3008,
Australia (a division of Pearson Australia Group Pty. Ltd.)
Penguin Books India Pvt. Ltd., 11 Community Centre, Panchsheel Park,
New Delhi–110 017, India
Penguin Group (NZ), 67 Apollo Drive, Rosedale, Auckland 0632,
New Zealand (a division of Pearson New Zealand Ltd.)
Penguin Books (South Africa), Rosebank Office Park, 181 Jan Smuts Avenue,
Parktown North 2193, South Africa
Penguin China, B7 Jiaming Center, 27 East Third Ring Road North,
Chaoyang District, Beijing 100020, China

Penguin Books Ltd., Registered Offices:
80 Strand, London WC2R 0RL, England

Published by Signet, an imprint of New American Library,
a division of Penguin Group (USA) Inc.

First Signet Printing, February 2013
10 9 8 7 6 5 4 3 2 1

ALWAYS LEARNING   PEARSON

As always, this book is dedicated to my husband, the man who makes me believe in fairy tales and happily ever after every day. This would not have been possible without his continued support and encouragement.

This is also dedicated to my daughter and my son. They sacrifice some "mommy time" each day for me to work on something that I love so much. Thanks for all the patience, my babies.

Chapter One

"Crapple Dapple, are you kidding me?" Suzy looked at her best friend, Claire, in horror.

"Crapple Dapple?"

Waving her hand in a vague way, Suzy said, "Oh, yeah. I'm trying to stop cursing so much at work. The new receptionist crosses herself every time I roll out a four-letter word; it's kind of creepy." Suzy gave Claire a few moments to recover from the laughter shaking her body, and got back to the question she'd asked. "Claire—earth to Claire—come back." Wiping the tears from her eyes, Claire finally composed herself enough to continue.

"Um, yeah, sorry, Suz, but you heard me correctly. Gray is going to take over daily operations at Danvers for the foreseeable future and Jason prefers that he relocate here to Myrtle Beach to do that. He trusts Gray, and although he will continue on as the CEO of Danvers, Gray will step up as the president of operations."

Last year, Danvers International had become the largest communications company in the United States when it merged with Mericom. Grayson Merimon, whom everyone called Gray, was the CEO of Mericom, which had been based in Charleston, South Carolina. Much to Suzy's chagrin, once the merger was completed, he'd been spending a lot of time at the Danvers headquarters in Myrtle Beach. Tall, dark, and handsome, Gray had it all. The man looked like sex on a stick and he'd made no secret of the fact that he was very interested in her. Suzy, however, wasn't interested in Gray—or so she kept telling herself. Her high school sweetheart, the man she thought she'd be spending the rest of her life with, had cheated on her, and now men were only good for one thing. And that one thing was something she wanted to avoid in the workplace.

"It's the kid, isn't it? It hasn't even been born yet and already it's turning my life upside down." Suzy groaned.

"Well, Jason does want to be able to spend more time with me and the baby when it's born so, yes, that has something to do with it."

"I knew it!" Catching herself lest she offend Claire, Suzy tried to get control. She also tried to understand why she was suddenly terrified at the thought of seeing Gray daily. She'd spent a lot of time in his company since the merger. She was always careful to have someone else present, though, when meeting with Gray. The strong, gutsy person inside her wondered why that was necessary, but the woman inside her knew. There was something in Gray's eyes that called to her, seemed to devour her soul every time she looked at him. He scared her; he made her want to run and do everything she could to save herself.

Suzy realized that Claire was watching her, a knowing look in her eyes. Quickly putting up her defenses, Suzy did what she did best: bluffed. "Ugh, well, no biggie I guess. Just another uptight geek to grace our presence here, right? I mean, why should it bother me? I haven't given him a thought since he was here annoying me last time. Maybe he will actually buy himself a pair of jeans or something though. Those uptight, heavily starched suits are so depressing and he should really lay off the hair products. Do you think a hurricane could move that hair?" Suzy ended her tirade and grimaced as she looked at Claire. Okay, maybe she should have limited her comments to no more than two. She was rattled, and when that happened, the words kept flowing no matter how hard she tried to stop them. She was grateful that she was talking to Claire, someone who would never judge her or try to peel the layers back to see what all the protests were hiding. Claire didn't have to, because she knew.

Years ago, Suzy had met Claire at Danvers International where they had both worked. Claire had been the personal assistant to the company president and CEO, Jason Danvers, while Suzy had handled all the many special events for Danvers. Two people couldn't be more opposite than the two women were, but it worked. Suzy's loud and outgoing to Claire's quiet and thoughtful. Claire wore her long auburn hair loose around her shoulders; thank God, Suzy thought, she'd given up the ponytails and buns she used to wear. Suzy styled her long red hair to suit her mood. She also dressed to suit her moods, and leather and stiletto heels played a large role. Suzy and Claire both were blessed to be a little above-average height and, Suzy couldn't lie, she loved her perky plump boobs. If you could take half of each, they would make the perfect person.

It was so hard to believe that the person in front of her now was married to Jason, the CEO of Danvers, and pregnant with his child. The fairy tale had come true for Claire and her Prince Charming had slain all of her dragons. Suzy couldn't think of anyone who deserved it more. After her sister and abusive father were killed in a car accident several years ago, Claire had struggled to support her ailing mother. When her mother suffered a stroke, her medication was altered and her recovery was miraculous. Now she lived next door to Claire in a house designed by Jason. Claire had given up the boring clothing and hairstyles she'd always favored and now she practically glowed. She was still Jason's assistant, until after the baby was born. If Suzy were a person prone to crying, this story would certainly have her sobbing.

Claire reached over and covered Suzy's hand with her own. "Suz, it'll be fine. Gray really isn't that bad when you get to know him. I'm actually quite fond of him. His brother, Nicholas, will also be moving here to assist with the daily operations."

"Nicholas? Stuffed shirt has a brother? God, please don't tell me he's smoking hot, too!"

Laughing, Claire said, "Well, I don't know what you consider 'smoking' but he looks similar to Gray in coloring and he's quite good-looking. Not as good-looking as Jason, because no one looks that good, but well above average."

Looking at Claire in horror, Suzy sputtered, "Geez, where do these guys come from? Jason, Gray, and Nicholas. If he looks even half as good, every woman here will stay in heat."

"Every woman, Suz?"

"Um, well, not you, obviously. I mean, except for Jason. And not me; my head isn't turned by a good piece of eye candy, but, for sure, every other woman here."

Suzy knew that her friend wasn't fooled for a minute by all of her protests so she wisely decided to change the subject. Even as she asked all the right questions about Claire's new life, her mind was on a tall man with dark hair and compelling green eyes that seemed to look through all of her defenses. Suzy was deathly afraid that the battle to storm the walls to her heart had already begun.

Chapter Two

Suzy stepped off the elevator at the fourteenth floor and the hub of the advertising department for Danvers International. Suzy's focus on special events required her to work closely with the department, so it was beneficial that she had her office on the same floor, which saved her considerable time running between floors. It would be nice to be closer to her friend Claire, but she was just an elevator ride away.

Suzy cringed as she saw the new receptionist up ahead waving frantically at her. Ella was someone she tried to avoid as much as possible. She couldn't possibly be more than thirty years old but had hair like a seventy-year-old church lady. Okay, not that there was anything wrong with that, but come on, this girl was never going to catch a man with that big old teased-up mullet hairstyle. If she could stand one second of extra time in her company, Suzy would insist on giving her a makeover.

"Ms. Denton, Ms. Denton, I didn't think you'd ever come back." Looking down at her watch in disapproval, Ella shook her head and stared at her as if waiting for an apology for being longer than an hour.

Just managing to keep from snapping at her, Suzy asked, "Was there something you needed, Ella?"

"Yes, I have a letter for you from Brittany." Dropping her voice to almost a whisper, Ella handed her an envelope and said, "I don't think you're going to like this at all."

Suzy, never one for patience, ripped the envelope open with Ella practically hanging over her shoulder and read the short paragraph inside. Feeling the smoke steam from her ears, Suzy yelled, "Fu—" but quickly substituted "Truck!" upon seeing Ella's eyes widen. *Truck, really?* Where was the satisfaction in that particular word? Even Ella looked like she expected the mother of all curse words.

"Ms. Denton, what is it? I saw Brittany take all her stuff with her, even her stapler." Ella seemed as repulsed as if she had mentioned that Brittany had stopped in the lobby and smoked a joint on her way out. "I knew she was up to something."

"Ella, it's nothing to concern yourself with. I'll handle it." Suzy gathered herself and walked toward her corner office at the end of the hallway. After she slammed the door behind her, Suzy let the curse words flow. Brittany had left her letter of resignation. She was going to elope with her boyfriend and would not be coming back. No notice, no nothing. She should have known better than to hire someone who popped bubble gum constantly and said, "like, you know" at least fifty times a day.

Under normal circumstances, replacing Brittany wouldn't be a hardship; she'd been fed up with her for some time. Since getting involved with her boyfriend, who played in a band, Brittany had gotten more and more unreliable. She was late almost every morning and had been calling in sick at least once a month.

The problem here was that the timing sucked. They

were in the middle of putting together Danvers's formal gala for their customers. Suzy spent at least two months preparing and planning the annual event. Now, with only a month left before the gala, her assistant had decided to quit without notice. Finding someone that Suzy could work with—who understood her vague instructions and wasn't offended by her artistic temperament—would be a challenge. Add in that she needed an assistant immediately and things were near impossible.

Taking a deep breath, Suzy called the personnel department to see if they had anyone they could send up right away. *Yeah that's about as likely to happen as Ella getting laid, but hell, stranger things have happened.* "Personnel, this is Ruth."

"Hey, Ruth, it's Suzy in events. My assistant has decided to fly the coop today, and I needed someone, like, yesterday to replace her. What can you do for me?"

"Hi, Suzy. I'm sorry to hear about that. Let me see if we have anyone available." Drumming her fingers against her desk impatiently, Suzy waited to see what Ruth would find. "Oh, you're in luck. We have someone who has already applied for the position, and it looks like she's qualified."

"Wait, how could someone have already applied for the job? I just found out myself ten minutes ago."

"This young lady works in your section, so maybe Brittany let her know she was leaving. You're familiar with Ella Webber, aren't you?"

"Oh, hell I, um, mean heck no! No way. That wouldn't work, and I can't believe she'd even apply. We would never get anything done; she'd spend her entire day crossing herself and reading me scripture."

Suzy heard Ruth's chuckle before she managed to cover it. "I'm sorry, Suzy, but I have no one else right now. With the expansion the merger created, we are still short-staffed. If you don't feel that Ella would make a good permanent replacement, then I suggest you use her temporarily until we can have the employment agency send over some others to interview."

"See what you can put together and I'll get back to you," Suzy said. Slamming the phone down in disgust, she laid her head on her desk. Just as she was considering throwing herself from her fourteenth-floor window, her cell phone rang. Suzy answered the call with a warm, "Yeah, what now?"

"Wow, please stop, all of this sentiment is making me uncomfortable," Beth replied drily. Beth was Suzy's younger sister by two years and was, up until recently, an elementary school teacher. Thanks to the constant cuts in the education budget, Beth had been laid off a month ago. Other than Claire, Beth was the only other person who truly seemed to get her, and Suzy loved her dearly.

"Ha-ha, very funny. It's been a rough day. My ditzy assistant decided to walk out without any notice while I was at lunch, and now I'm screwed. The big gala is a month away, and I have no possibilities for replacing her other than the Holy Roller receptionist, and that will never happen."

"Ah, I'm sorry, sis. Is there anything I can do to help?" Suddenly, it was as if a lightbulb flashed in Suzy's head.

"Hey, there just may be. Has anything turned up on the job hunt yet?"

"Ugh, no, nothing."

"How would you feel about being my assistant at

least until after the gala is over? I know you're a teacher and that's what you love, but you'd be saving my life if you could help me just for a while."

"Wow, I don't know anything about what you're doing, so I might hinder you more than I'd help you."

"You'd be great, Beth. You get me, and that's half of the job. Please say you'll do it. At least you'd earn a good salary while you're job hunting."

"Okay, I'm in! When do I start?"

"I'd say right now, but that's probably a bit sudden, so how about tomorrow?"

"Sure. Um, sis, how would I need to dress? I know since we are sisters everyone will be shocked that we look nothing alike."

Her heart squeezed at the insecurity she heard in Beth's voice. Suzy said brightly, "Yeah they're going to wonder why you got all the class in the family, and I dress like a street walker. Wear whatever you like, you always look great." Before Beth could protest further, Suzy quickly ended the call.

Beth called herself a "former fatty." Suzy had never liked that label and still didn't. Yes, Beth had been overweight for most of her life, and Suzy knew that her life had been easy compared to what Beth had endured. Suzy had tried to protect her and had gotten into many fights at school defending her sister.

She'd always told Beth that she was beautiful, and she truly felt that way. Beth, however, hadn't and decided to do something about it. After moving out of their parents' house two years ago, Beth had taken control. She'd joined a gym and started counting calories. It took her almost a year, but the two sisters were now close to the same size.

Suzy was so proud of her. Beth looked like a model but seemed to have no idea how beautiful she truly was. She was a small person trapped in the mindset of her former self. She simply wasn't capable yet of seeing herself as the rest of the world saw her. Suzy hoped that with time and maybe the right person in her life, Beth could finally open her eyes and see that the beauty on the inside was shining on the outside as well.

Maybe this job would be good for Beth. Her job as a teacher was a safe zone for her, but working at Danvers would require her to meet a lot of new people and leave her comfort zone, something that Beth almost never did. She gave Ruth in HR a quick call to let her know that she had someone coming in for the job tomorrow. Ruth seemed relieved that she had found someone on her own. *Hasta la vista, Brittany!* Suzy felt the smile spread across her face as she pondered putting Beth on the dating market.

"Now that's the smile of a woman on a mission if I've ever seen one," drawled an amused voice.

Suzy jerked around and was floored to see Gray standing in her doorway. "How . . . How did you get in?"

"I did knock and since I knew you were in here, I decided to peek in to make sure you were still upright after the flow of curse words I heard earlier."

Suzy could feel color creep up her cheeks and was horrified at the display of emotion in front of Gray. "When did you get back in town?"

Still watching her, Gray allowed his gaze to leisurely run the length of her body. For once, she wished she'd worn something a little less attention-getting. When she was getting dressed this morning, the short black suede skirt, tights, and leopard-skin heels seemed to go well with the matching leopard-skin tank top. Now, under his heated gaze, Suzy had the uncomfortable desire to cross her arms over her chest.

Gray, as usual, looked perfect. He was wearing an obviously expensive dark-colored suit that only enhanced the trim, athletic body underneath. His thick, dark-brown hair was perfectly groomed, and his eyes were framed by long lashes that a girl would kill for. His strong jaw had just a hint of stubble beginning to appear. She tried not to think of how that rough texture would feel under her hands, and against her body. Gray was well over six feet tall and there wasn't an ounce of fat on his superb body. *Down, girl. Put your tongue back in your mouth and get control of your body.*

"I just got in actually. You were my first stop."

"Wow, goody for me. I feel so special."

"You most definitely are, Suzanna."

"It's Suzy, not Suzanna. Suzanna was who my mother hoped I'd be before I shattered that illusion. Suzy is who I am."

"I know who you are, Suzanna, and it's exactly who I want you to be; I wouldn't change a thing."

Knowing she was in serious danger of pulling him against the wall of her office and gripping that hot butt, Suzy turned toward the window and asked, "Was there something you needed, Gray?"

"Now that's a loaded question if ever I've heard one. There are many things I want, but the first is dinner tonight."

"Then you're out of luck; I'm busy."

"You're lying but I'll play along. When are you not busy?"

"For you, I'm always going to be busy. I'm not interested in starting something with you, Gray. Why can't you accept that?"

Mocking laughter erupted as he said, "Because we both know it's not true. You want it as much as I do."

Feeling as if her soul were exposed, Suzy laughed his comment off and said, "Sure, whatever you say, but it doesn't change the fact that I'm not going out with you."

"Well, since you only object to a relationship, let's not have one of those. I'll pick you up later for sex, just plain old sex. You can even leave as soon as it's over."

Suzy spun around in shock. She looked to see if he was joking but his expression looked perfectly serious. "You don't have it in you, Gray; you're too straitlaced to be someone's sex buddy."

"Oh, I think you're wrong, Suzanna. I'm nowhere near as straitlaced as you seem to think I am. The question here is, are you a relationship girl or are you willing to put your money where your mouth is, so to speak? If you're who you say you are, then you'll jump at the opportunity for great sex with no strings." After throwing the gauntlet down, Gray stood there waiting for a response.

Boy, was my mother right; my big mouth has finally gotten me into trouble of the oh-so-hot variety. So if I sleep with him and he's lousy in bed, I can move on—perfect. Even as Suzy finished her thought, she wondered what in the world she was getting herself into. "Okay, Gray, you win. Let's scratch the itch once and for all and get it out of our system. No clinging or crying when it's over, though. I'm not going to make an honest man out of you or anything afterward."

*   *   *

Gray was surprised, maybe *shocked* was a better word. When he'd thrown out the challenge, he hadn't really expected Suzy to take it. Suzy, as she liked to be called, had haunted his dreams for well over a year now. Truthfully, he only continued to call her Suzanna because he knew it was guaranteed to get under her skin.

He'd first met her last year in a restaurant called Ivy. He was dining with Jason Danvers, and Suzy had been dining there with Claire Walters, who was actually Claire Danvers now. Both were very beautiful women, but Suzy had taken his breath away. She was so vibrant and pulsed with energy. Most of the women he'd dated were born to a certain class and had only one thing on their minds: marriage. The husband mattered little as long as he had a healthy bank account.

In truth, he'd made a lot more trips to Myrtle Beach in the last year than had really been necessary. He knew the first time he met Suzy that there was more to her than the world saw. Under her tough exterior was a caring, compassionate woman who tried hard not to let anyone see that side of her.

A few months after they'd first met, he had been working with Jason for a week at the home office. He'd asked her to spend the day with him that Saturday. She'd laughed and said she already had a better offer. Later that day, Gray decided to eat in the cafeteria downstairs. He smiled when he saw Suzy a few feet ahead of him talking to George, the man who ran the cafeteria. George was probably in his late sixties and Jason had mentioned that George had worked at Danvers for over thirty years. In the short time he had known him, Gray had grown fond of George and everyone at Danvers adored him. He always had a ready smile and a nice word for everyone who came through the cafeteria line.

Gray was curious when he saw Suzy grip George's arm and start what looked to be an intense conversation. He moved closer to hear what she was saying.

"George, I mean it, you'd better not touch that lawn mower. Neither you nor Sara should be trying to cut grass right now. You know the doctor said that the horrible pollen this year was making your asthma worse, and with Sara's back problems it's crazy for either of you to try when you have me." George had tried to protest, but Suzy had quickly, but gently, insisted that she didn't mind. "I'll be over Saturday morning as usual to do it. You know how much I enjoy that glass of fresh lemonade you always have for me. You wouldn't deprive me of that now, would you?"

Gray could see that George was no match for a smiling Suzy. Gray pulled back quietly, not wanting to intrude. He smiled as he headed to a table in the back of the room. Suzy had just confirmed what he had already suspected. There was much more to her than what she wanted everyone to believe. The time that had passed since then only reinforced that knowledge. Suzy was apparently somewhat of a modern-day Robin Hood at Danvers. Instead of giving the gift of money to those who needed it, she seemed to give the gift of assistance.

Through the months, Gray had learned that Suzy had picked up groceries for Cindy in accounting for two months after she'd had surgery; she'd watched Jim's dog when his mother was sick and he had to quickly leave town to care for her; and she spent a weekend helping Lori clean her basement after a water leak. He knew that the event planner would be horrified to know how people at Danvers talked about her, almost in awe. It just made Gray that much more determined to get through her tough shell to the woman he knew was there. He had no idea why she wanted everyone to believe that she didn't care about anyone else, because, obviously, she couldn't resist a person in need.

He wasn't going to delude himself; he wanted her in his bed any way he could get her. It wasn't just about the sex, though; he also wanted the relationship along with the sex. He couldn't deny that lust had been the first thing he felt for her and, although it was still there, he could also see a future with her, which he knew would scare her to death. He had planned to approach her carefully. But, if they needed to jump ahead past dating and go right to sleeping together, then, hey, he was a guy, and that would suit him fine. He'd allow her to believe she was calling all the shots. But Gray knew that sooner or later Suzy was going to be scratching her head and wondering what had hit her.

"So, my place or yours?" Gray asked with a twinkle in his eyes.

Suzy tried to maintain her cool façade. She clasped her hands behind her back so that Gray wouldn't notice them shaking. *Suck it up and put your big-girl panties on. It's time to either stand and deliver or run and hide.* "Um . . . Where is your place exactly?"

Propping a hip against the corner of her desk, Gray said, "Home is here right now. Jason is letting me use the penthouse until I find something to buy. I think I could probably sneak you up in the elevator without anyone noticing." Wiggling his eyebrows suggestively, he continued, "Have any elevator fantasies we could take care of on the way up?"

"I . . . um . . . don't think your place is a good idea, then." *My God I've turned into a blubbering idiot. The man starts talking about elevator sex, and I'm tripping over my tongue like a virgin schoolgirl. Get some composure. Geez.* "How about my place? It's a bit more private." Suzy walked over to her desk and wrote the address down for him and handed it over. As their fingers touched, fire seemed to fly from their fingertips.

Seeing the flush on Gray's cheekbones, she knew he'd felt the same zing she had. "So, how about dinner around seven and then back to your place?"

"Dinner? I told you this wasn't a date, Gray. You're getting lucky tonight; there's no need to wine and dine me," Suzy replied drily.

Chuckling, Gray said, "We both have to eat, so we might as well do it together. I'll meet you in the lobby around six if that's okay with you?"

Suzy knew it would do no good arguing and she was desperate to have him out of her personal space. "Yeah, yeah, whatever, I guess I can do that. Now, don't you have a job or something to do here?"

After another leisurely inspection of her, Gray smiled and blew her a kiss. "You will be on my mind all day, Suzanna." With that, he turned and left.

Suzy's knees were in serious danger of giving out so she slid into her seat and tried to slow her breathing. How could something as simple as an air kiss make her melt? She would not get attached to this man, and she sure as hell wasn't going to fall in love with him. *Please, please let him be terrible in bed, pretty please!*

Chapter Three

Suzy spent the day trying to put out fires and handle all the small details that Brittany would have normally handled. She seemed to be messing up everything she touched today. She was more nervous than she could admit, even to herself. She might talk a good game, but in reality, she wasn't that experienced in matters of the opposite sex. She'd been with Jeff for so long that she'd never really dated anyone else. She'd only slept with one man in her life, and she'd been engaged to the scumbag.

She wanted Gray with an intensity that she'd never experienced with Jeff. Things were familiar with Jeff, and their sex life had been good. But she was more excited at the thought of sleeping with Gray than she'd ever been about doing the deed with Jeff. Her thong sizzled when Gray was anywhere in the vicinity. Could she really pull off the worldly woman routine with him? She'd talked herself into a corner. She didn't want a relationship, because she didn't want to get hurt. Unfortunately, she had made sure Gray would never see her as anything other than a roll in the sack.

A check of her watch showed it was now close to six. It was time to suck it up and meet Gray. She hoped that Ella had already left for the day. She'd like to avoid any unpleasant conversation over the assistant's job that Ella apparently wanted for some unknown reason. Maybe Ella saw Suzy as someone in desperate need of saving. Poor thing. That would really be setting herself up for failure. At least with Beth coming in tomorrow, hopefully Ella would get the message and that would be the end of it.

Suzy pulled a small spritzer of perfume from her purse and gave herself a few sprays. *Hey, a girl has to smell fresh, right?* She knew she looked like someone on her way to meet the firing squad as she made her way down the hall. She was greatly relieved to see Ella's desk empty. All too soon she was in the lobby, where she spotted Gray immediately. *So-o-o unfair. One man shouldn't look so good. I want to drag him down here on the lobby floor and rip that uptight suit right off him.*

Suzy tried to hide her blush as Gray's eyes traveled the length of her body. Heat blazed in their green depths as they lingered on her breasts. She could feel her body responding to his, her nipples peaking in pleasure at the admiration so evident in his gaze.

"Have I told you today how beautiful you are, Suzanna?"

Clearing her throat and trying not to let her pleasure show at his statement, Suzy said, "You don't look too bad yourself, cowboy."

"Cowboy, huh? I like that." Lowering his voice, Gray leaned over and whispered in her ear, "I'll try my best to ride you all night."

Heat blazed through her, liquid pooling between her thighs as the image of Gray doing just that flashed through her mind. Trying to sound flip, Suzy said, "Yeah, we'll see if your game is as good as your talk."

Gray put his hand at the small of her back and led her toward the door. "Oh, I promise you, I give very good game, Suzanna, exceptional . . . game."

Gray led her across the street to a parking lot. Apparently, he didn't want to leave his vehicle in the parking deck on the lower floor. They approached a silver BMW sedan, and Gray clicked the locks and opened the passenger door for her. Although Suzy's small SUV was comfortable and dependable, this car was pure luxury. She gave an appreciative sigh as she slid onto the soft leather seats. "Whoa, why am I riding with you? I need to get my car since we're going to my place."

"Don't be silly, Suzanna. We might be having a sex evening, but I still intend to have a bite to eat first, and I also intend to stay the night." Holding his hand up to silence the protests she was forming, he continued. "Rushing out in the middle of the night is something you do after a quickie, and I have no intention of being quick with you. You don't have to worry, dinner will be very casual since I don't have to wine and dine you."

Suzy actually felt offended at that last comment, but what could she say? She'd told him exactly what she wanted, and he was following along to the letter. *You can do this; it's only sex. It's only sex.* Maybe if she kept repeating that enough, she'd actually believe it.

Finally, Gray pulled into a parking area near the beach and walked around to open her door. Suzy wondered where they could possibly be going. Gray took her hand and led her up a flight of stairs to the boardwalk that ran along the Atlantic Ocean. Several shops and restaurants lined the walkway. Gray led her inside a small restaurant that advertised the world's best foot-long hot dogs. He followed her up to the counter and said, "Order anything on the menu, princess." Then, lowering his voice, he said, "Maybe we could skip the onions, though."

Suzy ordered the house specialty—the foot-long dog—and even though she was tempted, she passed on the onions as Gray suggested.

"Do you want to eat in here or outside?"

"I think outside; it's a great evening," Suzy said.

Taking their purchases, Gray led them to a table in the corner of the boardwalk and pulled out a seat for her. Suzy had to admit, they did make a great hot dog. Gray also ordered the same thing, as well as a funnel cake. As she finished her hot dog, she looked longingly at his cake. Finally taking the hint, he broke a piece off and held it up to her lips. Having him feed her was one of the most sensual moments of her life. *Oh, good grief, get the hormones under control; it's funnel cake, not your wedding cake.*

Suzy could feel her hands starting to tremble as they finished their meal, and she knew the time was fast approaching for the main event of the evening. There was no backing out now, and she really didn't want to. She just hoped she was everything that Gray imagined she was. Could she live up to her image or would Gray discover the sentimental heart under the tough exterior?

"If you're finished, Suzanna, I'm more than ready to go to your place," Gray said.

"Um . . . yeah, sure." Gray gave her a puzzled look but luckily didn't question her.

He dropped their things in the wastebasket and turned to follow Suzy toward the stairway. Before he could reach her, a gang of teens on skateboards came roaring around the corner, and, in almost slow motion, he saw as Suzy jumped forward to avoid a collision. She teetered at the top of the stairs. He yelled her name as he tried to reach her and watched in horror as Suzy fought for control in the impossibly high heels. Gray recognized the exact moment when Suzy knew she would fall. Panic gripped her and her body visibly braced for impact.

The fall wasn't a simple fall, however. The heel of one of her shoes wedged into a crack in the steps, and Gray could see her ankle twist, almost stopping her fall. Then her foot separated from the shoe, and she continued her tumble. He saw her head bounce once as it slammed into the sidewalk at the foot of the stairs. Gray pushed his way through the teenagers and ran down the steps after her. A crowd of people was already gathered at the bottom. When he finally reached her, he turned her over and was alarmed at the pallor of her face and the obvious haze of pain in her eyes. There was blood running down the side of her face from a gash on her forehead. Gently pushing the hair back from her eyes, Gray yelled for someone to call 911. He took the corner of his shirt and dabbed the blood before it could pool in her eye.

Looking at him in alarm, Suzy said hoarsely, "No . . . Gray, please, you take me, I'm scared of being alone."

"Suzy, I'm afraid to move you."

"Gray, please, I'm hurting, please help me!" Suzy cried.

Gray leaned down and put his arms under her, lifting her as gently as he could. A couple who had stopped to help offered to carry her purse and insisted on getting his keys and bringing the car to the curb. At that moment, Gray would have trusted anyone as long as they would help him. He gladly handed the keys over, along with a description of the car and asked them to hurry.

Whispering words of encouragement to Suzy, he tried to question her about her injuries. He was afraid her ankle was at least sprained, if not broken, and he hoped that she didn't have other broken bones as well. She was trying to be brave; he could see the resolve in the tight set of her chin. Tears trickled from the corners of her eyes, and Gray's heart was breaking. God, he adored this woman. He had from the moment he'd laid eyes on her, and nothing had or would ever change that.

At that moment, his car came to a screeching halt at the curb and Gray hurried toward it. The couple who had retrieved the car for him climbed out and opened the back door for him. Gray hesitated as he approached, now unsure of how he could take care of Suzy and drive the car.

"Sir, I know you don't know us, but we want to help you. If you'd like to get into the back with your wife, my wife and I will drive you to the hospital and then catch a cab back for our car later."

Gray almost wept with relief. At this point, he didn't care if these people were axe murderers as long as they got Suzy to a hospital along the way. He thanked the couple profusely and slid into the back as gently as he could with Suzy on his lap.

Her eyes flickering open, hazy with pain, Suzy quietly said, "You called me Suzy."

With a tender smile, Gray caressed the curve of her

cheek and whispered, "You have always been Suzy to me, baby. You're right, it is who you are."

Smiling at him one last time, Suzy grimaced in pain and seemed to drift off. Gray was alarmed until he felt the even pattern of her breathing. Maybe he should be trying to keep her awake in case of a concussion, but he hated to make her endure the pain if she could have some respite from it.

"Sir, how's your wife doing?"

Gray cleared his throat, not bothering to correct the assumption that Suzy was his wife. "She's drifted off and seems to be resting peacefully. How much farther to the hospital?"

"Should be just another couple of minutes. I'm Frank, by the way, and this is my wife, Margie."

"I'm Gray and this is Suzy. I can't thank you enough for everything you've done for us; I don't know what we would have done without you two."

Finally, Gray saw them approaching a huge hospital, and soon they were pulling up to an emergency entrance. Frank offered to park the car and meet him in the emergency area with the keys. As far as Gray was concerned Frank could have the damn car; he just wanted to get Suzy inside.

Chapter Four

Gray rushed up to the receptionist and was relieved when she jumped into action. He was half afraid she'd start shoving forms at him, but instead she led him through a set of double doors into the hub of the emergency room. The receptionist stopped for a moment to inquire about a room, and soon he was laying Suzy on a gurney in a small room with very little privacy. A nurse followed closely behind them and was already firing off a rapid series of questions before he even had Suzy settled.

Asking her name, the nurse started waking Suzy up. Finally, after her name was called loudly several times, Suzy blinked her eyes open in confusion, and then Gray could see the pain literally taking her breath away. "Ms. Denton, can you tell me where you're hurting?"

"My . . . my leg and back, and hell, just about everywhere." Suzy gasped.

Gray was glad to see her make a small attempt at humor, even though it was obvious that the effort had cost her. Reaching over, Suzy held her hand out to him, seeking his touch and comfort. Gray wrapped his fingers around hers, using his other hand to rub her arm gently in reassurance. "It's going to be okay, baby, just hold on. Can she please have something for pain now?"

"I'm fixing to run an IV, sir, but we can't give her any pain medication until we know the extent of her injuries." Pulling Suzy's arm to lie flat, the nurse felt for a vein and, apparently satisfied, smoothly slid the needle in and taped it in place.

A short dynamo burst into the room and immediately began asking questions and giving orders. Walking over to him, the lady he assumed was the doctor held her hand out to him.

"Mr. Denton?"

"Actually no, it's Merimon, Grayson Merimon."

"This is Suzanna Denton, correct?"

"Yes, I'm her fiancé," Gray lied smoothly. Luckily, Suzy was too far out of it to dispute this fact, but Gray didn't intend to be dispatched to the waiting room while she was here alone.

"Okay, Mr. Merimon, I'm Dr. Mills. Can you tell me what happened to your fiancée?"

"She fell down a flight of stairs and, as she was beginning her fall, the heel of her shoe caught between an opening in the steps, so she may have injured her ankle before the fall even started. Her head then slammed into the sidewalk at the bottom of the steps causing the cut on her forehead."

"Did she lose consciousness at any point?"

"She drifted in and out on the way to the hospital."

Making a few more notes on her chart, Dr. Mills said, "I'm going to send her for a CAT scan first, Mr. Merimon, and then we will go from there. I don't want to risk injuring her further by doing a physical exam until we know what, if anything, is broken. You're welcome to accompany her and stay in the waiting room there."

Suzy looked at him in panic as they started to wheel her bed out into the hall. Gray walked quickly beside her so that he'd be in her line of sight. Soon they were taking her to X-ray and he was left on his own waiting. He decided to give Jason and Claire a call because he wasn't sure if she had family locally that would need to be contacted.

Jason answered the call on the first ring and Gray filled him in on what was happening. Jason promised that he'd let Claire know and that they would be at the hospital as soon as possible. Gray also called his brother, Nick, who was due to arrive in town at any moment. He'd made no secret of his feelings for Suzy to Nick; hell, everyone knew how he felt about her except her. Of course, she knew that he was attracted to her and she fought that attraction at every corner.

"Hey, Nick," Gray began as his brother's voice came onto the line, "just wanted to let you know what was going on. Suzy had an accident, and we are at the hospital."

"Oh, shit, you didn't get your chance to sleep with her and give her a heart attack or something, did you?"

"Funny, smart-ass. No, she fell and is having tests done right now."

Gray heard Nick take a deep breath, and then all joking was gone. "Man, I'm sorry. Is she okay?"

"I don't really know anything yet. She took a pretty ugly fall though." Gray gave Nick a brief rundown of what had happened, and even though he assured him that it wasn't necessary, Nick insisted on getting the name of the hospital and told Gray he was only minutes out of town and would come there first. Gray was glad for all the support he could get.

Finally, after what seemed like years, a nurse came out and told him that Suzy was finished and was on her way to a private room. Gray rushed back, not wanting her to think he'd left her. When he entered the room, Suzy's eyes locked on him, and she held out her hand.

Gray took it and pulled the seat up beside her. The nurse told him that they were just waiting for the results and that the doctor would be back in as soon as she had them. Gray leaned over the bed and brushed a kiss on Suzy's forehead and asked, "How are you, baby?"

"Besides feeling like I've been beat with a baseball bat, I'm just great. You sure know how to show a girl a good time, cowboy."

"Hey, I aim to please. I wanted to give you the most memorable night you have ever had, and I think I succeeded, right?"

"Oh, yeah, I'm not likely to forget this. I want to make it known right now, though, that all my clingy behavior here is totally due to my accident, so don't get any ideas. We aren't dating or anything."

"Duly noted. As soon as you're healed, I'll sex you up, just as we planned."

Suzy choked on a laugh, grabbing her ribs as if it hurt her. "Ugh, no jokes, laughing is torture right now."

Just as Gray was getting ready to go find the nurse for pain medication, Dr. Mills walked in. "Got your results here, Ms. Denton, and, as suspected, you have broken your right ankle. We will get a soft cast on your ankle tonight and then have the hard cast put on within a few days. As for the pain you're having in your ribs, there is no sign of any broken bones, which is very good. I suspect that you have bruised your ribs, which can be very painful as well. There was no indication of anything abnormal on the CT of your head, and due to the level of your alertness, I will allow pain medication. I assume that your fiancé will be on hand to care for you?"

"You assume right, Dr. Mills. I'll make sure that my fiancée is completely taken care of, rest assured. Will you be admitting her to the hospital?"

"Yes, she'll be admitted tonight for observation, due to the head injury, and could possibly be released as early as tomorrow. Of course, depending on how she's doing. I'm going to start the process of having Ms. Denton admitted. How's your pain level?"

Before Suzy could speak, Gray said, "She's hurting, please give her something."

"I'll send the nurse right in with pain medication. Ms. Denton, I'll see you in the morning when I make my rounds. Please have the nurse on duty page me if you have any concerns."

The nurse returned with the promised medication and, soon after, Suzy was resting comfortably and drifted to sleep, her fingers curled tightly around Gray's. A light knock sounded at the door and Claire stuck her head around it. "Oh, Gray, thank goodness. I just couldn't wait another moment. I finally played the pregnancy card, and rolled out some tears so the nurse would agree to let me come back. How is she?"

"She has a broken ankle and is just really banged up. They have her pretty heavily medicated right now so she's much more comfortable than she was. The doctor wants to keep her overnight for observation."

Claire's hand flew to her mouth and the tears this

time were real. "Oh, no! Poor Suz, she must have been so scared. I'm glad you were there with her. No matter how she protests, I know she cares about you. Her sister, Beth, is in the waiting room going crazy, and your brother just got here as well." Walking over, Claire leaned over and kissed Suzy on the cheek and Gray heard her whisper, "I love you, my friend."

"I'm going to walk back to the waiting room and let everyone know what is going on. Beth and I will go buy some personal items for Suzy, a gown and some toiletries that she might need. Can I get anything for you, Gray?"

Looking at Claire with gratitude, Gray said, "If Jason or Nick could loan me a change of clothing I'd appreciate it. After sleeping in these all night, they won't be too great in the morning."

"Of course. Don't worry about a thing, Gray; we will get you both everything you will need. As soon as they allow visitors, please give Jason a call so that at least Beth can come back to see her sister."

Claire walked over and gave his shoulder a quick squeeze. "She'll be fine, there is no way she'd be caught in that horrid hospital gown for any longer than necessary, trust me," Claire joked. Giving his shoulder one last squeeze, Claire went back to the waiting room.

A nurse arrived and informed Gray that Suzy's room was ready. He walked alongside the gurney as she was transferred to a room with more privacy. As soon as she was settled and the nurse was gone, Gray called Nick and let him know what room number they were in.

Within moments, the door opened quietly. Nick and a woman he didn't recognize came in. Gray assumed that this must be Suzy's sister, even though they didn't resemble each other at first glance. Nick walked over to his side as her sister approached the hospital bed. Leaning down, she picked up Suzy's other hand and said, "Suzy-Q, is there nothing you won't do for some attention?"

Gray was shocked at the comment and was opening his mouth to defend Suzy when her sister continued on in a voice obviously laced with affection and concern.

"I leave you on your own and look where you end up. You're in a hospital surrounded by hunky doctors and also have a hunky man sitting vigil at your bed. The thing I hate the most, though, is that even after wiping up the pavement with your body, you still look like a million bucks. That's so unfair, sister dear. I guess you're too high on the good stuff to answer me, right?"

Finally, Gray found his voice and asked, "I take it you're Beth, her sister?"

Turning to face him as if she'd forgotten him for the moment, a shy smile settled on her lips, and she said, "Ye . . . Yes, I'm Beth." She thought to herself, *Oh, good grief, I'm stuck in this tiny room with two of the best-looking men I've ever seen in my life, and this outfit makes me look like a cow.* Beth tried to discreetly smooth down the dress that she was wearing, terrified that it was riding up in the back and stuck to her butt.

Gray took a moment to study Suzy's sister. Now that she was standing closer, he could see the resemblance. Suzy had red hair and Beth had dark brown hair, but their eyes were the same and the curves of their faces were very similar. Whereas Suzy was stop-traffic beautiful with her bold dressing and smoldering sexuality, Beth was more of a quiet beauty. Her dress was conservative and, unlike her sister, she obviously didn't want or seek to be the center of attention. She was someone you would want to nurture and protect. Suzy was someone you would want to arm wrestle after a hot night of sex unless you took the time to know the woman behind the façade.

Gray released Suzy's hand and walked over to Beth. "I'm Gray Merimon. It looks like you've already met my brother, Nick." Beth shook the hand that he offered and turned back to her sister. "You must want some time alone with your sister. Nick and I will walk down for a cup of coffee so you can have some privacy. Can we bring you something back?"

"Oh, no. No, thank you." Giving him a grateful look, Beth slid into the seat he'd vacated, clearly relieved that they were leaving.

Chapter Five

"How're you doing, bro?"

"Better, now that I know Suzy will be okay. Did you get me a new cell phone?"

"Oh, yeah, got it right here." Nick reached into the pocket of his jeans and pulled out a sleek black cell phone. "How often are you going to change phones before you admit you have a problem?"

"I can handle it, Nick; just let it go."

Nick gave him a disgusted look and said, "You haven't thought this out, bro. You're going to be here playing house with Suzy now, and what happens when she finds out? You need to go ahead and tell her and then deal with it. Trying to ignore it hasn't worked too well."

Gray ran his hand through his hair and expelled a deep breath. Fatigue edged the corners of his mouth as he looked at his brother. Gone was the cocky grin that Nick usually wore; in its place was a look of concern.

"Nick, this is a first for me, and I don't know what the hell to do. I just kept hoping she'd get the message without this getting ugly. I can't figure out how she keeps getting my new number. I hate to think it, but someone within Mericom has to be leaking my personal information. Right now that's our starting point. See if you can find a connection."

Gray lowered his voice and said quietly, "Nick, you know how I feel about Suzy. This could not have come at a worse time. She's been hurt before, and I'm afraid this will cause her to run and never look back. I need your help to get this taken care of before she finds out about it. I'm so close to getting through to her and I won't let some nut job take that away."

Nick clasped a hand on his shoulder and said, "You can count on me, bro. I'll get right on it. None of this is your fault, so there is nothing for you to feel guilty about." With a mischievous smile, Nick added, "It's just the curse of the good-looking Merimon Brothers; it drives some women a little crazy."

Nick left to get checked into a hotel, while Gray made his way back to Suzy's room. He was surprised and pleased to see that she was awake and talking to Beth. Gray walked over to the bedside and was relieved to see the color was back in her face. Beth had also helped her change into a gown that was much more . . . Suzy. The woman did like the leopard skin.

Suzy felt her heart skip a beat as Gray walked in the door. Here she was lying in a hospital bed in complete disarray, and he looked like he'd just stepped off the pages of *GQ* magazine. She felt a little better since changing out of the horrid hospital gown, but there was only so much leopard skin could do. Her hair was a mess, her makeup was gone, and she was pretty sure she smelled. She looked like she'd been rode hard and put up wet.

Suzy cleared her throat and tried to come up with one of her usual smart comments. The fact that it wasn't coming naturally was out of character. It must be the damn drugs. "Hey, slick. Sorry about the date disaster and all."

"Couldn't be helped, Suzanna. You might want to check into some more sensible shoes though before our next date," Gray said.

"Yeah, right. I don't do sensible; you should know that by now," Suzy sniffed.

Gray walked over and picked her small hand up from the top of the hospital sheet and rubbed his thumb slowly back and forth over the sensitive nerves of her palm. He locked his gaze with hers and lowered his voice to a sexy timbre. "Oh, I know you, Suzanna, better than you know yourself."

Beth shifted in place awkwardly, clearly uncomfortable with the tension in the room. "Um . . . sis, I'm heading home now. Are you sure you don't want me to call Mom and Dad?"

Tearing her gaze from Gray's, Suzy warned, "You better not unless you want me to send them your way next."

Beth held up her hands in surrender and said, "Okay, okay, but we might actually need their help. How are you going to get to the second floor of your condo on crutches? And I also live on the second floor."

"Beth, don't worry about it; Suzy will stay with me," said Gray.

"The hell I will," shouted Suzy. The sudden movement jarred her injured ribs and pain flooded through her.

Gray saw Suzy's face pale and pressed the call button for a nurse. He rubbed her arm in a soothing pattern and said, "Baby, calm down. We can talk about all this later."

A nurse came in and soon Suzy was floating again. As she was drifting away, she wondered when she had started letting Gray call her "baby," and had he always smelled *this* good?

Gray watched Suzy's eyes grow heavy and soon the fight left her body. It was going to be a battle to convince her to move in with him until she was recovered. If he had his way, she'd be living with him permanently. This kicked things into overdrive a bit on the house front. He knew Suzy would use the excuse that he was living in the penthouse of Danvers to avoid moving in with him. He planned to take care of that in the morning. If there was one thing having money had taught him, it was that things that usually took weeks could be accomplished in days or hours. He'd call a real estate agent tonight and look at homes in the morning.

Gray noticed Beth fidgeting, clearly uneasy about being in the room with him. Beth was a stunning woman, but obviously not comfortable taking center stage. Suzy not only took it, she owned it.

Giving her a smile, Gray said, "Beth, I'll see that Suzy is taken care of when she's released—you don't have to worry about anything in that regard. I'd like to ask a question, though. Why is Suzy so against contacting your parents? I'd think they would want to know about her accident."

Giving him a shy smile, Beth said, "Our parents are a little . . . different. Actually, they're a lot different. I get along okay because I don't rock the boat, but Suzy has battled with them for all of our lives. They're both professors, quite brilliant really. They live, eat, and breathe higher education. Our mother is a history professor and our father is a biology professor. I caved to pressure a bit, which is one of the reasons I'm a teacher.

Suzy rebelled from early on and they clashed at every turn. Don't get me wrong. I'm sure they love us in their own way, but they aren't warm, nurturing people. If they came here now, they would spend the entire visit lecturing Suzy about her job, her clothes, and how her lifestyle caused her injury."

As if realizing that she'd been talking to a near stranger, Beth's face flushed a pink shade.

"Thank you for telling me, Beth. I appreciate the honesty. I'll in turn be honest with you. I'm crazy about your sister and have been for quite a while. I realize that it will take some time for her to be able to trust again after the emotional damage that Jeff inflicted on her, but I'm not going anywhere."

Surprised, Beth asked, "So she told you all about Jeff?"

With a wry smile, Gray said, "Yeah, she did. A while back when I was trying to convince her to go out to dinner with me and not taking no for an answer, she snapped. She told me about Jeff and all of the reasons that she wasn't interested in getting involved again. I'll spare you the colorful descriptions that she used to describe him, but I know that he broke her heart and you can rest assured that I have no such intentions."

Beth appeared to study him for a moment as if testing the sincerity of his words. Finally, she seemed to come to some decision and he could see her face softening. "Gray, I believe you. My sister comes across as fearless and unbreakable but that's just a façade. Don't get me wrong, I fully believe that she could conquer the world if she wanted to. Very little stops her. She can, however, be hurt. Jeff did a real number on her and I watched her fall to pieces over it. She got up and brushed herself off, but, make no mistake, inside she's still torn apart. I know she has feelings for you too even though she has tried to fight it." With an affectionate smile, Beth added, "She can never hide anything from me. Don't let my quiet demeanor fool you, though, If you hurt my sister you will have two Denton sisters after you, and that, my friend, would not be pleasant."

Wow. Gray could see the family resemblance now. Beth practically glowed as she laid down the law to him. Gone was the quiet, shy person and in her place was a lioness protecting her cub. Even though she was calling him on the carpet, he couldn't help but be impressed.

"Beth, I know this sounds a bit cliché, but I only have the best of intentions where your sister is concerned. You have nothing to be concerned about. I intend to find a house that Suzy will be comfortable in while she recovers, and she'll have everything she needs. If you would feel better living with us, I'd be more than happy to have you."

The spark seemed to leave Beth as fast as it had come and she returned to her former quiet manner. "Thank you, Gray, but I'll be fine. I will be over daily to help, though, and I'll be here tomorrow morning to help you, um . . . finalize your plans with her."

Gray laughed as he read the underlying message in her expression: *Good luck with that.* "Thanks, Beth. I plan to go look at houses, so if you could be here that would be great. We don't want to leave your sister alone to inflict damage onto the nursing staff, do we?" As Beth leaned over the bed to give her sister one last kiss before leaving, he stood, prepared to escort her to her car.

"Beth, I'll see you out. Suzy would have my head if I let you walk to your car in a dark and probably deserted parking lot."

He could see the protests forming on her lips. Beth obviously wasn't comfortable yet in his company. He opened the door and held it for her to precede him out. She was quiet as they walked down the hall to the bank of elevators. Gray decided to break the ice and asked her about her job.

"Well, I'm actually supposed to start working for Suzy tomorrow, but that doesn't look great right now. You do realize that she isn't going to stay at home while she's recovering, don't you? I'd give her maybe two days max before you are carting her to the office. It's not going to be pretty, but my sister isn't an idle person. In fact, she'll probably be the patient of your nightmares." Beth chuckled.

Gray laughed along with her, knowing she spoke the truth. "We will cross that bridge when we have to, Beth, and thanks for the warning."

They reached the parking garage and Beth walked toward a bright red convertible VW. Gray was a bit surprised. Like her sister, there appeared to be more layers to Beth than he'd originally thought.

Beth turned to say good night to Gray. As she was getting in the car, she asked, "Your brother, he is just visiting, right?"

Gray stifled a groan at her question. *Dear lord, please don't let anything happen between Beth and Nick. Suzy would kill Nick and then move on to kill me.* His baby brother was a love-'em-and-leave-'em type of guy. He was so charming that women seemed to love him even as he showed them to the door. Somehow he didn't think the Denton sisters would feel that affection for Nick should he do the same to Beth.

He pondered lying to her but knew that if she was going to work with Suzy she'd be seeing Nick around the office. "Actually, Beth, we are both moving here. Jason wants us at headquarters now, especially with Claire having the baby soon. Jason plans to take time away to spend with his family and I'd like for him to be able to have that."

Beth felt her heart drop. She'd just met Nick tonight; why did she care whether he was coming or going? Now Gray probably thought she had a big crush on him as well. The way Nick stared at her made her self-conscious. She felt like the old Beth again, wondering if her clothes made her look big or if her dress was clinging to her hips. Nick was drop-dead gorgeous and she was Beth, a frumpy, former fat girl with nothing to offer a man like that. She noticed Gray studying her, almost as if reading her mind. "Good night, Gray, I'll see you in the morning."

Gray watched Beth buckle herself in the car, and with a quick wave, she was gone. He walked back into the hospital and made a mental note to have a serious talk with his brother in the morning. Better to stop trouble now before it came calling later.

Chapter Six

Suzy woke up feeling as if her bladder was going to explode. She looked around the darkened room in confusion. Where the hell was she? When she tried to sit up, pain stabbed through her. She stifled a scream as she noticed a dark head lying on the side of her bed. Suddenly, it all came back to her, and she knew who was sleeping at her bedside. Gray, always Gray. She couldn't escape him any longer. He'd haunted her every waking moment for months and now here he was in the flesh. Fate is a cruel mistress. Instead of a night of hot sex as planned, she'd fallen down a flight of steps like some klutz. Apparently, Claire was rubbing off on her. Her friend had at least one accident a day, which Suzy had always found rather amusing; now the shoe was on the other foot.

"I can practically hear your mind racing from here."

Suzy snorted. Did he always have to sound so sexy? Just once couldn't he have a squeak in his voice or something? That deep, sexy rumble made her want to start panting. "It's not my mind racing, babe; it's my bladder. If you could step out for a moment, while I go to the bathroom that would be great."

Gray flipped on the bedside light and she blinked like an owl, trying to adjust to the sudden brilliance. He walked over to the bedside and started lowering the side bar of the bed. "What're you doing?"

"Well, unless you want to pole vault out of bed, I'm going to help you." When Gray had the side lowered, he leaned down and started sliding his hands under her hips.

Suzy stiffened in shock, sputtering, "What do you think you're doing, slick?"

"Relax, princess. I'm not attacking your beautiful body. I'm carrying you to the bathroom." Then lowering his voice, Gray murmured, "When I want your body, you will know it, I promise."

Shivers ran down her spine as she cleared her throat. "I can walk to the bathroom, Gray. I'm not an invalid."

"Baby, just let me help you. You're going to cause yourself a world of pain trying to prove your point, and I don't want to see that happen. I'm going to pick you up and set you inside and then carry you back to the bed. Are we clear?"

Being the intelligent person that she was, Suzy knew when to pick her battles. When you were about to pee all over yourself and it felt as if someone had stabbed you was not the time to stage a standoff. She closed her mouth and linked her arms around his neck as he gently picked her up. He held her against him with one hand and rolled the IV stand with the other. At the best he could do, it was still an excruciating trip, and she stayed on the toilet longer than necessary trying to recover enough to return to the bed.

Suzy had to give Gray credit. He made an incredible nurse. He was gentle, caring, and smelled good enough to eat. If not for all the pain she was in, she'd be seriously tempted to pull him down in the bed on top of her and finally take care of this ache she had inside whenever he was near. Heck, she could almost have an orgasm just hearing his sexy voice on the phone. She could only imagine how good the real thing would be.

When Gray had her settled back into the bed, he called the nurse and asked for more pain medication despite her protests. She needed to think clearly where he was concerned, and how could she do that when she was constantly in la-la land? The nurse came in and quietly injected medication into her IV. When she left, Suzy looked at Gray in a haze and said, "You know I'm not staying with you." She tried to hang on a little longer to finish her sentence, just barely managing, "And I'm not falling in love with you, Gray."

As she finished those last words, Gray held her hand to his lips and pressed a kiss against the palm, whispering, "I'm afraid you have to. From the moment we met, I ceased to exist without you. You've put me off as long as I can take. Ready or not, Suzanna, I'm coming for you, and I don't intend to stop until I have you . . . forever."

The next morning Gray left the hospital when Beth arrived. He'd convinced a real estate agent to show him some properties bright and early. Within two hours, he was signing papers to make the third house his. The house was unoccupied, so he'd be able to move in immediately. Gray's offer well above the asking price had the Realtor and the owner anxious to accommodate anything that he needed, so he could keep all the furnishings, for the time being. Later, when Suzy was settled in, he'd be happy to let her change anything that she wanted. But for now, it was a bonus to be able to move right in. He called Nick and asked that he handle having his personal items moved from the penthouse to the new place and also to stock it with supplies. He'd then talked to Beth about packing some items for Suzy.

As he was getting into his car, his cell phone rang. Afraid it was the hospital, he didn't even glance at the caller ID, instead answering it on the first ring. His blood ran cold as a mocking voice filled his ear. "Well, hello, my darling. Have you missed me?"

"Reva, how did you get this number?"

Laughter filled his ear as she said, "You should know by now, Gray, what I want, I get. I told you when you broke up with me that I wouldn't just tuck my tail and run like all the other women you have thrown away."

"I didn't break up with you, Reva. That would imply that we had a relationship, which we didn't. We went out for less than a month." What Gray didn't add was the only reason it had lasted that long was because he was desperate to take his mind off Suzy. It hadn't taken long to figure out the whole "love the one you're with" thing didn't work for him.

He'd met Reva at a launch party for an author friend four months ago. Warning bells should have been ringing wildly at the way she pursued him all evening before he finally agreed to have dinner with her the following evening. Truthfully, he'd had little interest in Reva, and he was paying the price now for letting it get out of hand. They'd gone out to dinner a few times, and he'd been her escort to various charity functions over the course of a month. Finally, after several weeks of pressure from her, they had ended up in bed together. Gray knew that it was a mistake as soon as it had happened, and he ended things afterward. Even if Suzy wasn't in his life, he had no desire to become seriously involved with Reva.

That had been the start of months of hell. To say that she hadn't taken it well would be an understatement. Gray had tried to be understanding because, in truth, he felt guilty for letting it go that far to start with. Unlike his brother, Nick, Gray wasn't the type to sleep around. When he was involved with a woman it was exclusive and they always parted as friends. Never had he been faced with a woman who hated him afterward.

After several weeks and hundreds of phone calls, emails, and appearances at his office, Gray had had enough. He tried one last time to reason with her on the telephone and then had notified security back in Charleston to nicely but firmly turn Reva away when she showed up at Mericom. He'd changed his home and cell phone numbers and had informed security at his condominium. For a week, life was peaceful. Then Reva somehow had his new cell phone number, and the phone calls and threats had started again. He'd changed his cell phone number at least five times, and each time she had it within days. He also received various hate mails at his office and home. Friends looked uncomfortable and embarrassed as they told him the latest lies that Reva had spread within their social circle.

Still, Gray was hesitant to involve the police. He felt as if he'd somehow caused the problem even though he'd never been anything but honest with Reva. There had been no promises made and he'd always treated her well. He'd also wanted to avoid the negative publicity that was sure to come when something like this came out. Even though Jason had encouraged him to take proper steps to protect himself, he still hated to open Danvers up to this type of publicity so soon after the merger. The most important reason, however, was his fear of Suzy finding out. Logically, he knew she couldn't expect that he hadn't seen other women since he met her. They were not dating; hell, he'd never even kissed her. Their foreplay had spanned over a year, and he thought maybe she was coming to terms with the inevitability of their involvement.

Something inside him said that she'd feel betrayed by his sexual involvement with another woman. Truthfully, he even felt that he'd betrayed her when there was no reason why he should feel that way. To his knowledge, Suzy hadn't been involved with anyone since her breakup with her fiancé. He'd dated a few times casually since meeting her. In the beginning, he saw her very little and they lived miles apart so it was more of an infatuation. As the merger between Meri- com and Danvers became reality, he was in Myrtle Beach at the Danvers headquarters at least once a week, and suddenly he was seeing Suzy regularly. He asked her out each time he saw her and, each time, she told him no.

In the last few months, though, something seemed to have changed. Even though she hadn't spoken the words, Gray could feel the softening in her attitude toward him. She still tried to hide behind her sassy mouth, but much of the heat had gone out of her com- ments. When he had asked her out yesterday he'd known that something would happen between them that evening. Of course, instead of sex, Suzy damn near broke her neck. Boy, couldn't a guy catch a break?

Apparently, the silence on his end of the phone line

had finally irritated Reva enough to end her rant and hang up. Gray knew it was just a matter of time before the next call. Another phone number would soon be required. He was starting to question whether he was doing the right thing trying to handle this on his own. He hoped that with his permanent move to Myrtle Beach, Reva would soon lose interest when he was no longer easily harassed.

Chapter Seven

"For God's sake, Beth, if you don't help me get in that bathroom to bathe and wash my hair I'm going to kick your butt all the way to kingdom come when I get off these damn crutches."

With a sigh, Beth said, "I don't know why I thought pain medication would make you a pleasant patient. It obviously hasn't done a thing for your disposition. If you fall and break your neck along with your ankle, I don't want to hear any complaining." With that remark, Beth walked over to the bed and leaned down so that Suzy could loop an arm around her neck. "Geez, and I thought I was the fat one. Does this cast add like fifty pounds or something? I thought it was a soft cast."

Beth received an obscene hand gesture for her comment. "You're not fat, Beth. If you get any thinner, I'll be able to hold both your feet together and pick my teeth with you. Now zip it and let's get this party started."

Flattered by her sister's assessment of her thin size, Beth was ready to carry her over her shoulder if necessary. They made it to the bathroom and she helped Suzy sit on the shower seat. "Umm, how are we supposed to keep the water off your bandages?"

Crap, she hadn't thought ahead. After making it this

far, Suzy wasn't going to be denied a shower. "Okay, unroll the bandages, Beth. As soon as we finish we can just put them back on. We are two pretty intelligent women. I know we can do this."

"Suzy, I don't know. I think there is actually a reason for them."

Waving her hand impatiently, Suzy said, "Suck it up, sis, and start unrolling. What're they going to do if they find out, break my leg or something?"

"All right, but please note that I'm doing this under protest." Beth started with the ankle first, trying not to show her reaction to the swollen and discolored nature of her sister's usually dainty ankle. It looked like it could pass for one of Barney's ankles or cankles now. Beth was starting to feel confident as she made quick work of the ankle bandage and turned her attention to removing her sister's nightgown. When she was halfway finished, Suzy suddenly screamed and her face turned white. "Oh, God, did I hurt you?"

Suzy's hand was trembling as she raised it as if to brace herself. Suddenly, the bathroom door flew open and Gray stood in the doorway, disbelief on his face. "What in the hell are you doing? Have you lost your mind? Beth, go press the button and tell the nurse to get in here, now!"

Even though his tone was hard, his hands were gentle as he grabbed Suzy's robe off the hanger on the wall and gently wrapped it around her shoulders. He ran his hand down her cheek, his eyes bright with something that she couldn't look away from. "Baby, what have you done? I can't leave you alone for a minute, can I?"

At that moment, Beth returned with a nurse in tow.

She brushed them both aside to survey the damage. "Ms. Denton, what were you thinking? You could have seriously injured yourself. Let me call another nurse so that we can lift you back into bed."

"No," Suzy mumbled. She looked at Gray in the doorway and lifted her arms. No matter how much she denied her feelings for him, she knew he was her safe haven. She needed him right now like she needed to breathe. *It's probably just the drugs; no way does he look this good all the time; that wouldn't be fair to the rest of the male population.*

Gray gently lifted her and took slow steps until he deposited her back on the bed. The nurse left and returned with more bandages and pain medication. Soon Suzy was drifting away as the nurse began the task of replacing what they had removed.

With Gray staring a hole in her, Beth lowered her head and said, "I know what you're thinking, and you're right. In my defense, though, you don't know how hard it is to say no to my sister when she makes up her mind."

Gray softened because he knew just exactly what Beth had been up against. Suzy wasn't a woman to take no for an answer. "I know, Beth. I'd have had a hard time saying no, too. I believe she's probably learned a lesson. How's she been today?"

"She's better. This is the first pain medication she's taken even though they've stressed that she needs to keep it at a constant level for pain management. I know she's hurting, but she's determined to fight it. Were you able to find a house today?"

"Yes, the papers have been signed and it's move-in

ready. I was able to keep the furnishings so Suzy should be comfortable. Did you bring a suitcase with you for her?"

"Yes, I have it in my car. When they release her, we can transfer it to your vehicle."

"Beth, I meant what I said. You're more than welcome to stay with us. I don't want you to feel like you're being excluded. Your sister needs you."

Touched by his concern for her, Beth smiled and said, "Really, Gray, it's fine. You don't have to worry about me. I should be the one worrying about you. This isn't going to be easy. I'm going to give you my cell number, and when you're settled in I'd appreciate a phone call to let me know how the patient is faring."

The doctor arrived, and with one final check and a list of instructions, Suzy was cleared for discharge. By this time, Suzy was awake and Gray braced himself for the arguments that were surely coming over her new living arrangements.

"Oh, thank God. I'm so ready to get out of here. The décor is circa 1980s and it smells funny. The nurse keeps giving me an evil look. I think she spat in my fruit cup this morning. Please tell me your place is better than here, although it must surely be, because the bar hasn't been set very high."

Gray was temporarily at a loss for words. Prepared to threaten, plead, or bribe her to be reasonable, he was surprised that she was going along with the program so easily. Whatever she was taking must be good stuff. He decided to hurry before it wore off. Luckily, the nurse arrived and soon they were moving smoothly down the hall. Suzy and the nurse waited at the front door while he and Beth went to collect Suzy's suitcase and Gray's car.

Gray thanked Beth and promised to call her that evening. Soon he was pulling his car to the front and he then walked around to help Suzy into the passenger seat. It took some adjustments with the seat and some colorful cursing from Suzy before they were heading toward his new home.

Suzy tried to focus on her surroundings and wondered when exactly she'd lost her mind. She was in the car with Gray on her way to his house, where she'd apparently agreed to live until she recovered. Her hormones kicked into overdrive as she risked a side glance at him. Gray was one major hunk. He looked good and smelled even better. She had the desire to shut her eyes and just inhale his fragrance. He might think it a little strange if she suddenly started sniffing so she controlled the urge.

Gray had been wonderful since the accident. A part of her heart that she thought had been broken beyond repair by her sleazeball ex-fiancé, Jeff, had started to heal. Surely Gray had a flaw. She'd yet to find it, but it had to be there. Maybe living with him for a while would show her what type of person he was. He probably left the seat up on the toilet, the cap off the toothpaste, and his underwear on the floor. She knew she was attracted to him, and even though she didn't sleep around, she fully planned to have sex with him. There was just something so powerful between them. Suzy was having a hard time walking—or hobbling—away.

Chapter Eight

Suzy jolted out of her thoughts as Gray slowed the car at an intersection. Suzy recognized the tourist area as Garden City Beach. This was one of her favorite areas. Only a few miles from the huge crowds of Myrtle Beach, Garden City was small and quaint and attracted mainly families looking for a vacation spot with more family-friendly amenities and the freedom to enjoy the beach with a little more privacy than Myrtle Beach offered.

They were now heading away from the main hub of the hotels of Garden City and to the section with many privately owned houses on the beach. As they got farther away, the houses became more elaborate and more private. Suzy felt as if her heart would stop as Gray pulled into the drive of what she could only call her dream house.

When she was little, her parents hadn't really encouraged the whole fairy-tale thing. She'd always wanted to be a princess, but her parents only purchased practical, educational books for them and refused to buy any of the more fanciful ones that she and Beth preferred. Luckily, the school library provided an endless supply and, as most little girls do, Suzy had read them and dreamed of one day being one of the princesses from the books.

As she'd grown older, she'd buried her dreams and gone for the shock value of leather and lace. At least this was always guaranteed to get a reaction from her parents. Through the years, her provocative attire had become her signature and her shield. No one messed with a girl who could run a mile in six-inch heels.

The house where they pulled in brought all those hopes and dreams back from where she'd buried them long ago. It was a beautiful Victorian, complete with gables and a turret. The façade was a blue-gray with white trim and a veranda along the side of the house that disappeared around the back. It was, quite simply, the house of her dreams and something she'd have never believed that Gray would choose. She pictured him in glass and steel, very contemporary and modern. Come to think of it, that was probably what he thought she'd select. This house was beautiful, unique and, yeah, she had to admit, almost magical. It was a castle for the modern girl who didn't require a moat or drawbridge.

Suzy realized that Gray had cut off the ignition and was studying her reaction. She forced herself to shut her mouth, which she knew was hanging open, and gave him a nervous smile. There was simply no way she could insult this house. "Gray, it's beautiful, but I'll admit, I'm surprised."

"Why is that? Were you perhaps expecting something with pink flamingos?"

With a chuckle, Suzy said, "Not exactly. I'd have expected something more modern. You're a big, rich, single guy on the prowl. This type of home might send the wrong message to your female fans. This house, although breathtaking, says, 'I want two-point-five kids and a new minivan in the driveway.'"

Gray studied her intently for a few moments and Suzy was powerless to turn away. He whispered one word that sent shivers down her spine: "Perfect."

Gray walked around to the passenger side and opened the door. "I'm going to run and unlock the door, and I'll be back to carry you."

Suzy tried to edge her way toward the door, hoping to at least be standing when Gray returned. The sharp pain took her breath away. When Gray returned, her face was white and her uninjured leg was hanging out the car door.

"Damn it, Suzanna. Couldn't you stay still for just two minutes?"

Unable to think of a snappy comeback, Suzy settled instead for sticking her tongue out at him. Childish, maybe. Satisfying, definitely.

Gray slid his hands under her as gently as he could and eased her out of the car. Each step he took caused a jarring pain in her ribs, but she kept her lips tightly pursed, determined not to look weak.

If Suzy thought she was in love with the house from the outside, the interior made it pale in comparison. The house had an open floor plan and soaring ceilings. The walls were painted a warm, pale yellow and a chandelier in the foyer bounced light off the shining hardwood floors. "I know you would like to look around, but I think for now it would be best to get you settled in for some rest. Maybe later if you feel up to it, I'll carry you around for a tour. Would you prefer the bed or couch in the family room?"

"The couch, I think. I'm tired of lying in the bed."

Gray carried her through the foyer and into another

brightly lit room with the same color scheme. There was a floor-to-ceiling stone fireplace on one wall with built-in bookshelves on the connecting wall. A row of windows framed in a light-colored wood made up another wall. A set of double French doors was situated in the middle of the windows and appeared to lead out onto a back deck. Suzy could see some lounge chairs and patio furniture arranged in seating areas around a barbeque grill and the sparkling waters of the Atlantic Ocean in the background.

Gray walked over to a tan leather sofa and gently deposited her onto it. He carefully arranged two decorative pillows behind her head and then took another pillow and propped her injured ankle on it. Next, he grabbed a chenille throw from a nearby chair and covered her. When he was finished, he stood back to survey his work, but Suzy could no longer hide her grimace of pain. Seeing it, Gray squatted down beside the sofa and took her hand.

"You're in pain. Will you please take some medication now?"

Suzy wanted to say no. She was tired of the drugged feeling that the pain medication gave her. The ride from the hospital and then the trip into the house had been painful and much worse than she'd imagined. She nodded her head to Gray in agreement and decided that there was always tomorrow to be strong and take a stand; the only person to suffer today for her stubbornness would be her.

Gray soon returned with a glass of water and a pill. He used his hand to support her head so that she wouldn't have to jar her body again. Suzy murmured a quiet thank-you and snuggled back into the couch cushions as best she could. Gray went to collect her luggage and she was dimly aware of him calling Beth and telling her that they had made it home. When he came back into the room a few moments later, Suzy's eyes were getting heavy and her thoughts were spinning.

With what she was certain was a dopey smile, she looked at Gray and said, "Thank you for everything. You've been so good during this mess, and I've never done anything to deserve your kindness." As if by great effort, she whispered, "I do care about you, though, but you scare me, Gray. You scare me so much."

With those final words, Suzy slipped off to sleep. Gray stood beside the sofa looking down into the face of the woman he loved more than life itself. The words that Suzy had spoken were a great admission for her. She wasn't likely to remember them when she woke again, but he would. He also knew what she'd said was true. He felt certain that Suzy more than cared for him—she loved him. Her heart, though, was damaged. She gave it years ago to her parents and they treated it with nothing but criticism and indifference. Then she'd taken one more chance and given it to Jeff and he shattered it. Repairing that heart and taking it as his own had been a long road and was far from over. He'd not have wished her harm in a million years, but the one positive to come from this accident was that Suzy's running days were over. She was here with him now, and he intended to show her that they were each other's forever after.

Suzy awoke to a wonderful smell, and her nose twitched in appreciation. At first, she was disoriented from the unfamiliar surroundings, and it took her several minutes to put the pieces together again. She was with Gray at his home. Apparently, he'd either left for takeout or had something delivered, and whatever it was, it smelled delicious. Her stomach rumbled in appreciation.

Soon, the object of various fantasies and a lot of denial came into view. "Oh good, the patient is awake. I thought you might be hungry by now."

Suzy surveyed Gray's casual attire and hadn't thought it possible for her mouth to water any more than it already was. . . . She was wrong. The man might look like a *GQ* model in a suit, but in jeans he was drop-dead gorgeous. He was wearing a Nike T-shirt and jeans that were faded from use and lovingly hugged his physique. *Great. I look like a hag, smell even worse, and he looks as fresh as a daisy. Where is the justice in the world?*

"Are you ready for something to eat? It's just simple vegetable soup and grilled-cheese sandwiches. I thought we would have something light and then maybe a slice of lemon pound cake later this evening if you like."

"Wow, I'm impressed. When did you go out to pick all that up?"

Gray looked at her and laughed. "I didn't pick it up, I made it."

Impressed despite herself, Suzy said, "Wow. Now, opening the soup can and making a sandwich I can see, but actually using a cake mix is more than most men I know could handle."

Obviously amused by her statement, Gray said, "Prepare to be blown away then. I didn't open a can—its homemade soup—and I didn't use a mix; I made the cake from scratch. Now, while you tuck that bottom lip that's hanging open back in, I'm going to go collect our trays."

When Gray returned, he set two trays containing steaming bowls of soup, sandwiches, and iced tea on the coffee table. He grabbed another pillow, and positioned it behind her head as gently as possible. Then he picked up a tray and arranged it on her lap.

Suzy looked down at the tray, "Holy shit, you have got to be kidding me! There is only one thing that I haven't seen yet that could be wrong with you."

A smile of supreme masculine confidence crossed Gray's face as he leaned over her on the couch and put his lips to her ear. "Sweetheart, if you're looking for a flaw, I promise you, it's not *that*. As you will soon find out." Shivers ran down her spine as his warm lips paused to trace the contours of her ear and then dropped a brief kiss onto her lips before straightening up.

Her heart raced, and heat rushed through her body at the feel of his lips on hers. *Good grief, girl, get it together. He barely touched you and you're ready to roll your injured body off the couch and ride him like Seabiscuit. Geez.* Suzy hoped the throw would hide the fact that her nipples were now standing at full attention. If a simple kiss could do this to her, she could only imagine how it would feel to have Gray inside her. *Stop, before you experience your first thought-induced orgasm.*

Suzy cleared her throat as she looked down at the tray that Gray had arranged on her lap. "I'm impressed, slick, I really am. If I didn't know better, I'd say you actually cut up all these vegetables yourself."

Gray sat in a chair and tried to settle his tray over the throbbing bulge in his jeans. The feel of her lips still burned on his. To think that if not for the accident, he'd already know her body as well as he knew his own. Living with her and being unable to make love to her would be equal parts of heaven and hell.

Gray pointed to the large, flat-panel television mounted over the fireplace and said, "If you aren't too tired, I thought we could watch a movie after dinner. I'm even willing to do a chick flick for you."

"Hey, it's Thursday, right? What time is it?"

Gray quickly checked his watch, worried by the urgent tone in her voice. "It's just after seven. Did you have prior plans? I'll grab my phone when we finish dinner if you need to make a call." *Surely, she didn't have a date. Damned if I'll have her in my home making her apologies to another man.*

"No, nothing like that, the Gamecocks are playing tonight on ESPN. Do you mind if we watch that instead? I have season tickets and I never miss a game if possible. If you don't like football, maybe I could watch it in the bedroom."

Gray couldn't help it; he threw his head back and laughed. Here he was trying to earn points with her by watching a romantic movie without complaint and she wanted to watch a college football game. If he didn't already love her, this would do it for him. Every time he thought he knew her, he found another layer. What you saw with Suzy wasn't even close to what you got. "I really had my heart set on *Sleepless in Seattle*, but for you, I'll sacrifice. Meg Ryan will always be there tomorrow."

"You're messing with me, right?" Suzy took a bite of her soup while waiting for his answer and almost swooned in pleasure. "You know what? I don't even care if you're a little light in the loafers, this soup more than makes up for it. Where did you learn to cook like this?"

"Light in the loafers—now that's something I've never been accused of." Gray couldn't remember laughing this much in an evening in years. The things that came out of her beautiful mouth were a constant source of amusement. She'd questioned his manhood at least twice this evening. That had to be some type of record. He'd so enjoy showing her that he was all the man she'd ever need.

"My mother believed that we should never be dependent on someone else to take care of us. Nick and I learned to cook at an early age. My parents, although financially secure, didn't believe in having others take care of them. Nick and I planned, shopped for, and prepared dinner once a week for the family. Everything had to be made from scratch and sandwiches were not allowed. My mother loved to cook, and I find I enjoy it as well. It's a great stress reliever. Of course, with my busy schedule, I don't have time to cook every evening, but when I do, I much prefer it to dining out."

Despite herself, Suzy was impressed. Gray was nothing like she'd imagined. She always pictured him as an uptight rich guy with an uptight rich family. While she enjoyed the rest of her meal, she said, "Tell me more about your parents. What was it like growing up?"

A warm feeling spread through Gray at Suzy's interest in his life. She'd always been so careful to maintain a distance between them. He knew she was trying to protect herself from being hurt again and he'd tried to give her the time that she needed. She'd knocked him on his ass the first time they'd met and time had done nothing to change that.

"My parents are wonderful. Nothing like you'd expect. You will love my mother. You never know what's going to come out of her mouth. She's outspoken, funny, and always finds a positive in something or someone. She's very affectionate, but doesn't mind busting our balls . . . um, giving us a piece of her mind when she feels we deserve it. She reminds me a lot of you actually, well, minus the leopard skin. My father is her opposite. He's quiet and dotes on my mother like some poor sap. She in turn treats him like a king. Don't get me wrong, my father can be ruthless in business and is very shrewd, but where my mother is concerned, he's putty in her hands. Even after all these years, you would swear they're newlyweds."

Suzy smiled at the love she could hear so plainly in Gray's voice, and waited for him to continue. "My mother's favorite quest of the moment is to see her boys, as she still calls us, settled down and happy. She feels that there may be hope for me, but she has a long road ahead with Nick. He's the baby of the family, and even though he has a hard time keeping his pants zipped, she can't stay mad at him. Nick's charm makes him a favorite with all the ladies, even our mother." Affection was apparent in his voice; there wasn't a hint of jealousy that Suzy could detect.

"It sounds like you have a wonderful family, Gray. You're very lucky." With a smile, she continued. "I don't think anyone could ever accuse our parents of doting on each other or us. Displays of affection make them uncomfortable." She paused to gather her thoughts, and said, "They aren't bad people. Work is their life and I accepted that long ago. Like most kids, I rebelled as often as I could, but it doesn't change anything. I think at one point, they seriously considered trying to get a grant to study me because I so confused them. But after many years, we all adapted to each other and the rest, as they say, is history."

Gray didn't think it was as simple as Suzy made it out to be, but she clearly didn't want to talk about her parents anymore, and he respected her wishes. "If you're all done, I'll clean up and find your football game on the television."

Suzy let out a groan and said, "If you don't help me to the bathroom, Gray, I'm going to christen this couch for you in style."

He grabbed her tray and set it back on the table. "I'm sorry; it's been a while."

"Maybe I could try to walk this time if you help me up?"

With a leer, Gray said, "I don't think so. Give a guy a break. This is the only thrill I'm getting right now."

Suzy couldn't help herself—she laughed and then clutched her ribs as the pain pierced her. *Okay, note to self, no fun of any kind until I'm well.* She waved Gray off as concern filled his eyes. "It's okay. Just try not to be so amusing. Now, please carry me to the bathroom before I embarrass myself right here."

Gray gently picked her up and Suzy finally got a glimpse of more of the house as he carried her down a long hallway with the same color scheme as the living area they had just left. The hallway appeared to only have one set of double doors at the end. Suzy was intrigued. Surely, the bathroom didn't take up one entire end of the house. As they approached the doors, Suzy could see that the room was plainly a bedroom and, obviously, the master.

"Wow, now this is impressive." The room was huge and contained a full seating area with a leather couch, matching chair and ottoman, and built-in bookcases. A king-size bed dominated the center of the room, with a wall of windows to the right. The room was painted a taupe color with white trim and a gray ceiling. A wrought-iron chandelier was suspended from the ceiling in the middle of the room. There appeared to be matching wrought-iron bedside lamps. The room was cozy, yet elegant. You would feel comfortable kicking off your shoes and cuddling up with a good book on one of the couches, but still be proud to show off this room. A fireplace, similar in design to the one in the living room, stood on the wall at the foot of the bed. Another huge, flat-panel television dominated the space above the mantel. You gotta love people who know how to enjoy television.

Gray paused to let her look around for a few moments, and continued on to the master bath. "You do know that I'm going to have to, um . . . help you here, right?"

Suzy wanted to laugh again; Gray was actually almost stuttering. Had the man never seen a woman in panties before? He did it at the hospital, but she'd made him leave the light off until he left the bathroom. She was also wearing a gown then and didn't need his help pulling her pants back up. Oh, shit, no wonder he was stuttering, this was going to get bad.

"How about I get your nightgown from your bag? We might as well get you changed while we're in here."

As he started to leave, Suzy stopped him. "Hey, I'm all for changing, but I have to use the bathroom now; I can't wait. We can figure the clothes thing out next. Put me next to the wall, and I can lean against it on my good ankle while you pull my pants down. Then maybe you could help me sit." *Did I actually say that with a straight face? I just asked Gray to pull my pants down and put me on the toilet; I'm officially in hell.*

Gray moved toward the wall closest to the toilet and put Suzy on her feet. He felt her wince as the move jarred her body. He squared his shoulders and tried to stop the shaking in his hands. He'd helped her at the hospital, but that was different. Being in this house alone with her was much more intimate. This was like opening the Christmas present you had always wanted and then being told not to play with it. *Get a grip, man; you don't lust after someone who is hurt. Think like a doctor; you aren't affected by a pair of panties. Please let them be granny panties, please.*

He avoided eye contact as he leaned down and grasped the edge of her jogging pants, easing them along her legs. *Holy mother, a thong!* Gray could feel sweat starting to break out on his forehead. The thought of hooking his fingers under the edge of her lacy black panties was almost more than he could bear. Averting his gaze, Gray pulled her panties down, helped her onto the toilet and then fled the bathroom like the hounds of hell were after him.

He stopped outside the bathroom door, panting like he'd just run a marathon. This wasn't the way he'd envisioned removing Suzy's clothing. He kept telling himself that she was hurt and he shouldn't be standing outside the bathroom door with a hard-on so painful the zipper of his jeans was almost cutting him in two. As much as he loved having her here, there was going to be more than one person suffering while she recovered.

Wow. Suzy had never seen a man run from a half-naked woman so fast. After being used to Gray taking every opportunity to touch her, this was a little surprising. If she had to, she'd crawl to the shower tomorrow. Skip bathing, brushing your hair, throw on sweatpants, and the man ran like hell. Was she really such a turnoff right now? Glancing down at herself, she knew the answer was yes. There was no way she'd want to do her if she were a guy.

So, okay, she had a broken ankle, and her body felt like it had been run over by a tanker truck, but was that any reason to let herself go? Where did these sweats even come from? She had a strict policy against pants with elastic. She'd make an exception for a pair of skin-tight leggings. But come on, there was nothing sexy about what she was wearing now. Surely, Beth packed some of her better clothing.

Suzy was determined to stand and pull up her own pants before Gray returned. She managed to hold on to the wall and pull herself up. With a lot of pain, and even more cursing, Suzy finally had her pants up. She gave a shout of victory and was in the middle of a fist pump when Gray burst through the door with her nightgown clutched in his hand. She was probably a bad person, but she couldn't help it and started laughing at the absurdity of the situation. She was standing in the bathroom with the man who had haunted her dreams for months. He looked hot enough to make her one good ankle buckle, and she'd picked better-looking things than her off the bottom of her shoes. She hurt in places she didn't know existed, but she just wanted to feel his mouth on hers, right here in this bathroom.

Gray looked into her eyes, and couldn't miss the heat there. He had been terrified when he heard her shout as he walked back to the bathroom with her gown. He fully expected to see her sprawled on the floor, further injured. When he threw the door open and saw the triumph on her face, and her fist waving in the air, he was captivated. His throat had swelled as his emotions took over. She'd never looked more beautiful to him than at that moment. He could see the answering desire in her eyes as her laughter faded and her gaze locked on his. He walked slowly toward her, reaching up to caress her cheek.

"Baby, I'm going to kiss you, and I really don't want our first real kiss to be in the bathroom." His voice going husky, Gray continued. "Let's get you changed and whatever else you need to do in here and then I'm going to tuck you into bed."

With Gray's help, Suzy was soon changed into a comfortable, lilac, silk baby-doll gown that ended above her knees. Gray stepped back and studied her, saying wryly, "Couldn't be a granny gown, right?"

As Suzy leaned against the corner of the vanity for support, she smiled up at him and said, "Besides today's sweats, have I ever given you a reason to think I'd own or wear something with the word *granny* in it?"

With a laugh, Gray said, "No, you certainly haven't. Let's get finished up in here so you can watch your game."

"Sure, that sounds good." *The only game I have any interest in right now is rounding third base with you, tight buns.* Suzy did her best to hide all the naughty thoughts racing through her mind as she brushed her teeth and Gray took a washcloth and gently wiped her face. *If he doesn't take me in the bedroom and kiss me now, I'm going to suck his bottom lip between mine before he can set that washcloth down.*

Gray reached down to pick her up and, even though she protested, he insisted on carrying her to the bedroom, where he deposited her gently on the bed. He'd turned the covers back and had a mountain of pillows propped up for her. He sat down on the edge of the bed beside her, reaching out a hand to stroke the line of her jaw before finally moving to her lips. His thumb rubbed gently back and forth as his eyes locked with hers as if waiting for her to pull away. Suzy reached up and put her hand over his, telling him better than words how much she wanted his touch.

Gray leaned over, never breaking eye contact, and gently pressed his lips to hers. Suzy felt her heart skip as a wave of heat threatened to incinerate her. Gray nipped lightly at her bottom lip, seeking entrance into the moist heat within. With a moan, Suzy opened her mouth to his, and shivered at the first contact of her tongue sliding against his. Gray laid siege to every corner of her mouth, as if discovering a treasure he'd long been denied. At that moment, Suzy wanted nothing more than to pull him fully against her and wrap her legs around him. Heat pooled between her thighs and desire ripped through her. She'd never known this burning desire, bordering on frenzy, to join her body with another. Gray released her mouth and was slowly trailing a line of kisses down her neck as his big hand came up to palm her breast through the thin silk of her gown.

The feel of Gray's hand on her breast was driving her insane. She reached up for Gray to bring them into closer contact and gasped as pain ripped through her. He jerked back as if scalded. "Oh, God, baby, I hurt you, didn't I? I'm so sorry." His face was flushed, and his eyes were wild as he looked down at her trying to locate the source of her pain.

Suzy's heart broke at the obvious guilt on his face. She took his hand in hers, softly saying, "It's not your fault, Gray. I was so, um . . . excited that I twisted the wrong way trying to get closer to you." Looking him directly in the eye, she added, "I don't regret it, though. It was well worth the pain to feel your mouth on mine and your hand against me." She pulled his hand to her breast so he could feel the hard peak of her nipple, leaving him no doubt that she spoke the truth.

Gray brushed a soft kiss against her mouth, leaving his hand on her breast another moment before removing it. He went to the kitchen to get a glass of water and her medication and soon returned to her side. Despite her protests, he finally got her to take a pill and settled her back onto her pillows.

"Hey, how about putting the game on now. I'll curse like a sailor, argue over all the officiating calls and ignore you for hours. How does that sound?"

With a smile, Gray asked, "Isn't that supposed to be my line?"

"I believe in equality, slick; get used it to."

Gray turned on the television and found the game for her. He walked over to his own suitcase and removed some fresh clothing. "Do you think you'll be okay for a few minutes while I take a very cold shower?"

Suzy smiled at the rueful expression on his face. Her

gaze automatically dropped to the crotch of his jeans, and her eyes went wide. There was no hiding the outline of his arousal and Suzy had to fight the urge to moan. "Um . . . yeah, you do seem to have a big problem there." Wiggling her eyebrows, she continued. "I'd love to help you with that; I was a Girl Scout, you know. I learned how to use a big stick to make fire."

Gray threw his head back and laughed until tears came to his eyes. This little slip of a woman continued to surprise him. She'd looked so small and fragile just moments ago, and now she sat in the bed with mischief dancing in her eyes, and she practically glowed. She was trying to take away the guilt that she knew he'd felt at her pain. "That's great to know, baby, but my stick already catches fire every time you're near." With one last look, Gray walked to the bathroom and left the door cracked to hear her if she needed him.

Chapter Nine

Gray stood in the shower, gritting his teeth as the icy jets of water blasted his overheated skin. He hadn't been kidding about the cold shower. He had been so consumed with his need for Suzy that he'd barely been able to leave the room. The reality of feeling her against him had been much more than any of his fantasies. Her tongue had tasted of pure honey as it hesitantly sought his, twirling around him as if finding a long-lost lover. His palm still tingled from the feel of her firm breast straining against it. If not for her cry of pain, he wasn't sure when, or if, he'd have been able to get control of himself. He'd always known there were hidden depths within her; he'd just had no idea how hot they burned.

After toweling off, Gray looked through the suitcases that Nick had dropped off for him earlier. Normally, he slept in either boxers or nothing at all, but tonight that would be dangerous. He was grateful that he kept a pair of lounge pants to wear around the house in the evenings. He pulled them and a T-shirt on. He toweled his hair enough to get by without digging through some suitcases for a dryer.

Reluctantly, he pulled his cell phone from the front of the toiletries bag where he'd stored it earlier. He had turned the ringer off, afraid that Reva would go on one of her mad calling sprees. Sure enough, there was a string of missed calls from a number he recognized as hers. He had to talk to Nick tomorrow to see if he'd found out anything. He was so tired of dealing with the whole mess. His life was finally going just as he'd hoped, and Reva could send it all crashing down. He could handle her messing with his life, maybe he even deserved it, but he would not allow her to cause Suzy any more pain. Reva would find out just how ruthless he could be if she threatened someone he loved.

Gray packed his phone away and went back into the bedroom. Suzy's eyes were barely slits as she struggled to hold them open. She plainly wanted to watch her game, but sleep was doing its best to claim her. He walked over to the bed and smoothed the hair off her brow. "Baby, why don't you let me turn this off so you can get some sleep?"

With a tired smile, she touched his arm and said, "Mmm, okay. I'm so sleepy."

Gray reached for the remote and clicked the television off. He'd thought he would sleep on the couch, so he'd be close enough to help Suzy if she needed him during the night. As he was walking away from the bed, Suzy whispered, "Gray, please stay with me."

He walked back to the bedside and said, "Baby, I am. I'm going to be right over there on the couch."

"No, Gray, sleep in the bed with me." With one last tired smile, she teased, "I promise not to feel you up during the night."

He knew this was going to be equal parts torture and bliss, but he was helpless to stop the anticipation of sleeping next to Suzy all night. He walked around and climbed in the other side of the bed. He wished he could pull her onto her side and snuggle, but settled instead for lying close to her and enfolding her hand in his.

Suzy woke him up one time during the night for a bathroom trip, and soon they were both back in bed soundly sleeping.

The sun gleaming through the windows woke Suzy early the next morning. Her first realization upon waking was of all the aches and pains in her body; the second was the male arm draped possessively over her stomach. She turned her head and studied Gray as he slept beside her. Just looking at him took her breath away. If a man could be called beautiful, he most certainly was. Even the shadow of stubble on his face just made him more handsome. His kiss last night had completely blown her away. Her reaction to him was something she'd never come close to feeling with Jeff. Gray had started a slow burn inside her the moment his lips met hers. If not for her damn injuries, there was no way she'd have stopped. She ached from frustration afterward just as he had.

Things seemed to be getting more intense with Gray. Part of her welcomed it, as if they had both known it was always destined to happen. The other part of her was still fighting the desire to run. Had she learned nothing from Jeff? Hadn't she told herself when he broke her heart and ground it under his heel like dirt that she'd never be put in that position again? Now, here she was lying in the bed with Gray, and Jeff was barely a distant memory. In another month, she'd probably be saying, "Jeff who?" Gray seemed to care about her; hell, he seemed to love her. Jeff, although considerate, had never acted as if she were the center of his world the way Gray seemed to. Jeff had often claimed to be too busy to go out to dinner or shopping, while Gray, even though he was a rich, powerful man, had dropped everything in his life to take care of her. Jeff would have never done that.

She had feelings for Gray; she'd known that for some time. Actually, she'd been denying that for some time. It wasn't just because he was handsome, although his hard, trim body was enough to make her toes curl; it was the man. He teased her, he pampered her, he cared for her, and he seemed to know what she needed when she needed it. With a sigh, Suzy continued to study Gray. *Yep, you still only have one hope left, girl. You better hope the main course is nowhere near as good as the appetizer. If it is, you're finished, game over.*

Gray slowly opened his eyes and allowed yesterday's events to surface. His arm was asleep and as he flexed it to get the circulation going, he felt the warm body underneath it. He became aware of two things at once: first, he was sleeping beside Suzy and, second, his morning wood was doing its best to drain every last drop of blood from his body and pool it there. Maybe he could sneak out of bed and get control of his body before Suzy woke up to see yet another tent in his pants. One more crack from her about making fire with a big stick would probably be his complete undoing.

Just as he was preparing to slide silently from the bed, a small hand settled across his arm, rubbing slowly. Gray sucked in a breath, and fire raced through his body. He decided that modesty wasn't going to get him anywhere. Rolling over on his back, he reached over and stopped Suzy's hand as it started up his arm. "I wouldn't start anything you can't finish, sweetheart, because as you can see, I'm already a loaded gun this morning and you're my trigger."

As Suzy followed the direction of his gaze, she could feel her face flush. Wow, if the size of that tent was any indication, her last hope that he was less than perfect was over. Gray was impressive in every area of his life apparently. *Come on, how much pain could hot, sweaty sex with a broken ankle cause? No pain, no gain, right?*

Gray slid a hand to her thigh, gently caressing it as he asked, "You look better today. How are you feeling this morning?"

When he touched her like that, she was unable to feel anything but pleasure and desire. "Bet— Better, as long as I don't move too much."

With an indulgent smile, Gray said, "If you're a good girl, I'll help you shower today. Beth is bringing by some things, including a shower seat, so we can get you bathed. Not that you need it or anything," he said, smirking. "I'll also call the hospital and find out when your hard cast will be put on. The doctor said you would have more mobility when you got the cast and the walking boot. Nick is coming over today as well to go over a few things from the office. I guess I should get dressed. Are you ready for your ride to the bathroom?"

With a dramatic groan, Suzy said, "Oh, yes, please. I'll never take going to the bathroom for granted again."

Gray slid out of bed and was thankful for baggy lounge pants. They didn't provide complete cover, but it kept things R-rated at least. He walked over and picked Suzy up, enjoying the feel of her warm body in his arms. He resisted the urge to kiss her until he'd at least brushed his teeth. He deposited her near the toilet with her assurance that she could take it from there. He left the door slightly ajar so that he could hear her if needed. Within a few moments, he heard the water in the sink running. Opening the bathroom door, he scowled at her. "How, might I ask, did you make it all the way to the sink?"

Obviously pleased with herself, Suzy said, "I hopped."

With an exasperated sigh, he said, "Suzanna, are you trying to kill yourself? You knew I was right outside the door. Didn't it hurt to jar yourself like that?"

"Well, kind of, but I can't depend on you for everything, Gray. I need crutches or one of those cool, jazzy chairs. You don't happen to have their eight-hundred number handy do you?"

Gray walked over to the double sinks and grabbed his own toothbrush, careful to keep an eye on Suzy in case she started to slip. When they were both finished, Gray picked her up again and returned to the bedroom. "I'll find us some clothing in a moment, but first things first. Good morning, baby." He lowered his head, fastening his lips onto hers.

Suzy sighed in pleasure at the first touch of his tongue against her teeth. She parted them for him and he slid inside. The cool taste of mint from his toothpaste invaded her mouth and Suzy thought she'd never tasted anything so good. No corner of her mouth was left unexplored as Gray's tongue ravaged her. She reached up and buried her hand in the springy softness of his dark hair, teasing his scalp with a scrape of her fingernails.

Suzy felt a shudder run through his body as he pulled his mouth from hers. He laid his forehead against hers, breathing deeply. "That's why I kissed you standing up; I knew I couldn't let it go too far in this position. If we were sitting or lying, I'd have my hands all over and inside that beautiful body right now, and you're not well enough for that yet."

"Oh, Gray, I . . ."

Suddenly, an amused voice boomed out in the room, stopping Suzy in midsentence. "Hi, boys and girls. What's going on here today?"

Almost dropping Suzy in his haste, Gray spun around and glared at his brother. "Don't you know how to knock?" he snapped.

Unruffled by the tone of his brother's voice, Nick smiled and said, "I did, brother dear, but for some reason, you guys didn't hear me. Now I know why. It looks like you're both in bad shape."

Suzy couldn't help it, she knew she should be embarrassed, but she burst out laughing. "This would be Nicholas, I presume?"

Eyes so much like Gray's twinkled back at her. The resemblance didn't stop there. The Merimon brothers both had the same dark hair and athletic build. Nick wore his hair a bit longer than Gray, and it was obvious who was the serious one and who was the prankster.

Nicholas started into the room, extending his hand. "Call me Nick, and I must say, it's nice to finally see . . . er, meet you, Suzy." Gray didn't miss the quick sweep of his brother's eyes as he took in the length of leg exposed by Suzy's short gown.

Gray clenched his jaw and all but yelled, "Out, now!"

With one last smirk in their direction, Nick dropped his hand and strolled out, saying he'd go make some coffee. Gray quickly sat her on the edge of the bed, taking a deep breath. "Sorry about that. My brother doesn't have an ounce of class. Sadly, you're stuck with him. He's crude and rude, but he's family."

With a smile, Suzy said, "Nick seems great; he has my same offbeat sense of humor. Although, I'd have preferred he saw a little less of my naked butt than he probably just did in this short gown. Maybe we should dress before he comes back."

Gray grabbed her suitcase and put it on the bed beside her, and then looked through his own for fresh jeans and a polo shirt. He looked over his shoulder, giving her a questioning look as she swore. "More sweatpants? Are you kidding me? Where the hell is Beth getting this crap? These aren't my clothes."

Gray couldn't help but laugh as Suzy held a pair of blue sweatpants up as if they were a snake about to bite her. "Honey, I think she was just trying to get something you would be comfortable in. Your usual, um . . . attire might not be so . . . functional at this point."

Her eyes shooting daggers at him, Suzy snapped, "Gray, I have a broken ankle, not an allergic reaction to denim, leather, or suede. I can lie on the couch in anything. The last time I looked, I hadn't completely given up on fashion." Hanging her head, she said, "Go ahead and get me some Geritol and put me out to pasture. It's all over for me."

"I know what will cheer you up. I don't know how many times I've dreamed of asking you this, so here goes. Do you want to take a shower with me?"

Suzy's head jerked up in surprise. "Is this really the

time for shower sex, Gray? Your pervert of a brother is somewhere in the house, you know."

With a chuckle, Gray said, "I'm well aware of that, but I have to shower and I promised you one as well. I was going to wait for Beth to bring the shower seat, but I don't see why. There's a built-in seat in there and the showerhead is detachable. We can put a garbage bag around your cast to keep it from getting wet. You can sit and I'll wash your hair, and, baby, I'll be glad to soap you as well."

Suzy was torn. She wanted to bathe more than she wanted anything at the moment, but full-on nudity in the shower with Gray—that was a bit more intimate that she was ready for.

"I can see the wheels turning in that mind. I'll wear my boxers, and you can take a towel with you to cover up anything you need to. How about that?"

Suzy's smile dazzled him with its brilliance. "That sounds wonderful. Let's do it, Gray. Let's shower to-gether."

Gray went to the kitchen to get a trash bag and when he returned, she said, "Please lock the door; I don't want to have to face Nick again in a compromising po-sition."

Gray gathered their clean clothing and went to start the shower. He soon returned for her, and after wrap-ping her ankle in the bag, he insisted on once again carrying her into the bathroom. He gently placed her against the wall beside the shower while he stripped down to his boxer briefs. Suzy's mouth went dry as she took a good look at a nearly naked Gray. *Oh, baby, if I were a dog, I'd be wrapped around his leg right now. Yum, yum!* There wasn't an ounce of fat anywhere on his lean body. He had six-pack abs that men would kill for, broad shoulders that were muscular but not bulky, and a narrow waist that connected to the most gorgeous set of buns she'd ever seen. In dress pants and jeans, his physique would stop traffic. In nothing but boxer briefs, he could start a riot. Suzy's palms itched to reach out and cup his butt, to see if it felt as firm as it looked.

Gray gritted his teeth at his body's reaction to Suzy's intense gaze. He didn't even think she was aware that she was staring and had been for what seemed like hours. He slowly reached out to grasp the hem of her gown to pull it up over her head and jerked her out of her dreamlike trance. She averted her gaze and asked him to hand her a towel. As he lifted her gown, she put the towel in its place. It was probably just as well; he wasn't sure he could handle being in such a confined space with her nude. He picked her up and placed her on the shower seat. "Are you ready to get started?"

"Oh, yes! Hit me, baby." Gray handed her a bar of soap and directed the water toward her chest. *Okay, so maybe that wasn't the best target area.* Suzy's breasts and nipples were clearly outlined through the towel. He tried his best to avert his gaze as she soaped the parts of her body that she could reach. He shifted her to the side and tilted her head so that he could wash her hair. By this time his heart rate had picked up considerably, and he was trying his best not to pant. Suzy had her eyes closed and had moaned in bliss a few times as he massaged the shampoo into her hair. With every moan she made, his boxers got a little tighter. There was no way he was making it through her recovery without a serious case of blue-balls. He quickly finished her hair and washed his own. When she handed him the bar of soap and asked him to wash her legs since she couldn't reach them, he thought he'd pass out.

In probably one of the most cowardly acts of his life, he put the bar of soap down and picked up the shampoo bottle. He aimed it at her legs and squirted a stream onto both of them. He then turned the spray of water toward them and washed the shampoo off. Suzy was staring at him, her eyes blinking at him like an owl. Holding up his hand, he said, "Don't ask. I'm only a man, baby, and not a very strong one right now." Gray reached around and turned the water off. Suddenly, a thought almost sent him into a panic. *I have to pick her up, and she's wet and naked. I'm going to embarrass myself.* No sooner had Gray finished that thought than he heard a knock at the bedroom door.

"Suzy, Gray, can I help you guys with anything?"

Gray had never been more grateful to hear Beth's voice. He told Suzy to stay put and jumped out of the shower. He stuck his head out of the bathroom door and yelled for Beth to give him a moment. He quickly dried off and dressed. He knew Suzy thought he'd lost his mind. He practically ran to the door and pulled Beth inside. "Perfect timing. Suzy just had a shower, and we could really use your help. Maybe you can dry her off and put a towel around her and I'll lift her out."

Beth tried to stifle the smile that threatened to overtake her face. This was the first time she'd seen Gray look anything other than poised. Even when Suzy was in the hospital, he still had an air of authority, a can-do, take-charge attitude. Now, he looked visibly disheveled. Apparently, one day of taking care of her sister had brought the poor man to his knees. Beth decided to take sympathy on him and briskly walked into the bathroom and retrieved a towel. She carefully stepped into the wet shower and smiled at her sister. Suzy had a smirk on her face and held her finger up to her lips. "Beth, I still have some soap on my legs and breasts, could you turn the water on and wash it off, please? You may need to use a washcloth to get it all."

Suddenly, something crashed and the sound of the bedroom door opening and slamming could clearly be heard. Beth looked at her with wide eyes, obviously wondering what was going on. "Um, okay, sure," she said.

Suzy burst into laughter, knowing she was an evil person but still unable to resist the temptation to torture Gray. She waved her hand to stop Beth from turning on the water and took a deep breath trying to control her laughter. "I'm fine Beth, just help me dry off."

Realization dawned in Beth's eyes as she too started laughing. "You're a bad person, you know that, right? That poor man has gone to hell and back for you." Between fits of laughter, she continued, "Let it be known that I object.

"So, evil one, how are you feeling today?" Beth asked. "You look better; the spark is back in your eyes. Oh, God, you didn't have sex last night did you?"

Suzy snorted and said, "Duh, thanks for your faith in me. But even I'd have found that impossible eight hours after getting out of the hospital. I sure wanted to, though. That man sets my underwear on fire anytime he's near."

"Um, yeah, thanks for all the sharing. I really need that visual when I look at him. I'd like to at least be able to be in the same room with one of the Merimon brothers. His brother, Nick, he gives me the creeps."

Surprised, Suzy looked at her sister. "Nick, why? I like him. Is he hitting on you or something?"

"Ugh, no. I'm not his type, I'm sure. He's just always staring at me like I'm some type of science experiment. No doubt, he's never spent much time around a woman who was bigger than a size three, and he's probably terrified I'll eat him or something."

Not for the first time, Suzy wondered if her sister's constant fat humor hid a serious problem. She studied her intently as Beth was leaning over to dry her. If possible, she looked even thinner, and despite her joking about women who were a size three, Suzy wondered if Beth was much more than that now. When they were alone without Gray and Nick being in the other room, Suzy vowed to have a serious talk with Beth. She didn't want to see her sister end up with an eating disorder.

"Bro, what're you getting yourself into here?" Gray looked over at his brother leaning against the kitchen counter and walked over to pour a cup of coffee. "In little more than twenty-four hours you have set up house."

"What's your point, Nick?"

"No point, really. Just hope you know what you're doing. I know how you feel about her, but your life is a little complicated right now. If you plan to continue, you need to come clean with her about Reva before she finds out on her own."

Gray's head jerked sharply up and he turned a steely gaze on his brother. "How would she find out? I know you aren't threatening to tell her."

"Chill out. Of course I'm not. I'm nervous, though, because we are no closer to finding out how Reva keeps getting your number than we were before. I just have a bad feeling about this, man. I don't think that woman is dealing with a full deck. I think we should get the police involved before this gets out of hand."

"Nick, what're the police going to do? She hasn't done anything other than make a nuisance of herself. Just keep at it and see if you can find out anything." Walking over to his brother, he laid a hand on his shoulder. "I appreciate the concern, but it's going to be okay."

Nick still looked like he wanted to argue, but wisely changed the subject. "Declan Stone is flying in today. Jason wanted to know if you could possibly get away for a few hours this afternoon so that the three of us could meet with him."

"If Beth is free to stay with Suzy, I should be able to. I need to pick up some papers at the office anyway. I'd like to see Declan in person. I think it's important to close the deal with him and bring him on board. He's more likely to do that if I'm there."

The merger of Danvers International with Mericom had created a communications giant headquartered in South Carolina. Both he and Nick had been pulled away from their base in Charleston, and were relocating to the corporate headquarters of Danvers in Myrtle Beach. Even with the promotion of key personnel in both Charleston and Myrtle Beach, the company was still short-staffed and he, Nick, and Jason were constantly being pulled in a million directions. The addition of Declan would be huge. He and Declan went way back. They had been college roommates and, even though Declan had made California his base for the last several years, they still remained in touch.

Declan had served two tours with the Air Force. Gray knew he'd spent a lot of that time in Afghanistan and Iraq. The Declan who came out of the military was a much darker and harder man than the friend he remembered from their younger days. He came from power and money, and after he left the military he'd used both as a base to launch his own consulting business. His specialty was mergers and acquisitions. He could smell a weak company a mile away and knew when it was prime for a takeover. He rarely considered a long-term assignment, and the fact that he was even willing to talk with Danvers about a permanent position was a testament to their friendship. With someone like him in place, Danvers would continue to grow and prosper beyond their wildest dreams.

Gray jolted as Nick said, "Hey, I think the princess is calling you."

Gray quickly set his coffee cup down on the counter and grabbed a chair from the kitchen table. He hurried back toward the bathroom and prayed that Suzy would be covered from head to foot now. Gray walked in the bathroom and set the chair down in front of the vanity. He stepped over to the shower and said a prayer of thanks that Suzy was indeed sufficiently covered for his peace of mind. He stepped into the shower and, almost as if by habit, dropped a quick kiss on her mouth as he put his arms underneath to lift her. "Hey there, beautiful, you from around here?" he joked.

Suzy smiled, grateful to Gray for lightening the mood since Beth was standing not two feet away. "Sorry, babe, I'm way out of your league so save the charm for someone else."

Gray looked down into her eyes, his expression

growing serious, and said, "It's all for you, Suzanna, everything I am is yours." Suzy stared back at him for a moment, surprised by the change from teasing to seriousness. Gray sat her down on the seat he'd brought into the bathroom with him, and the moment was gone so quickly Suzy had to wonder if she'd imagined the whole thing. One look into the sappy expression on Beth's face, though, convinced her that it had been real.

Beth cleared her throat and said, "Gray, my sister needs something for pain. Could you get it for her?" Suzy looked at her in surprise. She thought she'd been hiding the misery she was feeling pretty well but apparently her sister read her better than she thought.

Gray frowned down at her. "Baby, why didn't you tell me you were in pain? I should have known this shower would be too much for you. I'll be right back with the medication. Just stay here."

Both she and Beth laughed as he hurried out. "Um, exactly where did he think you were going to go?" They both tried their best to hide their smiles as Gray rushed back in with a glass of water and her medication. He shook one out into his palm and handed it to her. He absently rubbed her leg through her towel while he waited for her to finish and hand him the glass back.

"Gray, I'm going to dry Suzy's hair and help her get dressed." As he started to protest, Beth said, "I'll call you if we need your help. Go have some male bonding time or whatever it is that men do when they're together."

With one last look at Suzy, Gray reluctantly left the bathroom, and the bedroom door closed quietly behind him. Beth looked at her sister when he left and said,

"You know he loves you. Is there any doubt left in your mind after all this? I've never seen a man look at a woman the way he looks at you. I love you, sis, and I know you better than anyone else, so I'm saying this with nothing but love: don't screw this up. Don't run away from him or try to chase him away. He's the best thing that ever entered your life so grab on to him with both hands and don't let him go. He's not Jeff, he's a good man."

"You're forgetting, Beth; Jeff was a good man too and look how that turned out. Maybe I turn good men into bad people."

With an unladylike snort, Beth said, "Jeff was a spineless weasel, and I have no idea what you ever saw in him. I'm all for equal rights, but wouldn't you like to be with a man who actually wears the pants in the relationship at least part of the time? Jeff never seemed to have an opinion of his own; he was always in your shadow. I'm surprised he had enough ambition to cheat on you without someone advising him to." Suddenly, as if realizing she'd said too much, Beth's hand flew to her mouth. "Oh, God, I'm sorry. Oh, crap, I was just running off at the mouth. Please forget I said all of that."

At first, Suzy was surprised. Beth rarely said anything negative about anyone and she'd no idea that she viewed Jeff in this light. Now that the wounds were less raw, she could actually admit that Beth was right. Jeff had always deferred to her, and sometimes she'd felt more like his mother than his lover. If they had ever been equals in their relationship, it had been long ago. Maybe she just couldn't let anyone take care of her. As soon as she had that thought, she pictured Gray. She'd actually loved having him to lean on the last few days and never once had she felt threatened or annoyed by it.

She smiled at her sister and reached over to squeeze her hand. "You go, girl. I think you have more of me inside you than either of us imagined. Never apologize for being honest with me, and by the way, I agree. Now, about these ugly clothes you packed for me—where the hell did they come from?" As they both doubled over in laughter, Beth admitted that they were hers, and she'd just been trying to pack things that would be easier for Suzy to relax in while she was healing. Beth promised she'd go pack some of Suzy's things that afternoon. Soon Suzy was starting to feel loopy from the pain medication, and Gray came back to carry her to the sofa in the living room, where he had a breakfast tray waiting for her.

Chapter Ten

Both Suzy and Beth looked at the tray and almost drooled. Gray had prepared French toast and bacon along with a glass of orange juice. He put the tray over Suzy's lap and gave her a playful tweak of the nose as he was straightening. "Beth, I made you a plate as well. Would you like to eat here or in the kitchen?"

Beth looked at Gray like he'd just announced he'd run over her cat. "I . . . I already had something before I came. Th-thanks, though." Beth turned away from the sight of her sister eating the mouthwatering French toast and murmured something about straightening the bathroom.

"Beth, you don't have to do that, I'll take care of it," Gray offered.

Gray looked puzzled as Beth hurried from the room, as if she hadn't heard him. He looked at Suzy in confusion. "Did I do something to offend her?"

"No, don't worry about it. She's funny about food. She used to be heavier, and she worries a lot about what she eats. I've always been able to eat like a horse without gaining weight, but it's been a struggle for Beth all of her life."

Nick had walked in from the kitchen and was obviously listening to their exchange. "Wow, that's hard to believe. She's really too thin now. I can't imagine she'd ever have a problem with weight. She should chill. Men like a little something to hang on to."

Suzy waved her fork at him in warning. "Don't mention anything to her about it, and you better not hurt her feelings or I'll club you upside the head with my cast when I get it."

Nick held up his hands in surrender. "Even I have my limits. I don't go around hurting feelings. She may not be able to see it herself, but I think your sister is beautiful. A little uptight maybe, but beautiful. Before you throw in the last lecture, I'm not going to hit on her, so don't get your panties in a twist."

Suzy looked over at Gray. "I like him; your life will probably be miserable with both of us in it."

Soon, Gray and Nick left for their meeting with Declan Stone, and Beth had insisted on cleaning every inch of the house even though it didn't need it. A medical supply company delivered items that Gray had ordered. Suzy was now the proud owner of a pair of hot pink crutches, the shower seat that Beth had been unable to find in a store, and a cast cover for showering. She could maneuver on the crutches with Beth's assistance enough to get to the bathroom and back. She was still so sore from the fall that using the crutches caused her some pain, but she was desperate to have some mobility.

With Beth's help, she finally got her first real glimpse of Gray's home. To the left of the entryway was a formal dining area, in white. The tall ceiling and exposed woodwork were all in white, as well as the built-in cabinets. "Now, this finally looks like a beach house. I feel like I should be wiping my hands and feet before I walk in here." A table for eight took up the center of the room with plenty of sunlight streaming through the huge windows dominating one wall. Next to the dining room was a beautiful, airy kitchen. The walls were a light, slate blue with white trim. Stainless steel appliances and a large island in white and granite sparkled in the afternoon light coming in through the floor-to-ceiling wall of windows on the opposite end of the kitchen. Even though everything in the room was high-end, it still had a comfortable, homey feel to it. Suzy eyed what was obviously a back stairway, but Beth put her foot down saying they'd explored enough for one day. Truthfully, by that point she was tired and her ankle was again throbbing.

She asked Beth to get her some over-the-counter painkillers; she was tired of feeling zoned out on the stronger medication. After Beth helped her settle back on the couch, Suzy could feel the urge to close her eyes for a few moments. *I'm napping more than a ninety-year-old lady now. What's next, bingo and support hose?*

Suzy awoke sometime later to the feel of a hand caressing her face. She opened her eyes and stared at the face of the man who was fast becoming the center of her universe. With a smile she said, "Hi, dear, how was your day?"

"It was a long afternoon; I was worried about you. I called to check on you and Beth told me you were sleeping. She also said your doctor called and you can have your hard cast put on tomorrow."

"Yeah." Suzy held up her hand to high-five him. "I think that will make life easier. Thanks for the pink crutches. Where in the world did you find those?"

Gray leaned over and put his finger across her lips, silencing her. "Talk later. I need to feel your lips against mine, now."

The touch of Gray's lips sent her blood boiling. Gray ignited a fire inside her with just a look. Her breasts strained against her shirt, her nipples desperately seeking his attention. Kissing a man had never been as erotic as it was with Gray. He nibbled, he sucked, he consumed. His tongue merged with hers as two halves of a whole meeting. His hand wandered down to her breasts, cupping them possessively before rubbing the nipples between his fingers. Suzy could feel the coil of desire pulling tighter as liquid pooled between her thighs.

Gray wrenched his mouth from hers, his eyes wild with desire. "We have to stop, baby; I don't want to hurt you and I'm about to lose control." He removed his hand from her breast and stood shakily to his feet. "You don't know how I've dreamed of seeing you just like this. Your lips swollen from my kiss, your nipples puckered against your shirt from my touch, and your face flushed with need. When I finally get to love you, though, there will be no stopping. We won't come out of that room until I've had you in every way I have dreamed of for the last year." Forcing himself to turn away from her, he laughed and said, "So, how about steaks for dinner?"

Suzy nodded her agreement, and without looking back, Gray strolled toward the kitchen. She let out the breath she'd been holding and tried to bring her body under control. She'd gotten to the point where she didn't care if she was in pain as long as Gray was inside her. Her body vibrated with need so strong, she had to grit her teeth to keep from calling him back. She knew physically she was hardly in the condition to make love, but she'd never wanted anything as badly as she wanted Gray. She needed to have that physical intimacy with him. Surely, if you could walk with a hard cast and a boot, you could have sex as well. *Excuse me, Doctor. If I can walk with a cast, can I also ride the man I'm living with?*

Suzy had to chuckle a little as she imagined Gray's and the doctor's expressions should she ask that question tomorrow. The object of her fantasy came back in the room looking like he'd just managed to get himself under control. "I thought you might like to eat on the patio. There is a nice table and chair set and I can grab some pillows to make you comfortable."

"Now that's the best offer I've had all day. Hand me my trusty pink crutches and I'll hobble right out there."

"Oh, no. I don't plan to be replaced by the crutches. Those are just for when I'm not here. I'm afraid I plan to take advantage of every opportunity to cop a feel, so I'll be carrying you to the table." As Gray picked her up, Suzy reached over and gave him a light kiss on the lips. His heart skipped in happiness at having her take the initiative in touching him. Carrying her around would ensure he stayed in a constant state of arousal, but it was a pain he was willing to bear to feel her body close to his.

Suzy took a moment to appreciate the beauty around her as Gray settled her in a comfortable patio seat facing the ocean. He propped her ankle on a padded stool and walked over to start the barbeque grill. The Atlantic Ocean stretched as far as the eye could see. The setting sun made a beautiful orange cast on the horizon as the day slowly became evening. Myrtle Beach in the fall was one of her favorite times of the year. The scorching days of summer were gone, and the days and the evenings were mild enough now to enjoy the outdoors without having to worry about a heat stroke. She loved the ocean. There was no way she could ever live without being close enough to feel the sand between her toes or smell the salt in the air. The beach brought her peace, and she'd spent a lot of time walking it and sitting on it when Jeff left her.

Gray studied Suzy as she dropped her head to the back of the chair and seemed to delight in the feel of the ocean breeze on her face. His gut clenched at the news he had to deliver tonight. He was going to be forced to go out of town for at least a week. He knew between Beth and Nick that she'd be taken care of, but he didn't want to leave her. With Claire being in her last trimester of pregnancy, Jason didn't want to be away from home, and Gray could understand that. They were finally close to closing a big contract they had been working on for months and to let it go now wasn't an option. Gray had always been known as the closer, and Danvers needed him on this. He could send Nick, but it wasn't really fair to the customer or to Nick since he hadn't been in on the deal from the beginning. They had thought they were months away from closing the deal, but when a big customer called, you dropped what you were doing and went. That was the nature of the business, and it couldn't be helped.

He felt like he'd gained valuable ground with Suzy the last few days, and he hated to leave now when they were getting so close. Maybe the timing was good.

Reva continued to be a problem and he was going to be forced once again to change phones. Maybe it was time to make some inquiries with the authorities as to what his options were there. With his relationship with Suzy progressing, it was becoming imperative that he deal with Reva once and for all.

He finished their steak and grilled vegetables and quickly set the table. Suzy opened her eyes and looked up at him with a sleepy smile. He dropped a light kiss on her lips. "I could really get used to this, you know, being waited on by a handsome stud while I recline in my chair. If you scrub toilets and take out the trash, I'll keep you on staff permanently," she teased.

"For you, sweetheart, I'll do whatever needs to be done. I'm especially good at handling matters in the bedroom. I'll be happy to audition if you would like," Gray said with suggestive wiggle of his eyebrows.

Suzy had no idea what had come over her, but as if her hand had a mind of its own, she reached out and slid it down one side of Gray's perfect butt. Of the two of them, she didn't know who was more shocked. Gray almost upended the entire plate of food he was carrying into her lap. Even then, she couldn't seem to remove her hand. Maybe she'd always secretly been an ass girl or maybe she still had too many drugs in her system. Whatever the reason, it was about the hottest moment she'd ever had while wearing all of her clothing.

Gray managed to set the food on the table without breaking eye contact with her. A smile tugged at the corners of his mouth as he said, "Find anything you like back there, baby?"

Suzy gave his butt a playful pat and dropped her hand. "I was just test-driving the merchandise a bit. Is there anything else you would like me to appraise, Mr. Merimon?" *This is it, I've officially lost it. I was just running from this man last week, and now I'm groping him like a horny teenager this week. I wonder if my health insurance covers mental health issues.*

"Hmm, I see. Did Beth medicate you before she left?"

Suzy held up two fingers, showing a small space in between. "Maybe a little bit. I told her I just wanted Tylenol. I was pretty sore after checking out the bottom floor of the house."

"You should have waited for me to get home. You don't need to overdo it, honey; it has just been a few days since your accident. I do like this affectionate new Suzy, though, and you're more than welcome to palm any part of my body if you want to."

They spent the rest of the meal enjoying their food and discussing the daily events at Danvers. Gray told her that he'd be going out of town and he was pleased to see the obvious look of disappointment that she'd been unable to hide quickly enough. He also told her that he had arranged for Nick and Beth to take her to get her cast the next day.

Later that evening, they settled into bed, just as they had the first night, with Gray close beside her, holding her hand against his chest. Suzy found it hard to fall asleep after a drugging good-night kiss from Gray left her body humming with sexual frustration.

All too soon, it was morning and Gray was leaning over the bed looking utterly sexy in a dark suit. Suzy was surprised to see the red tie. It looked like something she'd have picked out for him. She wanted to grab it and pull him on top of her. *Whoa. Down, girl. You can rip the buttons from his shirt another day.*

Beth called out a good morning from the other room, letting them know she'd arrived. She didn't come into the bedroom, probably deciding that they needed the privacy for their good-bye.

Gray sat down on the side of the bed. His hand traced the shape of her face as if memorizing every detail. "Promise me you will listen to Beth and take your medication when you need it. Nick will have my new cell phone number, so get it from him today."

Suzy held up her hand, stopping him. "Why do you have a new number?"

Gray shifted as if uncomfortable with her question. "I've just been getting some annoying sales calls and wrong numbers. I thought getting a new number would solve the problem, no big deal. Anyway, please take it easy while I'm gone, and I'll call you every chance I get." Before Suzy had a chance to question him further, Gray took her mouth in a kiss that left little room to concentrate on anything else.

All too soon he was gone, and Suzy was left with nothing but one very amused sister. "Go on, I know you're dying to say something, so let's hear it before you explode."

Laughter shook Beth's body, all attempts to act innocent lost. "It's just funny to see you over there mooning over some guy. I'm used to seeing men look at you with that same expression when you blow in and out of a room, totally oblivious to the drooling stares of every man in it."

"You're crazy; I've never been one to lead men on. I've been in a relationship for most of my dating life so I'm hardly the serial dater."

"Oh, sister dear, I'm not talking about going from

one man to the next. I'm just saying that wherever you go, men want you. I doubt you have entered a room in your entire life and not immediately had the attention of everyone in it. That's one of the things I love about you, you're totally clueless to the allure you hold for the opposite sex. You, of course, um . . . dress to impress, but you don't do it for anyone's benefit. It's just who you are. If you wore a sack instead of your usual attire, men would still be falling all over themselves to get your attention, and you probably wouldn't notice." With a fond smile, Beth added, "And that's what makes you so special. I feel sorry for people that never know that about you."

Suzy was touched by the sincerity in her sister's voice. It was true, she never really noticed attention from men unless they were very obvious about it. Most would probably say she dressed just for attention, when in reality she dressed like she did because she'd always enjoyed having her own style, and if she was honest with herself, she also knew her parents would be appalled so that made it even more rewarding.

The sound of the front door opening startled them both until they heard Nick's voice boom out, "Hey ladies, your chauffeur is here."

Beth looked downright panicked as she demanded, "What's he doing here?"

Before Suzy could answer, Nick walked into the bedroom, giving them both a dazzling smile. "Gray said your appointment for your cast is at ten this morning. If you behave yourself, we will grab some lunch afterward. I know you must be going crazy stuck in this house."

With that offer, Nick officially moved to the top of Suzy's list of favorite people. She still felt like she'd survived a fight with a pit bull, but the thought of being off the couch for a while today sounded heavenly. Beth's eyes were frantically darting around as if trying to tell her something. She didn't know what her sister's problem was with Nick, but for this one day, she was just going to have to suck it up. Apparently, she'd sell her sister out in a minute for a big, greasy cheeseburger.

Suzy insisted on using her crutches on her way outside to Nick's car. When they reached the curb where he was parked, she burst out laughing, while Beth looked around in confusion, obviously refusing to accept that the vehicle in front of them was Nick's. Sitting at the curb in all its glory was a blue minivan.

Nick had the grace to at least look embarrassed, which was probably a new feeling for him. "Okay, ladies, have your fun, but I'll have you know I lowered myself to this level for you. My car is in the shop and the only loaners available were either a two-door or this lovely family car. This baby comes complete with passenger airbags, a DVD entertainment system, and can go from zero to sixty in about five seconds."

Suzy could hardly catch her breath, she was laughing so hard. Beth had joined in by this time, and Nick stood next to them on the sidewalk looking at them in disgust. Suzy managed to get control of herself, saying, "Come on, Beth, let's load up in Nick's grocery-getter before we miss my appointment." As she reached for the back door, Beth was there, listing all of the reasons that she should sit in the back and Suzy should take the front. Finally, after she threatened physical violence with her crutches, Beth reluctantly took up the shotgun position beside Nick after helping Suzy settle in the back of the van.

Suzy spotted the DVD player and was unable to resist asking, "Hey, Nick, do you have any movies in here? Maybe *Barney*?"

With a chuckle, Nick said, "Very funny, but I wonder who would have been laughing if you and the princess up here had to fold yourselves in a two-door compact car."

From where she was sitting, Suzy saw Beth's head whip toward Nick at his "princess" comment. That's just what she needed, these two hating each other. She should talk to Nick about taking it easy on Beth; he probably didn't understand how sensitive she was to comments that she thought were negative in any way. Maybe it was time to give Beth the same advice she'd given Claire—"get laid." *That had actually worked out pretty well*, she thought with a satisfied smile.

Chapter Eleven

They arrived at the doctor's office with only a few minutes to spare before her appointment. Beth walked up to the window to let them know they had arrived and Nick helped her into a seat. Beth sat on one side and Nick on the other as if they were using Suzy as a buffer between them. Both Nick and Beth stood when the nurse called Suzy's name. Beth gave him her best eye roll and said, "I think I can take it from here. Why don't you go sit in your minivan until we're finished?" Suzy snickered, even though Beth wasn't usually so rude. The nurse tried to hide her smile, plainly amused by a man who looked like Nick driving a minivan.

Nick looked down at Beth and tweaked her nose, saying, "Chill, princess, there's no reason to get your panties in a wad. I'll wait out here."

By this time, the nurse could barely contain her amusement as she ushered them down the hallway to an examination room. Suzy studied her sister after they were left alone, asking, "What's the deal with you and Nick? You two can't be in a room together for more than a minute without biting each other's heads off." Good grief, she was sure that Beth actually just huffed at her question.

"It's nothing, Suzy; he just irritates me, that's all. Haven't you noticed the way he calls me princess all the time? I know he's just doing it to be insulting."

Confused, Suzy asked, "Why would you think that?"

"Oh, come on. By calling me princess, he's just trying to point out the fact that I'm anything but that. Kind of like if he called me beautiful or something. It's his way of making fun of the way I look."

Suzy was shocked, and even though she didn't know Nick that well, she felt certain he hadn't meant his comment in the way that Beth took it. "Beth, you're beautiful and if Nick called you that, he'd only be telling you the truth. I'll tell him that the nickname he's given you is bothering you."

Beth grabbed her hand, saying urgently, "No, please don't say anything to him. I'm sure you're right, he's just kidding, and it's no big deal."

Suzy wanted to argue, but at that moment, the doctor came in and she was forced to postpone their conversation. He explained the process of having the hard cast put on as he unwrapped the soft cast. He also gave her instructions for caring for the cast and advised her to call his office if she had problems or concerns. Soon the doctor and his nurse were layering thin strips of wet plaster over her ankle and calf. She was surprised at how fast the wet mixture appeared to harden. Suzy thought longingly of her stiletto heels and wondered when she'd ever be comfortably wearing them again. *Why do I care what type of shoes I'm wearing? I'm sitting here in sweatpants yet again. All I need is a pair of orthopedic shoes to complete the picture. I can tell everyone years from now; I used to be sexy until I broke my ankle. It was all downhill from there.*

When the cast was complete and dry, the doctor helped her to stand and she almost pitched forward when she tried to walk with her crutches. It was like trying to move a cement block with her toe. The doctor said if it didn't cause pain, she could use a special boot they made to go over casts for walking. The nurse put one on her cast and Suzy had to admit that using the crutches as well as putting weight on the cast was a much easier combination.

As soon as they got to the waiting room, a harassed-looking Nick held out a cell phone to her. "Please talk to my lovesick brother before he either freaks out completely or drives me crazy. He's been calling every five minutes for the last hour."

Suzy smiled as she put the phone to her ear. "What have you been doing to your brother? If you don't leave him alone, he's going to hop into his minivan and leave Beth and me stranded here."

The sound of Gray's voice in her ear sent a tingle through her. "God, baby, I've been so worried. What took so long? Is something wrong? Did they hurt you?"

Suzy's head was spinning at the barrage of questions Gray was belting out. Nick was right; he did seem to be freaking out. "Um . . . calm down, Gray. I'm fine. It takes them a little while to actually put a cast on, you know. Everything is okay, really. I have my cast now and the walking boot so I'm in much better shape than I was this morning when you left."

She could hear Gray expel a deep breath. "Thank

goodness. I've been out of my mind with worry. I thought something had happened to you, and my brother was no help at all. Why didn't you let him go back with you?"

"Gray, get a grip, I'm fine, I promise. How was your trip? Do you think you will have to be there all weekend?" Suzy had been surprised that Gray had been forced to leave for a business trip on a Friday. He'd explained that the customer they were trying to land was having a gathering at the CEO's home that weekend and he'd been invited. This was a chance to meet the other principals of the company and conduct business in a less formal atmosphere. He was hopeful that he'd be able to close the deal on the Monday following the gathering. The customer was located in Nevada, which meant hours of travel time and a time difference, as well.

"I hope I can wrap it up quickly. I don't like leaving you so soon after your accident." Lowering his voice, he continued, "I'm going to miss lying beside you tonight. I'm afraid I've gotten spoiled having you in bed beside me. I want your face to be the last thing I see before I go to sleep and the first thing I see when I wake in the morning."

Even though her heart was melting at the love she could plainly hear in his voice, Suzy kept it light. "You aren't going to make this easy for me, are you, slick?"

Gray laughed, always seeming to appreciate her sense of humor and know exactly what she was trying to say. "You might as well wave the white flag right now, sweetheart, because there will be no retreat."

"I'd be disappointed if there was," Suzy admitted.

"I've got to run, baby. Please be careful today and I'll call you tonight."

When Suzy pushed the End button on the cell phone and handed it back to Nick, he was making a gagging motion with his finger. Since she couldn't take her hands from the crutches to hit him, she settled for sticking her tongue out, to which she got nothing but laughter in return.

Soon Suzy was settled in the backseat and Beth was forced into the front beside Nick again. Claire had called Nick while they were in the doctor's office to check on Suzy and he'd invited her to lunch with them. They were going to eat at the sandwich shop around the corner from Danvers.

Claire was waiting for them in the parking lot when Nick pulled up in his minivan. Suzy had to admit that seeing a pregnant woman laugh that hard was almost scary. Nick gave them all a look of disgust and walked ahead to hold the door of the restaurant open.

After they were settled at a table, Suzy looked at Claire and bluntly asked, "When is that bun coming out of your oven? You look like you're about to explode." Claire choked on the drink of tea she'd just taken and Beth had to pat her on the back until she could catch her breath.

"By bun, I assume you're referring to my baby, and he or she's due in about three more months." Rolling her eyes, Claire continued. "I'm sick of the swollen ankles, the fatigue, and the hemorrhoids are a real pain in the butt." As soon as the last word left her mouth, Claire seemed to remember Nick's presence.

Suzy wasn't sure if Nick's face was redder at that point or Claire's. They both looked like they wanted to climb under the table. Suzy jabbed her elbow in his ribs and said, "For heaven's sake, Nick, you have been around the block more than a few times. Stop acting like a convent girl."

Nick held his hands up, still refusing to make eye contact and said, "Ladies, I don't have many rules, but I have to draw the line at talking about hemorrhoids, tampons, or PMS. If you want to talk about sex, then I'm your guy, well, unless it's with my brother, but no talk of the female cycle or anything hanging out of your body, okay?"

They all laughed, and Suzy called the waiter over to order a beer for him. For such a ladies' man, the guy really needed to loosen up. She had to appreciate the fact that although he didn't know them all that well, he was still willing to spend his day taking her to a doctor's appointment and then spend lunch with three women. From what she could tell, like his brother, Nick was a good man.

All too soon lunch was over and they dropped Claire back at the front doors of Danvers. Suzy tried to convince Nick to let her go into the office to pick up her mail, but he adamantly refused. He did offer to pick it up on Saturday and bring it to her. By the time they made it home, Suzy was exhausted and her body seemed to be aching all over. She didn't want to admit it, but she'd overdone it a bit today. She was grateful when Beth suggested she rest on the couch for a while.

Nick offered to stay for a few hours so that Beth could go to the supermarket and pick up some of Suzy's clothing. She'd refused to wear sweatpants for another day, so Beth caved to pressure and promised that she'd have her own clothing by tomorrow.

Gray sat on the bed in his hotel looking down at his cell phone. He wanted to hear Suzy's voice, but according to Nick's text, she was sound asleep on the couch. Disappointment stabbed through him even though he'd just talked to her a few hours earlier. Running his hand across his face, he admitted that Nick was right about him, he was a lovesick sap. Being away from her was tearing him apart. He knew that once she was his, he'd be able to breathe easier when they were apart. Right now, with so much hanging in the balance, he was afraid of losing ground while he was away. He just couldn't start over again with her. It had been hard before, but now that he'd finally established intimacy between them, even though they hadn't had sex, the bond was there. He'd go to pieces if she walked away now. Giving someone this type of power scared the hell out of him. If he was smart, he'd probably run and never look back. He knew that he'd passed the point of no return—his life was with Suzy and a life without her was nothing at all.

The one thing still stopping him from relaxing was Reva. He wasn't naive enough to believe that the silence since changing phone numbers would last. She'd be back and it was high time he dealt with it. He couldn't start a life with Suzy with something like that hanging over them. It was also time that he came clean with Suzy and told her what was going on. When she'd asked about him changing his cell phone number that morning, he'd stumbled around like an idiot trying to find an explanation. Gray had always believed in being honest and he wasn't going to continue keeping something like this from her. He didn't want to tell her over the phone, but as soon as he got home, it would be time to level with her and hope that it didn't change anything.

He was surprised at how well things had progressed between them. The feel of her hand on his butt yesterday had both shocked him and almost brought him to his knees. He'd always desired her, even with the front she presented to him and the world. You couldn't be a male and not immediately take notice when she walked into a room. Suzy was a drop-dead gorgeous woman and she didn't dress to minimize it. It wasn't that she dressed specifically to draw attention to it; she was just unique and her style represented that. He wouldn't change anything about her. Just smelling the light fragrance of her perfume when she walked by him was enough to make him hard as a rock.

He'd been amused by her when they'd first met. She seemed to do and say a lot of things just for the shock value. He had a feeling being raised by such uptight parents had something to do with it. He'd bet that she'd spent her adolescence finding ways to get a reaction out of them. They probably about had a coronary the first time she walked out wearing an eye-popping animal print. Gray saw through the smoke and mirrors to the person underneath that camouflage. Suzy might seem tough, but she was breakable. She acted like she didn't want or need affection when, in reality, she craved it. She wanted someone to love her enough to peel back her layers and see the person inside.

As Gray started dressing to attend the party at the

home of their potential new customer, he was still uneasy and the feeling bothered him. He decided to text Nick again to make sure everything was okay. He hated having these gut feelings because they invariably drove him crazy until whatever was causing them finally presented itself.

Chapter Twelve

Gray had been gone for almost two weeks. Suzy had no idea it was possible to miss someone as much as she'd missed him. The simple trip that Gray had assumed would last no more than a week had run much longer than he'd imagined. He had been in Nevada for a little over a week and then in California dealing with a supply problem, which luckily he'd finally settled. The new guy at Danvers, Declan Stone, was flying down to California in the morning and Gray was handing the reins over to him. He thought someone should be there for a few extra days to ensure there were no other issues, and he didn't want it to be him. He'd wanted to fly home for an evening just to see her but she'd put her foot down, or her boot at least. As much as she wanted him home, she didn't want just a few hours. She had big plans for Gray tomorrow night when he finally made it home and she didn't want to be rushed.

Suzy was feeling much better than she had when he left. She'd learned to manage pretty well on her crutches and was much more mobile now. Things that she'd always taken for granted like showering or going to the bathroom still required more time, but she was getting the hang of it. Beth had finally brought over her clothing and it felt better to look more like herself.

Skinny jeans were out since she couldn't fit them over her cast, but skirts were comfortable even if she had to settle for ugly flat-heeled shoes to go with them.

Gray had insisted on Nick staying with her and Beth at night. She was glad to have him in the house, but Beth seemed to hate every moment of it and never failed to let Nick know. If Suzy didn't know better, she'd swear it was some form of foreplay between them. Beth had been working at Danvers for the past week. She went in to pick up messages and mail and returned the calls and handled correspondence for Suzy. Suzy planned to go back to work on Monday. She knew it would be a fight with Gray, but she couldn't stay home forever and with several projects in the works, she had to be there in person some of the time.

Suzy smiled as she thought of how many times each day Gray called her. Their last conversation of the day was usually at night when Gray was back at his hotel and Suzy was settled in bed. She'd never been one for phone sex, but their nightly talks had gotten pretty interesting. She was sure that Gray went to sleep each evening just as tightly wired as she did.

Even though she wore a heavy, awkward cast, she planned to finally give both Gray and herself what they had both been longing for when he got home tomorrow. She'd already told Beth and Nick that they should make plans to return to their own homes. Beth had blushed and Nick had given her a thumbs-up along with a wicked grin.

Today Suzy planned to go shopping for a special purchase even if it took her all day to hobble into the store. Beth would be appalled to be pulled into Victoria's Secret, but she'd not be deterred. She was a woman on a mission and that was to get something special for tomorrow night. Maybe it was time she also helped Beth pick out a few things for herself. If there was one thing she knew, wearing sexy undergarments just made you feel sexy. It was like a powerful secret that you carried, or in this case, wore with you all day.

Nick had invited Claire and Jason over for a barbeque that evening and Beth said she was going to invite a girl from the office that she'd gotten to know. Suzy thought it sounded like a great evening, and it would have been perfect had Gray been there.

Beth came into the bedroom to help her shower and get dressed. They had gotten the hang of using the cast cover and the shower seat, and after a few mishaps they had it down to a science. Suzy used the chair that Gray had put in front of the vanity for her while she dried and styled her hair and put on her makeup. Beth stood beside her doing her makeup as well. Soon they heard Nick yelling for them from the other room.

Suzy had come to adore Nick. He might tease, torment, and heckle her unmercifully, but he was such a good guy. He and Beth had taken turns fixing dinner each evening and, just as Gray had indicated, he and Nick did truly know how to cook. Nick helped out around the house, ran errands, and even kept the minivan so they could all travel in comfort. Suzy had to admit, he was a complete stud, as well. She could see why he had the reputation as a ladies' man because women admired him everywhere they went. To his credit, other than a lazy grin here or there, he hadn't gone out on a date nor had anyone over since he'd been staying with them. Someone like Nick was bound to have an active social life, but he seemed content to stay in with them each evening and watch a movie after dinner or just sit around and chat. She thought, not for the first time, that there was a lot more to Nick than she'd first imagined. She truly couldn't understand why Beth seemed to loathe him so much.

As great as Nick was though, he didn't make her heart beat fast when he entered a room or make her palms sweat or her thighs tremble when she heard his voice on the phone. He might be as gorgeous in looks as his brother, but for all of the attraction he held for her, he might as well be her brother too. Gray turned her on more from thousands of miles away than his brother would have walking through the bedroom naked. It just wasn't there for her.

Soon, the three amigos, as Suzy had taken to calling them, arrived at Broadway at the Beach. This was a shopping area of Myrtle Beach that she really loved. Dozens of shops and restaurants were built around a lake, and large bridges at each end allowed you to cross to the shops on the other side of the lake. The development also contained a movie theater, putt-putt course, and an aquarium. She and Beth often came here on the weekend to spend a day relaxing.

Nick had dropped them off at the curb so Suzy wouldn't have to walk so far on her crutches. They stood at the railing that surrounded the lake laughing at all of the fish that bobbed their heads from the water hoping to be fed. Beth took mercy on them and walked over to one of the feed dispensers that were located around the lake. The fish were soon in a frenzy, fighting for the food Beth was tossing in. Nick walked up beside them laughing at a small fish that was determined to beat his bigger brothers and sisters to the rest of the snack.

As the last of the fish swam away, they all took off at a slow pace, careful to give Suzy plenty of time to maneuver her crutches on the walkway. When they reached Victoria's Secret, Suzy turned to Nick with an amused look on her face. "So, comrade, does the all-for-one and one-for-all thing still apply when we are underwear shopping or do you need to sit out front with those retired gentlemen over there?"

Nick threw back his head and laughed. "Honey, Victoria doesn't have a secret left that I haven't seen. I'll not only accompany you ladies in, I'll help you pick out some stuff, if you like."

Suzy saw Beth clench her teeth, clearly not impressed with Nick's offer to help. Suzy, however, was amused and intended to see if there was anything the store had to offer that would embarrass him. She had to draw the line, however, at letting him help her pick anything out. Somehow it seemed really wrong to let Nick see what she was buying to wear for his brother.

Nick started off admiring the displays in the store and then led them over to see their new selection of micro-thongs. He held up a small black pair to Beth, saying, "Hey, princess, what do you think? Maybe a nice push-up bra to match? You can look for your size in the bra and I can look in the thongs," Nick offered helpfully. As Beth's mouth opened and closed like a guppy fish, Suzy took her chance and left them to their argument in the underwear aisle while she moved on her crutches toward the other side of the store where the nighties were displayed.

She looked wistfully at the display showing the

bustier with garters and stockings. There was no way she could pull that off with a cast. After browsing for a few moments, she found what she was looking for. It was simple, yet oh so sexy. She held up a black lace baby-doll top that would tie in the center of her breasts while the sides fluttered open to reveal her stomach and matching G-string panties.

She was grateful to see that Nick and Beth had moved on from the underwear aisle so she could go back and pick up a few new sets for herself. She cringed when she looked toward the back of the store and saw Nick holding up a red corset and Beth looking at him like he'd just grown horns. Those two were something else. She wondered how Gray had talked Jason into letting Nick be her babysitter while he was away. She knew that Nick worked at home a lot in the evenings and he was at the office as long as Beth was with her. Apparently Gray had been firm to Nick about not traveling until he returned home.

Suzy was surprised to see Beth bring some items of her own to the register beside her. Beth's face turned red as she noticed Suzy studying her purchases. She decided to walk away and give her some privacy. If her sister was finally trading in her cotton for silk, there was no way she was going to do anything to discourage her. She intercepted Nick as he was coming toward the checkout and steered him out the door so that Beth could have some privacy.

As Beth walked out the door, Suzy was surprised by the size of the bag she carried. If there was a moment she'd ever been prouder of her sister, she couldn't remember it. Could Beth finally be seeing what everyone else already saw? It was at least a good sign because she couldn't remember the last time Beth had actually bought something from a girly-type store. She didn't want to embarrass her or make her regret her purchases so she kept up a constant stream of chatter to distract Nick, and then they grabbed a burger at Johnny Rockets before heading back to the house.

Claire and Jason arrived around seven and Suzy was surprised to hear the doorbell chime again a few moments later. Beth came back in the living room with an attractive woman around their age that Suzy didn't recognize. This must be the new friend at Danvers that Beth had mentioned making. Claire walked toward them and, ever gracious, threw an arm around the new guest. "Ella, you look beautiful. I'm so glad you could come."

Suzy only knew one Ella and this wasn't her. Claire looked at her, saying, "Suz, you remember Ella from the office, don't you?"

As Suzy hobbled over to the trio on her crutches, recognition hit her, and before she could catch herself, she loudly exclaimed, "Holy shit, what happened to you?"

Ella blushed furiously, and Claire and Beth looked at Suzy like she'd lost her mind. Was she the only one here who remembered how Ella looked just a few weeks ago? "Your sister helped me, um . . . make some changes." Then blinking as if tears weren't far behind, she asked, "You don't like it?"

At that moment she saw Ella for maybe the first time. She tried so hard to be helpful because she wanted everyone to like her and she'd bet that there had been very few times in her life that she'd fit in. Whereas

Suzy had dismissed her at first glance, Beth had obviously bonded with her, and the result of the makeover was nothing short of astounding. Her teased beehive hairdo was gone and in its place her brown hair had been straightened and now hung past her shoulders in waves. Blond highlights had been added to accent the color. Wow, who knew she had all of that hair under the bad hairdo? Her eyebrows had been waxed and, instead of looking like one big eyebrow, now she actually had two well-defined ones.

Suzy noticed that Ella actually had beautiful skin and the only thing that had been added there was a light blusher on her cheeks and a glossy pink lipstick on her lips. Her hair and face were not the only changes though. She actually had a figure. She was wearing a sleeveless silk sundress in a light turquoise color that ended several inches above her knees and a low-heeled pair of beige strappy sandals. She looked pretty, fresh, and about ten years younger.

As her sister poked an elbow in her side, Suzy realized she'd been staring at Ella for several minutes without saying a word. Ella looked as if she were ready to bolt, obviously taking her silence as disapproval. Suzy reached out and took one of Ella's hands between her own. "You look beautiful, Ella, and you know I wouldn't say it if I didn't mean it. Now, come on in and let's get a drink. I want to hear all about your makeover."

A smile broke out on Ella's face as they all started toward the living room. The doorbell chiming once again stopped them. Suzy rolled her eyes, saying, "Geez, who is that?"

Claire stepped forward and walked toward the door

saying, "That's probably Declan; I hope you don't mind but Jason invited him. He thought it would be good for him to meet a few people from Danvers since he's new in town." As she finished her sentence, Claire opened the door and Suzy could see a huge figure filling the doorway.

As Declan walked inside, Suzy couldn't help the murmur of appreciation that escaped her lips. Beth and Ella both looked at her when the *Mmmm* escaped her lips. She arched an eyebrow and said under her breath, "Oh, come on, you were both thinking the same thing. There is nothing wrong with appreciating a good piece of artwork."

Claire led Declan over to them and took care of making the introductions. As Claire kept the conversation flowing smoothly with small talk, Suzy took a moment to study the new addition to Danvers. He was another prime piece of eye candy; there was no denying that. He was similar to Nick, Gray, and Jason, with dark hair and tanned skin. You could not be a woman and not appreciate the masculine beauty of Declan Stone. There was also almost a darkness about him that both pulled you in and made you want to run. Suzy had a feeling that there was a lot more to him than any of them knew. If there was one thing she was sure of, Declan would bring variety to their little group because she just knew that he'd never conformed to "normal" a day in his life.

They all made their way out onto the back deck, where Jason and Nick were drinking beers and arguing over who could grill the best steak. Beth had made a pitcher of daiquiris for the women and a virgin daiquiri for Claire. Suzy hobbled over to a seat and Beth helped her put her foot up onto a stool. Declan walked over to join the men and Claire motioned Ella to join the ladies at the table.

Claire smiled at her, saying, "You must be glad that Gray will be home tomorrow. I know he's been giving Jason hell about being gone so long. I'm glad we have Declan now to spread some of the travel to. Jason said he's flying out tomorrow to take Gray's place."

Suzy leaned over and took her friend's hand. "You don't worry about us. I've had two babysitters with me the whole time. Jason needs to stick close to you. I'm afraid you might pop at any second." Wrinkling her nose in confusion, she continued, "You don't think it's getting, like, overdone in there, do you?"

Claire burst out laughing. She'd so missed seeing her friend at the office every day. Suzy could make her laugh when nothing else in the world could. From the expression on her friend's face, she could tell that she was dead serious as well. "No, you can't overcook them, Suz; I think they have a self-timer or something that lets you know when they're ready. It's pretty normal for a first baby to go past its due date so it could still be quite some time yet." As she moved around trying to get comfortable in the chair, Jason walked up behind her and helped her put a pillow behind her back. He reached down and dropped a kiss on her lips, caressing her cheek with his hand before returning to talk with the men. Suzy was certain there wasn't a dry eye at the table at the obvious love that sparkled between Claire and Jason.

Suzy cleared her throat and steered the conversation to Danvers. She got caught up on the latest gossip just as the steaks were finished while Beth went to get the roasted potatoes and the salad from the refrigerator. Ella went to help her and soon they had the table set and everyone settled into a chair. Suzy sat between Claire and Beth with Nick on Beth's other side and Jason on Claire's other side. Ella somehow ended up sitting between Nick and Declan. She looked like she hoped the deck would open up and swallow her whole. She saw that Beth had also noticed the same thing and neither of them could figure out a way to save Ella from the seating arrangement without embarrassing her.

Luckily, Nick could always be counted on to keep the conversation going and, as if he'd also noticed Ella's discomfort, he took great pains to draw her into the conversation and make her comfortable. Suzy had to admit, Gray's brother was an all-around great guy. She thought she caught Declan studying Ella a few times from under his lashes but it was so fleeting she couldn't be sure. Ella was nowhere near in his league; he'd chew her up and spit her out, and that Suzy would never allow.

The evening passed far too quickly and Suzy was sorry to see everyone leave. When she went into the kitchen to get a glass of water before bed, Nick's back was to her and his conversation was completely out of character for the Nick she knew. "Listen, you nut job, you better never call me again. If it were me, you would be rotting in jail somewhere and if I have anything to do with it that will happen sooner rather than later. I meant what I said, don't ever call me. The sound of your voice makes me sick." With that last line, Nick roughly hit the End button on his call and swung around to leave the kitchen. Surprise colored his face as he saw an amused Suzy standing there.

"Wow, sounds like you have yourself a stalker there, Nick."

A strained laugh erupted from him as he lightly said, "Yeah, you know how it goes. Some women just have a hard time letting go of all of this. Sometimes you just can't be Mr. Nice."

Suzy laughed along with him, but was still unsure about exactly what she'd walked in on. Nick was far too nice and easygoing to let someone push him to the point of the rudeness that she'd heard. Whatever this woman had done, it was bad. Maybe she should mention it to Gray when he returned; she hated to think that Nick had to deal with something that was obviously upsetting him so much. They both said their good nights and Suzy settled in to wait for Gray's call.

As her cell phone rang, a thrill shot through her body. If a ring tone could turn her on this much, imagine how it would feel to have Gray in her bed tomorrow night. She could practically have an orgasm just thinking about it. She answered the phone, smiling as she heard Gray's voice.

"Hey, baby, how are you?"

"Hi, yourself. I'm good, how about you?"

With a chuckle, Gray said, "I'm much better for hearing your voice. God, I can't wait to see you tomorrow. I wish I could have gotten an earlier flight out."

"That's okay, all that matters is you will be home tomorrow." Dropping her voice to a whisper, she continued, "You better get some rest tonight because we aren't going to get much sleep here tomorrow night, big boy." Suzy smiled in satisfaction at the groan she heard on the other end of the line.

"You're killing me, babe. Everyone here probably already thinks I have some issues. I seem to keep a hard-on and I know you love it, you little witch."

Suzy laughed, admitting, "You're right, I do. Why should you be any better off than I am? I ache for you every minute of the day, Gray; I need you inside me to ease that ache."

After taking a deep breath, Gray said, "If we don't change the subject, the people next door might have something to talk about in the morning."

"Yeah, I agree. Nick and Beth probably don't want to hear me in here alone moaning. Oh, speaking of Nick, does he have some kind of girlfriend problem?"

"Baby, this is Nick we are talking about, so I'm sure he always has some girlfriend. As for problems, why do you ask? He hasn't had anyone over, has he?"

"No, nothing like that. I walked in the kitchen on him this evening and he was having a rather heated exchange with someone on the phone. He was threatening to have them arrested if they didn't leave him alone. I think he might have messed with the wrong woman this time."

Gray was silent for so long, she thought they had lost their cell phone signal. "Hellooooo, Gray, are you still there?"

"Oh, sorry, sweetheart. Jason was beeping in on the other line. Don't worry about Nick; I'm sure he will be fine. I'll talk to him about it when I get back. I've got to run and make a few calls before it gets too late. I can't wait to see you tomorrow."

"I can't wait either, Gray. Please be careful in your travels." As Suzy was starting to end the call, she heard Gray add one more thing as he hung up.

"Oh, and Suzy, it wouldn't offend me in the least if you were completely naked when I get home."

With a smile, Suzy set her cell phone on the bedside table and snuggled down in the bed. She could almost imagine Gray's arms around her as she tried to tap down the desire that threatened to consume her.

Chapter Thirteen

Suzy was in a great mood when she awoke the next morning. Beth helped her shower and dress, and after taking a few business-related calls she barged into the kitchen, making Nick and Beth jump apart from where they stood next to each other at the counter. *Oh, great. I probably interrupted yet another argument. Can't these two be in a room together for more than a few minutes without squaring off?* "Good morning, fellow campers, how are we today?"

Nick flashed his usual killer smile and said, "Well, look at you this morning, sunshine. If I didn't know better, I'd think someone already got lucky last night."

Beth started choking, spitting her coffee all over herself and the counter. Suzy walked over and whacked her on the back until she could get her breath. "Geez, sis, it wasn't that funny. Are you okay now?"

"Um, yeah, thanks. My coffee just went down the wrong way."

Suzy saw Nick give Beth a strange look and he actually picked up a towel to wipe up the coffee while Beth cleaned the counter. Maybe there was hope for these two after all.

Nick had made a breakfast of bacon, eggs, and toast. Suzy grabbed a plate and started eating with gusto. She was excited yet nervous about Gray's impending arrival. His plane was landing around eleven tonight and Nick was going to pick him up at the airport and drop him at home. Beth was also going home that evening and Suzy was looking forward to having the house to herself for a few hours before Gray arrived. She'd enjoyed Beth and Nick, but having some alone time sounded great.

"Hey, guys, I thought I could go to the office for a while today. I'm going back on Monday anyway so I might as well get my feet wet." Even as she finished her sentence, both Nick and Beth were shaking their heads.

"I don't think so, sis."

"I agree with the princess," Nick said. "There is no way I'm facing my brother and telling him you got hurt today because I let you go to work on the day of his return. Can you imagine how much damage a man with that much sexual frustration could do to a face like mine?"

Suzy gave a groan of disgust. "You guys are such wimps. Wait until I get this cast off. I plan to dedicate at least half of my time to torturing you."

With a chuckle Nick said, "I thought you already started that."

Suzy elbowed him in the ribs and grabbed his last piece of bacon, laughing at his protests. "Maybe I'll just work from home again today. I must admit there is something pretty sweet about lying on the sofa while you're handling business. Beth, if you could pick up those files I needed this morning it would really be great. What's your agenda today, Nick?"

"I've got a meeting with Jason this morning and some conference calls lined up for this afternoon. I'm going to head down to Charleston in the morning to check on a few things there at Mericom. The parental troops are also requiring a visit from at least one of their sons so I'm going to see them while I'm there. You're gonna owe me because this will stop them from coming here for at least a few weeks."

"Here?" Suzy squeaked. "Why would they come here?"

Nick pushed his chair back from the table and gave her a wicked grin. "I don't know, let's see, maybe they're a bit curious about the woman that both of their sons are shacking up with." Holding his hand up to stall her, he continued, "I mean, I know it sounds more exciting than it actually is, but Mom is probably already picking out baby names for her first grandchild. My father is probably the only thing that has kept her from showing up so far, and trust me, sweetheart, that won't last much longer."

"Ugh." Suzy shuddered. "Why can't all parents be as uninvolved as ours? I couldn't even explain this living arrangement to people that know me, much less to your parents. Please say whatever you need to say to keep them away for a while. When Gray gets home, he can deal with it."

Beth stood up and started clearing the table. "I'm going to get dressed and go to the office for those things that you need, sis. Can you be trusted here on your own for a few hours?"

"Uh, yeah, Beth, I think I've got this one. Maybe you can pick us up some lunch on the way back. I'd kill for a hot dog. No onions though."

Nick stood and left after saying he needed to get ready as well, and Suzy was left to her own devices.

She really hoped they would be gone soon. She didn't want to admit that she'd developed a secret addiction to *The Price Is Right*. She'd never live that down. She settled onto the couch and picked up her laptop from the coffee table. Beth and Nick came out a short time later dressed for the office.

Beth looked pretty in a floral dress with flats. Even though it was fall, the days were still warm. Suzy noticed a pink flush on her sister's cheeks and vowed to lecture Nick when they were alone. She was tired of him upsetting Beth all the time. She couldn't figure out why those two couldn't just get along. She gave them both a wave good-bye and settled back with her remote control. *What's next, soap operas? I'm home for less than three weeks and I already know the television schedule for every daytime show. Pathetic. Just pass me the box of bonbons and put me out to pasture.*

She smothered a curse as her cell phone rang. She didn't recognize the number, which wasn't unusual since several vendors had her telephone number. "Suzy Denton." She was met on the other end of the line by continued silence. "Hello?" After several other attempts, there was still no reply so she ended the call. *Great. If someone had to interrupt my TV show, couldn't it have at least been a heavy breather instead of a hang-up?* The same thing happened to her twice more that morning until she finally shut her phone off in disgust. Apparently some kid had her number and was determined to call her all day.

Gray had been working nonstop since early in the morning to wrap things up in California. He'd managed to book an earlier flight on another airline. It was going to cost him several hundred dollars just to get home a couple of hours earlier, but it was money well spent. He stepped outside to call Nick to arrange for an earlier pickup.

Nick answered the phone with his usual, "Hey, bro, what's up?"

"My flight is coming in around nine tonight; can you pick me up earlier than expected?"

"Sure man, no problem. Does Suzy know?"

"No, I want to surprise her. Just make up some excuse for you and Beth to be gone earlier. Make sure she has everything she needs before you guys leave, though."

With a tired sigh, Gray asked, "Nick, did Reva call you last night?"

"Yeah, she did, bro. I wasn't going to even mention it, but Suzy heard me talking to her and questioned me about it. I don't think she heard enough to connect it to you."

"Nick, I'm sorry you're being dragged into this. I'm going to tell Suzy when I get home and then I'm dealing with it. I'm tired of it. My damn cell phone rings constantly, and apparently she's been making a nuisance of herself at Mericom. The woman is just unbalanced. I'm going to talk to the police and see what my options are. I even thought about talking to her parents, which seems absurd considering her age. I don't think they would be thrilled to know that their daughter is stalking me."

With a laugh Nick said, "Yeah, there's something about finding out your daughter is a fruit loop. I'm just glad you're finally ready to take care of this. You're too nice, you always have been. I like Suzy, a lot, and I don't want anything screwing it up for you. I'll see you tonight."

As Gray ended the call with Nick, he placed another call to Declan. He was probably at the airport right now and hopefully had a moment to talk. Declan knew people from every walk of life. If anyone knew the best place to start to deal with someone like Reva, it was him.

Suzy flopped back against the couch cushions with a sigh of satisfaction. It felt good to be working again even if it was from home. She'd gotten the ball rolling on a formal cocktail party being held for a new customer in a couple of weeks and a training seminar for their telemarketing staff next month. She'd have never gotten so much accomplished away from the office without Beth. She knew it was selfish, but she hoped her sister would consider staying for at least a few months because she was the best assistant she'd ever had. Since they knew each other so well, Beth anticipated everything she needed without her having to ask. She also understood her offbeat sense of humor, so there was no offending her.

She was surprised at how fast Beth had caught on to her new job. Of course she was very intelligent so there was never any doubt that she could do the work, but Suzy had been unsure of how she'd feel in a different environment. They weren't on a regular schedule yet with her still working from home, but Beth had been going into the office every day for the past week and she seemed comfortable. Having made friends with Ella was probably a help. Apparently, if Ella's new appearance was anything to go by; their friendship was of great benefit to them both.

Suzy had told Beth to go home earlier. She and Ella were going to have dinner and Suzy was more than able to fix herself something. She'd also told Nick not to bother to come back that evening, so she finally had the house to herself. Taking a shower on her own might be a little challenging, but they pretty much had that down to a routine so she knew she could handle it. A quick look at her watch showed it was just after six. Gray would be home in just hours and her stomach was knotting in nervous anticipation.

How could you prepare for something you had wanted for so long? She wasn't even worried about being let down—she was worried about being consumed. After they had sex, Suzy knew it would be impossible to continue denying the bond between them. They were so involved in each other's lives now it was as if they had been a couple for years. When had she finally let her guard down with him? They had established so much intimacy between them since her accident that sex seemed like the next natural step in their relationship. Had there ever been this level of anticipation with Jeff? They had really just grown into a relationship. He was comfortable and reliable, kind of like a Toyota. She'd enjoyed sex with him, but never craved it so badly that her body ached as it did for Gray. Tonight she knew would be the turning point in her life; Gray had finally broken down all of her walls and there was nowhere left to hide.

Suzy prowled around with restless energy. It was just after ten and she'd showered, layered her body with scented lotion, and dressed in her new Victoria's Secret lingerie. She still had hours left until Gray was going to be home and was far too wired to watch television. She walked into the kitchen and headed straight for the one thing that always settled her nerves. There, sitting on a shelf of honor in the freezer, was her pint of Ben and Jerry's Chunky Monkey ice cream. She never made the mistake of taking it to the table or anywhere away from the freezer. If she did, she'd eat the entire thing. If she stood near the cold confines of the freezer, she could only stand so much before she had to put it up and shut the door. She grabbed a spoon from the nearby drawer and closed her eyes in bliss at the first explosive taste on her tongue.

Gray walked in the front door wondering if he should call out his arrival or try to surprise Suzy without scaring her to death. The house was quiet and there was no sign of her. As he was walking toward the bedroom he noticed the kitchen light was on so he quickly detoured there and stepped in the doorway to a sight that damn near made his heart stop. Suzy was standing in front of the refrigerator with the freezer door open and a pint of ice cream in one hand and a spoon in the other. A black thong showcased the cheeks of her ass and a matching black top in the same lace barely skimmed the top of the panties. Even the cast on her ankle looked sexy. Her crutches were leaning on the counter next to the refrigerator as she stood propped against one of the doors for balance. From his angle, he could see her eyes close as she stuck the spoon in her mouth and moaned in pleasure before slowly pulling it out to repeat the process.

Gray was afraid he was going to literally explode in his pants if he stood there for much longer. He dropped his briefcase on the floor, watching as her startled gaze flew to his. The air practically sizzled around them as he strode purposefully toward her. He took the ice cream from her hand and shoved it back in the freezer with the spoon still inside. He wanted her here and now, on the kitchen floor or the counter, he didn't really care which as long as he was inside her. The sight of the crutches reminded him that he'd have to be careful, but there was no way he was being denied.

Neither one of them spoke as he reached for her, pulling her close and taking possession of her mouth. His hands slid down and cupped the cheeks of her bottom, squeezing her against his rigid length. He'd no idea if he had enough control to make their first time last. He'd wanted her for so long that he felt incapable of gentleness. He reached down to hook his arms under her knees and carried her to the bedroom before he took her against the refrigerator.

Chapter Fourteen

Suzy felt like she was in the middle of a dream. One minute she was eating ice cream and the next minute Gray was carrying her through the house toward the bedroom. His jaw was clenched, and as she traced his bottom lip with her finger, his eyes blazed. This wasn't the planned seduction that she had in mind for the evening, but it was so much better. She was desperately aroused and so sensitive that the feel of her thong between her legs was coming close to bringing her to orgasm.

Gray lowered her gently to the bed, stepping back long enough to impatiently kick his shoes off and remove his shirt. Suzy sucked in a breath at the naked beauty of his broad shoulders with muscles rippling and his taut stomach with a thin line of hair disappearing into his slacks. His hand went to his belt buckle when she reached out and stopped him. With a hoarse laugh he said, "Baby, if you're trying to stop me, you might as well shoot me because it will kill me."

Suzy gave him a tender smile, keeping eye contact as she brushed his hands aside and slowly unbuckled his belt, sliding it from the loops of his pants. As she dropped the belt on the floor, she unbuttoned his slacks and stopped with her hand on the zipper. Never breaking eye contact, she leaned over and placed a kiss on his lower stomach below his belly button. She smiled as his stomach jerked in reaction to her touch. She lowered the zipper of his slacks and as she parted the fabric, his erection sprang forward, straining at the confines of his boxers. "Oh my, what have we here?" Encouraged by Gray's moan of pleasure, Suzy lightly scrapped a nail down his length and then back up. As she started to hook her fingers in the top of his boxers, Gray clamped a hand down over hers.

"Playtime is over right now, baby. If your hand touches me there again I'll do something I haven't done since I was a teenager: embarrass myself. God, I need to touch you."

Suzy shivered at the husky timbre of his voice. He put his hands under her arms and lifted her to the center of the bed. As he knelt beside her he said, "Tell me if I hurt you. I know we need to work around your cast, but I need to know if anything I do causes you any discomfort, okay?" Suzy nodded her head as she lay back on the bed, reveling in the sight of his masculine beauty. He propped a couple of pillows up under her head and then braced his knees on either side, straddling her body. His bulging erection rubbed against her stomach and the apex of her thighs as he lowered his head to take her mouth.

This kiss was so carnal it literally curled her toes. His tongue swept inside her mouth, staking claim to all it touched. Suzy lifted her arms, grasping his shoulders and running her hands over his biceps, before curling her fingers in his hair, pulling him closer and closer. The taste of his mouth was heady and rich, better than the finest of wine. He nipped lightly on the corner of her mouth and then licked it to take away the sting. He lowered his head, trailing kisses down her neck. His tongue circled the shell of her ear, causing her nipples to pebble unbearably hard as if demanding their turn.

As if heeding the call, he sat back on his haunches and cupped his hands around her breasts. "Ah, baby, a perfect handful." Locking his gaze on hers, he whispered, "These are mine, sweetheart, mine." Suzy could only nod in agreement; she was powerless to deny him anything at this point. A smile settled on his lips as he found the tie holding the lacy top together. With a flick of his wrist, the bow gave way and her breasts were laid bare. He looked at her for several moments as if mesmerized and then his fingers lazily started drawing circles around her erect nipples. Suzy whimpered as each stroke against her nipple sent a rippling heat straight down between her thighs. Liquid heat pooled there, readying her for Gray's possession.

He lowered his dark head and took one nipple into the dark recesses of his mouth, sucking the taut peak as Suzy arched her back, mindless with pleasure. She dug her hands in his hair, not certain if she wanted to push him away to stop the exquisite torture or pull him closer for more. She was helpless to hold back the moans escaping her throat at the rough texture of his tongue against her nipple. His mouth finally released one peak and he turned his attention to the other. His hand was lightly stroking her stomach, sliding lower to settle between her legs.

Suzy rotated her hips against his hand, desperate to feel it against her with nothing between them. With one last kiss against the curve of her breast, Gray moved to the foot of the bed, causing her to moan at the loss of his hand between her thighs. He leaned over, starting at her ankles and lightly ran his hand up her calves and then along her inner thighs. He gently spread her legs as he went farther, careful not to jar her broken ankle. When he reached her core, his hand traveled back down and he bent his head, using his lips to travel the same line his hand had just taken. Suzy's body jerked as she felt his warm breath against the lace of her panties. He trailed his finger up and over her mound, rubbing her lightly through the material. "Ah, baby, you're so beautiful. I want to kiss and lick every single inch of your soft skin."

Suzy was slowly going out of her mind. She was going to blow apart if he didn't come inside her soon and ease the ache. Suddenly, his hands grasped the dainty side of her panties and with a flick of his wrist the material gave way. Before she could recover from the shock, he'd taken the other side and ripped them as well. Sitting back on his heels, he gave her a sexy smile. "Sorry, baby, I didn't want to hurt your ankle trying to get them off you. You might want to consider giving up underwear permanently."

Gray sat back to look at the treasure he'd uncovered. With his finger, he eased open the folds of her sex, taking a deep breath at the sight of the swollen, pink nub glistening with the evidence of her need for him. As he ran his finger over the nub, Suzy bucked, a low moan coming from her throat. He could come right now just from looking at her like this. She lay open to him, giving herself completely. He wanted to rip his own underwear off and bury himself inside her. Some reserve that he didn't even know he had was holding him back, and demanding that he give her everything he had before he linked their bodies.

Reaching out, he circled her nub, letting her get used to the feel of his finger a few seconds before he slowly started to penetrate her with it. Her inner muscles clenched tightly around him, pulling him farther into her depths. He could feel the ripples beginning inside her and knew she was close to her release. He slowly slid a second finger inside her and she raised her hips, pulling him deeper.

Suzy's body was wound as tightly as a bow. Gray's fingers were bringing her equal parts of pleasure and torture. Her body was desperate for release. She could feel the moisture dripping from her thighs as his fingers continued to plunge into her. Just as she felt herself starting to crest, her orgasm shimmering on the horizon, Gray increased the pressure on her clit to mirror the speed of his thrusts into her and she blew apart. Her orgasm ripped through her body, taking her breath away as the contractions seemed to go on and on.

Gray felt her peak, her muscles clenching against his fingers as if holding him in place. He continued to thrust inside her until her muscles loosened some. Just as her body settled, he leaned over and before she knew his intentions, he took her glistening nub into his mouth. He had to use his arm to settle her body, afraid she was going to hurt her ankle as she bucked wildly beneath him. The taste of her was almost his undoing; she was just as he knew she'd be, sweet and spicy. Releasing her nub, he held her lips open so his tongue could follow the same path that his fingers had just taken. This time her orgasm flowed hard and fast. Her moans were now closer to screams and Gray knew that his control was gone.

He stepped off the bed and grabbed one of the condoms from his pants pocket that he'd thought to buy on the way home. Nick really had a good laugh over that. Locking eyes with Suzy, he lowered his boxers, his erection springing forward from the confines. Her eyes widened as she took in his size. When she licked her lips, he almost lost it. She opened her arms to him, her invitation clear. He quickly sheathed himself with the condom and settled back on the bed. He helped Suzy onto her side, leaving her cast on the bottom and pulled her back snugly against his chest.

So much for her hope that Gray was less than perfect in the penis department; she'd been off there by a long . . . long shot. She'd always thought Jeff was an average size but if that were true, Gray was well above average. She had doubts that she could even stretch enough to accommodate his size, but she planned to die of pleasure trying if she had to. She'd wondered what position they would use due to her ankle injury and it was now obvious that Gray had given that some thought as well. As he pulled her against him, he lifted her leg over his thighs and she caught her breath as she felt him probing against her entrance. She gripped the hand that he laid over her stomach and twined her fingers with his and pushed her bottom against him, whispering, "Now, Gray, I want you now."

With a hoarse groan, he started to ease into her. He gritted his teeth as he slowly advanced, inch by inch. She was so tight, he was trying to maintain control and go slow so that he wouldn't hurt her. When she moved her body against his impatiently, he could no longer hold back, and with a shout, he gave them both what they wanted and plunged in to the hilt. "Baby, are you okay?"

Suzy raised his hand to her lips and kissed the palm. "I'm perfect. Don't stop." When she took his thumb and sucked it into her mouth, he lost all control. He withdrew completely and plunged back in. Suzy moved her hips in tempo with his, meeting his thrusts and angling her body to take him even deeper. As the volume of her moans increased, he could feel the tremors start in her body. He released her hand to move to where their bodies were joined. As he flicked his finger against her nub, she screamed as her body started clenching. Gray tried to hold himself in check, to prolong the moment for her, but the feel of her small hand gripping his shaft as he pulled back to thrust in her again was his undoing. She gently gripped his balls as he plunged inside her once again and violent shudders shook his body as he came.

In the haze of passion, Gray felt an overwhelming wave of love flow through him for the woman he was joined with. He wanted to shout it to the world, but was also afraid of ruining the moment and having her retreat from him. He lay there for a moment, reluctant to separate from her heat. His body was spent or at least he thought it was, but a wiggle of her pert little bottom completely dispelled that notion. With a rough groan, he said, "Baby, you're going to kill me. I think I just lost five years of my life."

With what could only be described as a wicked laugh, Suzy took his hand and put it over her breast. She felt her nipple instantly harden as he tweaked the peak between his fingers. She felt like she should say something to acknowledge the single best moment of her life, but she was at a loss as to what. If she went with her heart, she'd be declaring her love now. Would he return the words or find an excuse to pull away? There was no way she could bear it if he made some excuse and left her now. She'd shatter. Lying there in his arms with his body still embedded within hers, there was no room left to hide. She loved him, and she knew the way a woman does that this was it for her. Whether they worked out or not, Gray was the love of her life. There would never be another man to hold her heart again. If she was honest, she'd admit that she had been his from the moment they met. Her running days were over; she only hoped that the keeper of her heart this time would cherish it and not stomp it to pieces.

She felt Gray stirring inside her. After the relentless way he'd pleasured her earlier, he seemed to be rising to the occasion for a repeat performance. His lovemaking was the stuff that legends were made of. His size had stretched every corner of her feminine core, but her body had lovingly adjusted as if welcoming its missing half. She started as she felt Gray's warm lips in the curve of her neck and his hand cupping her bottom, giving it a playful squeeze.

"I can practically hear the wheels turning in your mind, baby; I hope you're thinking of this." To emphasize what "this" meant, he flexed his hips, moving inside of her.

With a laugh, Suzy said, "You're pretty proud of yourself aren't you, slick? I must say, you have the moves. I probably won't be able to walk right for a week." She jerked in protest as Gray withdrew from her body. "Hey, no fair, where are you going?"

Gray pointed to his impressive length. "Just a condom change, babe; save my place for me." Soon he strolled back from the bathroom and she suspected he put a little more swagger than usual in his walk. She was powerless to avert her gaze from his erection as he came closer to her. Amusement lined his face as he said, "Can I show you anything in your size, ma'am?"

As he came to stand beside the bed, she leaned over and took him in her hand. His body jerked at the feel of her hand firmly clasping him. She pulled up into a sitting position on the bed and released his erection long enough to tug him onto the bed with her hand. With him on his knees, she leaned over and gripped his length again. His eyes widened as she led him to her mouth. Her tongue reached out and licked the tip of his penis like an ice cream cone. His big body shuddered, and heat slammed through him. With a few more soft licks, she slid her hands around to his butt and gripped a cheek in each hand. She used the position to drive his erection into her mouth.

With a harsh shout, Gray ran his hands in her hair, guiding the pressure of those soft lips as she licked, nipped, and sucked. The sight of her red hair flowing over his penis would have brought him to his knees if he wasn't already there. Her hand and her mouth worked as a team gliding up and down his shaft, sometimes so slowly it drove him crazy and then increasing the tempo until the blood was pounding in his head. When he knew he was close to the brink, he stilled her hand, wanting to be inside her before his release.

Gray donned another condom and slid onto the bed. "Baby, do you think you can do the good old missionary? I don't want to move your ankle, but I want to be able to look into your eyes when I enter you, and be able to kiss those beautiful lips when we're making love."

Suzy's heart melted at his words. She didn't care if she had to hang her cast behind her head at that moment; she wanted exactly what he did. She opened her arms and he lowered himself over her. This time there were no preliminaries. As he reached down to take possession of her mouth, he also took possession of her body with a firm stroke. Suzy moaned, her body stretching to welcome him again. She already felt herself on the edge of an orgasm as the friction increased with every stroke of his body.

Somehow this joining was even more intimate than the last. With Gray's body fully pressed against hers, she hooked her good ankle around his hips, driving him deeper inside her. She jerked her mouth from his, gasping, "Gray, mmm, faster, oh, God, faster!"

Her words were like gasoline on Gray's fire, the need for her pushing everything else from his mind. There was only here and now, this woman and the heaven of finally having her in his arms. Her ears rang as he increased the tempo, pumping harder and faster. Suzy's thrusts met his with equal vigor, both of them reaching for the ultimate pinnacle of pleasure. His heart swelled as she clutched him, screaming his name as she shuddered with pleasure. With a few more thrusts, his body joined hers in climax. Even though he didn't want to leave her body, he knew he was too heavy for her to take his full weight. He collapsed beside her on the bed, running his hand lightly up and down her stomach while he caught his breath.

Suzy turned her head to study Gray. With a devilish smile, she said, "Oh, baby, he has a big stick and he definitely knows how to use it."

Gray chuckled. He loved that he never knew what

she was going to say next. He leaned over and kissed the tip of her nose. "You're not so bad yourself, baby. If it weren't for being afraid I'd crack your cast open, I'd show you a few more tricks with my big stick."

Even though her body was spent, she still tingled at his words. She knew she'd be sore tomorrow, but she also knew it was worth every twinge. "Hey, slick, how about a shower?" At his hopeful expression, she held her hand up. "Um, no, not that, even though it sounds yummy. I'm afraid my cast cover wouldn't hold for a round of wild-monkey love, shower-style."

"Yeah, that sounds great. After traveling half the day and other pursuits, I could really use it. I'm afraid you wouldn't love me if I started to stink up the bed."

Suzy's heart thudded at his casual mention of love. *Get a grip; it's just a figure of speech. He's not on bended knee beside the bed with a ring. Stop acting like a twelve-year-old with her first crush.* She forced a light laugh, saying, "You got that right, spare the soap and spoil the mood." Her breath caught in her throat as Gray rose from the bed. She was actually afraid she'd swallowed her tongue for a moment. God he was beautiful. His tight butt just begged to be squeezed and his penis made her want to do a drool check. Such masculine perfection hardly seemed fair. Gray's parents must certainly be stunners to have produced children who looked like him and his brother. She bet that many a heart had been broken through the years. She just hoped she wasn't another one to add to his list.

Suzy shrieked in surprise as he leaned down and hefted her into his arms. "Gray, I can walk, put me down." He shut her up in a move that left little room for arguing. His mouth took possession of hers and his tongue swept aside every argument she had. By the time he was finished, she could barely hold a single thought.

She pointed him to the cabinet under the sink where she kept her cast covers and soon Gray had it on and gently seated her in the shower seat. He helped her wash, which was a lesson in torture with his hands seeming to be everywhere at once. She clamped her thighs around his hand as it wandered between her legs, steadily inching toward her core. "Stop that, you're insatiable," she said, laughing.

Leaning down to kiss her lightly, he looked into her eyes and whispered, "Only for you, baby."

It took quite a while to finish showering and drying off. They both had a hard time keeping their hands off each other, so the simplest of tasks took twice as long as usual. Finally, they were back in bed with Gray curved around her body, his hand on her stomach and her hand resting over his. How had she ever slept without the feel of his body against hers? As her eyes grew heavy, Suzy nestled back farther into the safety of his arms, smiling sleepily when she heard his groan as her bottom pressed against his groin.

Chapter Fifteen

Suzy woke up to the sun shining in the window. A quick look at the bedside clock showed it was just after nine. She looked down at the masculine arm draped across her hip. Even in sleep with stubble on his face and rumpled hair, the man only looked hotter. She'd love nothing better than to shrug off her covers, climb on top of him, and take him inside her. Liquid pooled and her muscles clenched at the thought. Unfortunately, immediate needs had to be answered. Her mouth was so dry that her tongue was stuck to the roof, and she was desperate to use the bathroom.

She decided to use the bathroom off the kitchen and then get a glass of water. Maybe she'd put together some breakfast for them. She wasn't nearly as talented as Gray and Nick in the kitchen, but she could at least fix some eggs. It took a few moments to struggle from under Gray's arm. He finally mumbled something in his sleep and turned to his other side, freeing her. She grabbed his shirt from the foot of the bed and pulled it over her head. She smiled, knowing he would like seeing her in it. She looked around for her crutches and then remembered that in their haste to make it to the bedroom last night, she'd left them in the kitchen. Luckily she'd acquired some mad balancing skills the last few weeks and she was able to hobble to the kitchen, keeping most of her weight on her other foot. She almost tripped over Gray's briefcase, which was still lying on the floor where he'd dropped it. She went straight to the bathroom and then hobbled back to the kitchen.

Her stomach was growling, reminding her of all the calories she'd burned the previous night. Humming under her breath, Suzy opened the refrigerator to survey the contents. *Hmm, okay, someone needs to go shopping.* It looked like it was going to be a simple meal of cereal and toast. She cocked her head, hearing a buzzing sound. She shrugged when the sound stopped, and poured a glass of water from the glass pitcher in the refrigerator. As she finished her first sip, she again heard a buzzing sound. It seemed to be coming from near the doorway. She walked in that direction and the sound once again stopped. She leaned against the wall, determined to find the source of the annoying sound. A few moments later, the buzzing was back and she looked down at Gray's briefcase. The sound appeared to be coming from there.

"What the heck?" As she opened the case, the sound again came and Suzy felt the front pocket vibrate. Sticking her hand in, she pulled out his cell phone. "Ah-ha, got ya! Pretty tricky aren't you?" *Okay, you're talking to a cell phone, maybe it's time for some breakfast. The low blood sugar is getting to you.*

The phone again buzzed in her hand. She frowned down, looking at the display. It showed fifteen missed calls and twenty text messages. Good grief, had something happened? Should she go wake up Gray and have him check his phone? She hated to do that, knowing he was tired from the travel and um ... other things. She didn't know his password to check the messages, but she could read the first few texts to make sure everything was okay. She hit the button to display the text messages and was even more concerned. They were all from the same person. Had something happened to Nick or his parents?

When she opened the first one, she felt the floor start to shift under her. She was back in her apartment a year ago reading Jeff's messages and having her whole world collapse around her. Somehow the pain she felt then was nothing compared to the pain she felt now. The first message simply said, *Call me, lover.* As her hand trembled, she clicked on the second message, *Remember that night in your house, we didn't get much sleep did we, lover?* She tried to stop herself from looking at another text, but it was like a train wreck she was helpless to avoid. With another click, the rest of her world fell away. *I'm lying here stroking my body remembering the feel of you inside me.*

Suzy dropped the phone as if it were a snake and hobbled to the bathroom, bile rushing from her throat in waves. She heard her name being called from another room, but was unable to get control of her stomach. Gray rushed into the bathroom, a pair of shorts riding low on his hips. "Baby, are you okay?" He pulled her hair back from her face as she was sick one last time. She tried to pull away from him but he held on to her arm tightly as if afraid she'd collapse. "Baby, what happened? Are you finished?"

Tears flowed out of her eyes and down her cheeks. Gray grabbed a washcloth from the vanity and wet it. He gently smoothed her hair back and cleaned her face.

His eyes mirrored his concern as he finished with her face and lifted her chin. "Would you prefer to go back to bed or maybe the couch?"

Suzy looked at the face of the man she loved and wondered how he could look so concerned for her when he'd apparently been with someone else while he was away. Maybe it didn't take him two weeks to finish up after all. He could have been in Charleston part of the time with whoever sent him the text messages. Did everyone know but her? Nick, Claire, Jason, and Declan had all mentioned his trip at dinner the previous evening. Had he fooled them all or were they covering for him? There was no way Nick didn't know; they were too close. That thought hurt almost as much as Gray's betrayal. She trusted Nick and had started to think of him as a brother. Had he been playing her, too, covering for his brother?

She used what strength she had left to pull away from Gray. She saw the confusion and concern as he tried to figure out what was going on. She hobbled back out to the kitchen and stood next to his cell phone that she'd dropped. Stopping to stand in front of her, he frowned. "Baby, what the hell is going on?"

She looked down at the phone and his gaze followed hers. She saw his shoulders stiffen as if calculating what she knew. When he looked up into her eyes, he knew. Was her life destined to be ruined by a cell phone again and again? First Jeff, and now Gray?

Gray felt his whole world falling apart. Last night had been the single most amazing night of his life and he'd awakened this morning reaching for Suzy. The love he felt for her overwhelmed him. He'd planned to tell her today, but that wouldn't happen now. She'd never believe him with the timing. He didn't have to look at his phone to know what she'd found. Reva had had his new number for several days now and since he'd planned to tell Suzy all about it, he hadn't seen the need to try to get the number changed again. He deleted the messages and texts each day without even reading them. He didn't think Suzy would dig through his briefcase looking for his phone for no reason. She must have heard a call or text coming through.

His gut clenched to see what that had done to her. There were tears on her cheeks and even worse, she'd been physically sick. He felt like the lowest piece of pond scum. His omission had done this to someone he loved more than his life. He should have trusted her and never let it get to this point. Squaring his shoulders, he prepared to do what he should have done weeks ago—tell her the truth. "Suzanna, let's go sit in the living room and talk."

As he tried to take her hand, she hid it behind her back, knowing it was childish, but if he touched her, she'd fall apart. Sarcasm was her only defense and she prepared to wield it for protection as she had so many times before. "Wow. Why am I only Suzanna when someone has screwed around on me? You know, I think Jeff called me the same thing when he saw me holding his cell phone and knew he was busted. It looks like you have committed a pretty big offense. Are you sure you wouldn't rather call me Ms. Denton?"

Gray saw through the flippant words to the hurt lying underneath them. She was close to the edge and if he had a prayer of saving what was between them, he had to get through to her now. The walls were going up and he knew that once they were firmly in place, he'd never reach her again. He had to get her to sit down long enough to listen and there was only one way to do that: make her his captive audience. He leaned down and scooped her up in his arms before she had time to dodge him.

Suzy sputtered, trying to twist out of his arms. "Stop it," Gray demanded. "You're going to hurt yourself. I'm putting you on the couch and you're listening to me dammit; you owe me that much."

When he sat her on the couch, she quickly scooted away, intending to go to the bedroom and shut the door until she could get Beth to pick her up. "I don't owe you anything, Gray; you screwed some other woman and then came straight back here to me. Should I be grateful that you had time to fit me in? I'll give you credit; you have some stamina there, slick. It's actually quite impressive."

Suzy was incensed when Gray actually put his hand over her mouth to stop the flow of words pouring out of her. He enunciated each word harshly, "STOP IT NOW!"

At that moment, the front door opened and Nick and Beth came walking into the living room, stopping in shock at the scene before them. "What's going on, bro?"

Gray threw them a look that had them both backing up. "Leave now." Then, as if almost an afterthought, he added, "Please."

Suzy started to struggle, trying to tell her sister to wait for her. Beth took a hesitant step forward before Nick put his arm on hers, halting her. Suzy knew by the look on his face that he knew what was going on and her heart broke a second time that morning. "Let's go,

Beth. They need some time alone." She could hear Beth protesting as Nick led her back out the door.

When the front door closed again, Gray looked down at her and closed his eyes wearily for a few moments before opening them again. "I know you're angry and I know you aren't going to believe me at first, but please just listen to the whole story. I promise you, baby, I haven't cheated on you, just please listen to me." As she started to protest, he held up his hand. "Please, if you care anything about us just listen to what I have to say." He started back at the very beginning from when he'd met Suzy and how drawn he was to her. He admitted that he'd gone out with Reva just to take his mind off Suzy. He'd been afraid that they were never going to be together and had decided to go out with Reva after she pursued him. There were never feelings involved and there were just casual dates. When he got to the part where he slept with her one time, the only outward reaction from Suzy was the clenching of her fists.

He took a moment to catch his breath, and studied Suzy's reaction. Her eyes were carefully averted from his as she stared out the door. He continued the story, telling her about breaking it off with Reva and the barrage of phone calls, texts, and visits. He admitted that he'd felt guilty for letting it go that far and had been hesitant to report it to the authorities. He also ended the story, telling her of his fear of her finding out and pulling away from him.

Suzy sat beside him not moving a muscle. Gray didn't know whether to be encouraged that she'd given up trying to get away from him or scared that she seemed so lifeless. He decided to stay quiet and give her time to work everything out in her head. She sat beside him looking incredibly small and fragile in his big shirt.

Suzy's head was spinning and her stomach was again churning. Out of everything she'd imagined, this was a scenario that had never entered her mind. It was too far-fetched to be made up. It hurt that he'd kept this from her, but what truly killed her was imagining Gray with the other woman, possessing her body just as he had hers. She knew that she'd no right to feel that way, but she did. There had never been a commitment between them and there certainly wasn't when this happened. Maybe in some part of her fantasy world, she thought Gray had been in Charleston for this past year pining over her when in reality he had been living his life, which included dating and having sex with someone else.

She still couldn't look Gray in the eyes. She knew he was waiting for her to say something and she could also feel his fear. Still looking straight ahead, she quietly asked, "Who else knows? Obviously Nick. I could see it on his face this morning, but who else?"

Gray's voice had taken on her same low tone, as if afraid he'd frighten her away. "Yes, Nick knows and also Jason. I'm sure there are others, such as security at Mericom and at my home in Charleston. It would have been impossible to hide it from Nick and Jason with Reva making a scene at Mericom on a regular basis. Don't be angry at either of them; they wanted you told before I went out of town." Gray took a deep breath and continued, "Sweetheart, I'm so sorry. This is exactly what I was afraid would happen and I've made it that much worse by letting you find out the way you did."

As he laid a hand on her shoulder, Suzy pulled away. "I can't talk about this right now, Gray. I need some time to think." At his look of despair, she added, "I'm not leaving; I just have to be by myself for a while. Could you please get my crutches for me?" She could tell that he wanted to argue, but he quietly got up and retrieved her crutches from the kitchen. By the time he returned, she was standing beside the couch and she took the crutches from his hands. When she reached the bedroom door, she turned around, finally facing him, and said, "Please just let me have this time. I'll come out when I'm ready. Go to work if you need to, I'll be fine." The door shut quietly behind her and Gray stood staring at it for a few moments before walking outside to sit on the deck.

Suzy closed the bedroom door and leaned against it, studying the room. The bed was still rumpled from their night together. Who would have thought that things would fall apart so quickly? She couldn't bear to sit there so she walked over to the chaise longue in front of the windows and settled herself against the cushions. Where did they go from here? She could pack her bags and have Beth pick her up. It would be difficult to navigate the steps to her condo, but she was more mobile now than she'd been a few weeks ago.

If she left though, was it the official end of whatever this was that she had with Gray? Was she ready for it to be over? She couldn't stay here with him if she felt as if he'd cheated on her. Maybe she was punishing Gray for Jeff's sins. Although, if she thought back, she'd never felt the crushing devastation that she'd felt when she read the messages on Gray's phone. Jeff had thrown her for a major loop. Maybe one of the main reasons, though, was she just truly never thought Jeff had it in him to be anything other than a straight arrow. Did it upset her because she had been in love with him or was it more shock that he'd dared deviate from who she thought he was? All that she knew was that it didn't hold a candle to the gut-wrenching pain of imagining a life without Gray in it.

Suddenly, a smile covered her face as she remembered a line she used to tell Claire often when she was encouraging her to get a life. *Put your big-girl panties on.* Well maybe it was time she took her own advice. She got up from the chaise and hobbled to the bathroom. She looked at herself in the mirror and wondered who the pathetic person staring back at her was. Her eyes were puffy, her hair was hanging in disarray, and she was as pale as a ghost. *Screw this! I refuse to be the victim again. That's my man out there and no whack-job woman is going to ruin my life again. She thinks she's crazy? Well she ain't seen crazy yet, but it's coming.*

It took her almost two hours to shower, dress, and pack, but already she felt more like herself. The pitiful creature of this morning was gone. In her place was a woman with a mission. She and Gray would go to Charleston and this mess was going to be taken care of. Their lives couldn't move forward with this hanging over them. She loved him, dammit, and even though it would probably scare the crap out of him, she planned to have him in her life for the duration. She was never one to back down from a fight, and this was a fight for the most important thing in her life. Stepping back from the mirror, she gave her reflection one last look. Black leather skirt? Check. Off-the-shoulder silk peasant top?

Check. One flat leopard-skin sandal? Yuck. Well, two out of three wasn't bad. She had her hair back in an elegant ponytail and her makeup was flawless. Stiffening her spine, she prepared to do battle if necessary with Gray, and with a smile she acknowledged that he wouldn't know what hit him.

Gray had just walked back into the living room from the deck when the bedroom door opened. Expecting to see a still upset Suzy, he was shocked at the person standing there instead. Gone was the pale, shaken woman in his big shirt. In her place was the beautiful, sexy, confident woman that he had fallen in love with. Hope took root inside him as he stepped toward her, his eyes desperately searching hers for some indication of her feelings. When she turned behind her and reached for the handle of her suitcase, his heart dropped to the floor.

He held a hand out to her, ready to plead if he had to. "Baby, where are you going? Please don't . . ." Before he could finish his sentence she interrupted him.

"*I'm* not leaving, Gray; *we* are leaving. Why don't you pack whatever you need. I'm ready to get on the road before it gets any later."

"Honey, I'm at a loss here. Get on the road to where?"

As she moved to stand in front of him, Gray thought, *My God, when have crutches ever looked this sexy?* "We're going to Charleston, Gray. We have a problem and we are going to solve it . . . together. I'm finished being left out of the loop. From now on, this concerns both of us. If you aren't comfortable with that, then there will be no us."

He was a man who made million-dollar deals over

breakfast, he was on a first-name basis with senators and congressmen, and he was proud of the fact that he was never at a loss for words. No matter what the situation or problem, he was smooth. It was his God-given talent and it had made him a very successful businessman. This woman in front of him, with her eyes flashing and her good foot tapping impatiently, had done what no one else could do; she'd made him speechless. He'd expected to grovel at her feet for days, hoping she'd give him another chance. He'd braced himself to see the hurt and betrayal in her eyes again and, God, the tears; those were like stakes through his heart. Yet here she was telling him to pack his bags so they could go handle Reva together. She was exceptional and she was still his.

"Um, honey, what do you have in mind? I don't think you're in any condition to go drag Reva out by her hair or anything. We can certainly go to Charleston and turn everything over to the police."

With a sigh of impatience, she said, "I'm not some redneck, Gray; I'm not gathering my kinfolk to go kick her arse. I do want to see her, though." She held up her hand to stop his protests. "She needs to know that you're taken, Gray, and trust me, she'll want to see that proof. As to how that will happen, we will decide when we get there. Now, please, can we go?"

Suzy stiffened as Gray walked toward her with a slow, sexy smile. Her body responded immediately, but her heart needed to keep its distance for now. To his credit, he didn't reach for her. He looked her in the eyes for a moment, and then quietly said, "I love you so much it takes my breath away." As she started to shake her head, he continued, "I know this isn't the time for this talk and we will put it on the back burner for now. I needed you to know that. You take my breath away."

Gray walked toward the bedroom, and Suzy heard him opening drawers as he packed. She quickly wiped a tear from her eyes, his declaration of love still ringing in her ears. She wanted to bask in the moment, the first time he declared his love, but she couldn't, not yet. The timing was all wrong and things were too unsettled between them. The desire to just give up and run was still there. If she did, though, would she ever stop running? This was a pivotal moment in her life and how she handled it could very well define her love life forever.

Chapter Sixteen

As if afraid she'd change her mind, Gray had packed a bag and was leading her out the door and into his BMW in less than an hour. He called Jason before they left, letting him know that they would be in Charleston for a few days. He'd also called Nick and, even though Suzy knew Nick was bombarding him with questions about what was going on, Gray kept the conversation brief.

He turned on the stereo in the car and Suzy's gaze flew to his when the first strains of Bon Jovi's "Always" drifted through the car. Gray's lips lifted in a grin at the shock on Suzy's face. "Claire told me you liked them. I've actually seen them in concert a few times. The first time was in Tokyo with my father, if you can believe it. It was the first time I traveled with him on business, and the customer there had gotten the tickets for us. It was on New Year's Eve 1990 and, man, what a night."

Mesmerized, Suzy watched the emotions flittering across his handsome face. "That was probably one of the highlights of my teenage years. I felt so damn important. I was out of the country with my father and he was treating me like an adult. I was also proud because my dad seemed like the coolest man in the world. He knew most of the songs and he sang and danced in the aisles along with everyone else." With a laugh, Gray said, "I suspect now he probably had some very strong alcohol helping him find his groove that night, but it was so great to see him let loose. I saw them again about ten years later in Fort Lauderdale with some buddies from college. We had a blast that evening, but it still didn't compare to that first concert with my dad. That was special." With a squeeze of her hand, he said, "Maybe you and I can catch a show the next time they're touring."

Suzy threw her head back and laughed until tears streamed down her face.

"You're starting to hurt my ego here, baby. A simple 'no, thank you' would have been sufficient. You don't have to laugh until you collapse."

"Sorry," she managed to choke out. "I wasn't laughing about going to a concert with you; I was laughing because I never imagined you going to one, period, unless it was a Harry Connick or Michael Buble. Not that there is anything wrong with them. I just imagined you would like quieter music. I told Claire once that I could never go out with you because you didn't even own a Bon Jovi Tour shirt and now I find out you saw them in Japan. How cool."

With a chuckle, Gray said, "Well, my conversation with Claire makes a little more sense now. I couldn't figure out why she was grilling me on my musical preferences and seemed greatly relieved when I mentioned liking a lot of the older rock music. With her being pregnant and all, I was terrified of letting her down and making her cry. She looked so serious at the time. Now I know she was just interviewing me to see if I was worthy of dating her friend."

They talked about other bands that they both liked

and Suzy was surprised to find that their tastes were pretty similar. As if by mutual agreement, they avoided talking about their argument that morning and about Reva. Looking at the road signs, she saw they were getting closer to Charleston. "So, where do you live in Charleston? I've been there a couple of times for weekend trips."

"I have a place in the French Quarter. Have you been there?" Gray asked.

"Wooo, baby, I'm impressed! Yes, I've been there. I bought a beautiful bracelet in a little shop there a few years ago. That's a gorgeous place. Are you keeping your place there even though you will be living in Myrtle Beach?"

"For now, yes. I'm sure I'll be going back and forth between the two cities a lot and I'm rather attached to my place there. There are only twelve condominiums in my complex and it's located in a residential area full of historic homes. I know most of my neighbors by name and there is nothing like strolling around in the quarter on a Sunday. My usual routine when I wasn't traveling was to stop at one of the outdoor coffeehouses there and have a cup of coffee, a pastry, and read the paper. I could sit there for hours during the spring and fall. During the summer, you have a brief window before the day starts to heat up."

Suzy couldn't help but smile at Gray's obvious love of the city. She could picture him doing exactly as he described and she also knew that she'd love to be with him some morning, holding hands and strolling through the city. Maybe when this whole mess was behind them, they could start over and be a normal, dating couple. *Ugh, when have I ever wanted to be normal?*

Okay, maybe I could settle for an unusual dating couple. Yeah that had a better ring to it.

Suzy looked out the window with interest as they drove through the city. Charleston was called the Holy City, and it was obvious when you drove around how it got its nickname. Churches were more numerous here than anywhere she'd ever traveled to. The architecture was breathtaking and the colors vibrant. Stately old houses kept in pristine condition gave you a sense of being transported to another time and place. Palm trees and colorful flowers surrounded each home. The Ashley River made a perfect backdrop for Battery Park. As they passed White Point Gardens and entered the French Quarter section, she sighed in pleasure.

This section of Charleston was probably the most suited to her personality. It had almost a hippie feel to it. She was surprised that Gray had a home here. This was probably the most expensive area to live in the city, but she would have expected something a bit more traditional for him. Gray wasn't the straight arrow she'd always thought him to be. When he pulled up to a gated building complete with a security guard, Suzy smiled as the guard addressed Gray by name. Gray pulled into an underground parking garage and turned off the ignition.

"Home sweet home, baby. Let me help you out and I'll come back for the bags later. I'm on the top floor, but luckily I have an elevator so it shouldn't be too hard for you." He opened his door and stepped out, opening the back door to get her crutches from the backseat. As he helped her from the car, he leaned over to give her a quick kiss as if afraid she'd protest the contact.

Soon they were in the elevator going from the garage floor to the second floor. The hallway they stepped out into was sleek, and she counted four other doors before they came to one at the end of the hall and Gray stuck a key card into the slot on the door. When he swung the door open, he stepped back to allow her to enter the hallway first. She instantly liked the clean lines of his home; everything looked modern, but not cold.

Just as she was turning to get a better view of the living room, she gave a shriek when a couple sitting on the sofa looked at her curiously. Gray almost barreled into her back, not expecting her sudden halt. "What's the matter, baby?"

As he peered around her, he groaned out loud. "Mom, Dad, what're you doing here?"

Suzy wanted to turn around and leave as fast as her crutches would carry her. Even as she seriously considered doing just that, his parents rose from the couch and walked over to where they were standing. Gray's father was an older version of Gray and Nick. He had dark hair with silver at the temples and he was tall and well built. He wore a pair of faded jeans and a blue polo shirt. When she looked at his mother she didn't know if she wanted to laugh or cry. *What is it that they say about the bond between little boys and their mothers? God, it must be true because Gray is dating his mother.* Suzy didn't look like his mother physically other than maybe height, but they could be twins in their choice of clothing. Gray's mother was wearing a pair of tight skinny jeans tucked into a pair of black spike-heeled knee boots. A button-down white blouse was left loose, and a cropped black jacket gave the whole look a fashion punch. She had long blond hair that flowed in waves down her back and perfectly applied makeup that showed off a set of eyes that looked exactly like Gray's.

When she felt Gray tap her on the shoulder, she realized that while she'd been studying them, Gray had been making the introductions. She felt her face flush in embarrassment. Luckily, Gray's father stepped forward and held his hand out. "Hi, Suzy. I'm John Merimon and this is my wife, Victoria."

Suzy shook his hand, returning his smile and then turned to Gray's mother. She was shocked when instead of taking the hand that Suzy had extended to her she stepped forward and threw her arms around her. She was holding her crutches and couldn't return her hug and truthfully she was too surprised to try. Victoria pulled back, still holding on to her shoulders, and said, "Honey, it's so nice to meet you. Nicky has told us all about you. Of course, being Gray's mother, I knew he'd been mooning over some girl for ages."

Suzy couldn't help but laugh at Gray's moan behind her. Gray's father walked over to his son and put a sympathetic arm around his shoulders. "Your mother is a force of nature, son, you just have to hang on and ride the hurricane-force winds out."

"Very funny, John." Gray's mother snorted, but Suzy could see the love in her expression as she looked at her husband. "Oh, geez, look at us standing here running our mouths and this poor girl is forced to stand here on her crutches and listen to us." Shooing the men out of the way, Victoria ushered Suzy to the couch. She pushed an ottoman over to the couch and insisted on propping Suzy's foot up on it. Standing back with her hands on her hips, she surveyed her handiwork with pride. "Now, Suzy, what can I get you to drink? Would you like water, soda, or something stronger like I'm fixing to indulge in?"

"Water would be great, Mrs. Merimon, thanks."

"Oh, God, please call me Vicky. When I hear Mrs. Merimon it makes me think of John's mother, which in turn gives me a serious case of road rash."

Gray's father rolled his eyes as he walked to the living room to take a seat. With a smirk, Gray clapped his father on the back as he walked by. "Force of nature, right, Dad? Guys, I don't believe I caught the reason for the ambush you staged today."

His mother had returned from the kitchen with a bottle of water for Suzy and a glass of wine for herself. She perched on her husband's chair and, after taking a drink of her wine, she said, "I told you that Nicky told us everything, and before you rip him limb from limb, remember you boys can't keep a secret from me. He tried his best, but I knew he was hiding something." Smiling at Suzy, she continued, "Every time they did something wrong growing up, I knew the minute I looked into their chubby little faces they had been up to no good."

Almost choking on her water, Suzy said, "Chubby?"

"Oh, dear, yes. Gray and Nicky were round as little butterballs until they were around ten or so. I think they got that from John's mother."

Suzy didn't know who was more horrified at this point, Gray or John. All she knew was that she loved this woman. She was so outspoken that she made Suzy seem tame. She'd never imagined she'd feel so at home with Gray's parents, but it was as if she'd known them for years.

"Mother, I'm sure Suzy is fascinated by my fat years, but you didn't finish answering the question about why you were waiting for us."

With a dramatic sigh, Victoria said, "He's always so impatient. So as I was saying, Gray, your brother told us about that tramp Reva and what she's been putting you through. I will say, Gray, that I'm not proud of you for sleeping with that girl."

Gray looked completely mortified to be having this discussion with his mother. If they hadn't been discussing him sleeping with another woman, Suzy would have found the whole conversation hysterical.

"Mom, I'm sorry that you feel that I didn't treat Reva well, but I don't think this is the time to discuss it."

"Gray, honey, I'm just pointing out that if you had listened to my pep talks all of these years, you would have remembered the most important one concerning people like Reva: 'If you roll with dogs, you will get fleas.'"

Suzy couldn't help it; she threw her head back and laughed until her sides hurt. Gray hung his head in defeat as his mother continued imparting more of her wisdom. When she finally caught her breath, John winked at her and said, "Welcome to the family, Suzy. Imagine our Christmas dinners each year.

"So what's the plan with this woman, son? We could talk to her parents, Bart and Jean, but I don't know how much good it will do. We aren't really friends, and frankly, I find them both obnoxious. Have you thought of a restraining order?"

"I'm thinking of talking to her first, Dad."

Suzy put her hand on Gray's arm and added, "He means that *we* are going to talk to her first. I told Gray that I felt that she needed to see us together so that she'd understand that he has moved on." With a dead-pan expression, Suzy added, "If that doesn't work, I plan to shove one of my crutches up her ass."

Victoria jumped to her feet and clapped her hands. "Grayson, you have found your match. There will never be a boring day in your life with this one; she and I are going to be the best of friends."

Gray looked as if he couldn't decide if that was good or bad news. He rarely ever stood a chance against his mother and now, with her firmly aligned with Suzy, the men in his family might as well wave the white flag now. "I think we are going to settle in, and Suzy needs to rest for a while after our ride. I'm going to arrange to meet Reva later on for a drink. I don't want her in my house and I don't want to go to hers. Hopefully this will be the end of it tonight."

His mother gave him a somber look, saying, "I'd like to think so, honey, but if she's anything like her mother, I can't see her giving up that easily. Jean is a lot like Reva and she's relentless when she wants something. I'm afraid, my dear, that the apple didn't fall far from the tree. If we need to, your father and I can make things very difficult for them socially. I don't really enjoy playing those types of games, but I also don't enjoy some tart stalking my son, either."

Gray's father stood and put his arm around his wife. "Your mother and I are going to take off and give you two a chance to relax. We would appreciate a call this evening after you speak with Reva." They each took turns giving both Gray and Suzy a kiss on the cheek. "Suzy, it's been a pleasure meeting you, and I think I speak for Vicky when I say we are both happy that you're in our son's life."

"Happy? Heck, we are thrilled, my dear. I was terrified he'd end up with some uptight socialite. I've taught my boys well, Suzy. If you love them, they will take care of you for the rest of your life."

"Um, Mom, it sounds like you're discussing a puppy." With more hugs, Gray's parents were finally out the door and Gray collapsed against it when it closed. "Oh, man. I'm so sorry, baby; I know you weren't expecting that. If you want to run now and never look back, I couldn't blame you. I'd follow you, though, so you have fair warning."

With a smile, Suzy said, "Are you kidding? I loved them! I wish my parents were like that. You have what I always dreamed of: cool parents. I wanted to ask your mother if I could borrow her outfit."

With a smile, Gray walked over to the couch and settled in next to her. "Yeah, I really lucked out. Mom and Dad are the greatest and even though Mom is a bit of a meddler you can't help but adore her. Of course, those boots of hers weren't just made for walking. She kicked our butts plenty growing up, and she was right, we never could lie to her. She's the original human lie detector. My dad has always been pretty easygoing and he was who you went to when you wanted to discuss technology like computers or phones or if you wanted to borrow money. Mom was who we went to when our hearts were broken or we were feeling guilty about something. She'd throw us in the kitchen and as we baked, we talked. When whatever we had made was ready, Mom would get us both a plate and a glass of milk and we would sit at the bar with her until we felt better again. She might not look like Betty Crocker, but that woman can wield a mean whisk."

Suzy couldn't help but think of how much better her life would have been growing up with parents who took that much interest in her life instead of just meeting her basic needs. She'd love to be able to talk to her mother or father as Gray did to his. Her parents had only visited her home once since she'd lived there. If you wanted to see them, then you had to visit. They took a little more interest in Beth's life, since she'd at least picked a career in education, although they considered teaching children to be pretty low on the pole.

Gray rubbed her hand, asking, "Do you want me to show you to the bedroom to rest for a while?"

Suzy had been dreading this discussion, but she had to make her feelings clear. "That would be great." As if sensing a "but" coming, Gray remained sitting, studying her expression. "Gray, I'd like space of my own. If you only have one bedroom, then I'll gladly take the couch. I know that sounds silly since we have slept together, but I need for this mess to be over before we continue that part of our relationship."

She braced herself, waiting for Gray's argument and was surprised when none came. He took it so well, Suzy wondered if she should be offended and then scolded herself for being silly. You couldn't lay down the law and then sulk when no one challenged it.

Gray stood and held out a hand to help her to her feet. Before she knew what was happening, he gave a tug and pulled her into his arms. He ran his thumb along her bottom lip as he stared into her eyes. "I love you, Suzy, and if I could spare you this I would. I regret the stupidity that made this thing with Reva even possible. I guess in my defense I was just so down over thinking it was never going to happen with us that I let my guard down. I want you in my arms. Hell, I never want you to leave them, but I do understand why you need the distance and I promise to let you call the shots. I want you so bad my teeth ache, but it's up to you, baby. Just know that I'm here waiting for you to come to me. My door and my arms are always open to you."

Suzy's eyes misted with tears at the obvious love in Gray's voice. He leaned down to settle his lips on hers and she felt her heartbeat kick into overdrive. She allowed herself to be pulled firmly against his hard body as he melded their contours together. His breathing was ragged, but his touch was gentle, as if afraid she'd push him away. His tongue sought entrance into her mouth, which she was helpless to deny. As her lips parted, his tongue swept inside, seeking hers and tangling with it. Suzy moaned, feeling liquid heat rush to her core as his erection pressed against her stomach. She knew in another minute she'd be too far gone to protest anything that Gray wanted to do.

Suddenly Gray wrenched his mouth away, breathing deep and ragged. With another deep breath, he rasped, "Baby, I'm sorry for getting carried away. I only meant to brush a kiss on your lips, but when I touch you, I go up in flames. Let me show you to the bedroom and I'll use the guest bath for a very cold shower."

Suzy chuckled at his expression of pain, but truthfully it wasn't that funny since she was suffering just as much as he was. *You made the rules so suck it up, Buttercup, and just hope that your panties don't burst into flames before this is over.* She could see that her nipples were pebbled and pushing against the thin material of her blouse. Since she had to use both of her arms for her crutches, she had nothing to cover them with. The flush on Gray's cheekbones as he looked at her said that he'd noticed them and was having a hard time looking away.

Finally, he cleared his throat and led her down a hallway into what she thought was the master bedroom. A huge bed with a low black headboard dominated one wall with matching nightstand tables on each side of the bed. An armoire stood against the wall at the foot of the bed and a writing desk sat in the front of a large picture window. The white plantation shutters on the windows made a contemporary contrast against the black furniture.

He walked over to another door and flipped on the light as she walked up behind him. The bathroom contained a large espresso-colored double-sink vanity with a matching mirror. A clear glass-enclosed shower took up one corner with a large spa tub against the back wall. Suzy smiled, giving Gray a thumbs-up gesture. "Very nice, Mr. Merimon, and very modern. I'm impressed. This is nothing like the beach house, though."

With a sheepish grin, he said, "That's because I picked the beach house myself. I was so busy when I bought this place that I picked it by location. It was already furnished and I just moved in. It's so . . . clean, though, that I feel like a complete slob if I throw my socks on the floor or leave a glass on the table. I always felt more like I was visiting a hotel than coming home. The house in Myrtle Beach can be our home and we can keep this for our visits to Charleston."

Suzy felt warmth flow through her at his casual mention of *their* home. God, it was impossible not to love this man. If not for the thought of him making love to some other woman months earlier and the fallout from it now, she'd have her body wrapped around his right now probably professing her love in every way imaginable. It was childish to punish him for something that happened before they were together, but this whole thing scared her more than she wanted to admit. After going through a hellish breakup with Jeff, she couldn't bear to be played for a fool again; her heart would never recover.

Suzy became aware of Gray leaning against the door where he'd been studying her while her thoughts whirled. "It kills me that I put that look of fear in your eyes. I'd give anything to take it all back."

She shook her head and forced a laugh. "I don't know what you're talking about, dear. I just remembered that Saks is having a huge one-day sale this week and I can't miss it. They have some leather pants that I've had my eye on for weeks."

Of course, Gray knew she was lying through her teeth, but she could tell he appreciated the effort to lighten the mood. She hobbled behind him back into the bedroom as he was setting her bag down, and with a brief kiss on the lips he was gone. She washed her face and used the restroom and then collapsed on the bed, where she fell asleep before she had time to dwell on anything else.

Gray had decided to pass on the guest room so he settled instead for a chair in the living room. Even though he was tired, his mind was still racing from everything that had happened in the last twenty-four hours. This morning had started off with such promise. When he'd rolled over and found Suzy gone from the bed, he hadn't been alarmed. He'd taken his time leaving the bed and wandering through the house looking for her. When he'd heard the sound of someone being violently ill, fear had almost choked him as he rushed toward the sound. After he saw his phone on the floor and put all the pieces together, he too had wanted to throw up. He'd never thought it possible to be vulnerable, but in that moment, he'd realized how much of his life was already in Suzy's hands.

Even though he was still worried, he'd started to relax today. Even the unexpected drop-in from his parents hadn't shaken him too much. Maybe that's how life sets you up. You suddenly start feeling confident and then something small slams you back to earth. For him that moment was when he saw the expression of terror on Suzy's face in the bathroom and knew that he was responsible for it. After what Jeff had put her through when he left her for another woman, he knew that to trust and love again was difficult for her. He didn't think she'd dated anyone in the year since that had happened. Due to the cold nature of her parents, Suzy needed to feel loved whether she could admit it or not.

He'd been so grateful this morning when Suzy had come out of the bedroom dressed and obviously ready to stand by her man. He'd have gladly followed her to the ends of the earth at that point without complaint. Now that they were here, though, he was starting to question the wisdom of taking Suzy with him tonight. He knew she was a strong woman, but Reva was a very nasty one. Was he making a mistake? He was banking on Reva not making a scene in a public place, but hadn't he already established the fact that she was pretty much crazy?

Dragging a hand through his hair, Gray pulled his cell phone from his pocket and grimaced as he saw a load of missed calls and texts all from a now-familiar number. He'd started saving them all a few days ago for evidence should he need to go to the police and file a complaint. He opened one message and his skin crawled as he read it. *Lover, I need what only you can give me. I'm burning up for you.* He forced himself to hit the Reply button on the message and send her a text asking her to meet him at Sorin's Pub later on that evening for a drink. He'd barely hit the Send button when her reply popped back. "Sorin's? You're here! See you there, lover."

In disgust, he tossed his phone on the coffee table and wearily leaned his head back on the chair. He realized he must have dozed off when a movement in front of him startled him awake. At first he wondered if he was actually still asleep and dreaming. Suzy stood between his spread legs completely naked. Gray sucked in a breath as he sat there and simply stared at the picture before him. She'd released her hair from the ponytail and it lay against her shoulders like fire. Her breasts were full and her dusky nipples puckered under his scrutiny.

He leaned up in the chair and put his forehead against the neatly trimmed nest of red curls and she shivered at the warmth of his breath against her core. Still neither of them spoke as she laid her hands on his shoulders and then pushed back. He lay back in the chair and caught fire as he saw the heavy-lidded desire in her eyes.

Suzy smiled into his eyes and said, "This next move isn't going to start out very sexy, but the main course will be well worth it." She gripped the arms of the chair and slowly—and rather awkwardly—managed to get on one knee while she slid her cast out to the side. *Oh geez, I should have thought this out better. I'm going to have to be good with my mouth to have any hope of making him forget this scalded-cat performance.*

Gray forgot to breathe as Suzy finally settled on the floor between his legs and reached for his belt and unbuckled it. Next she went for his zipper, and as she slid it down, her nails raked against the sensitive skin of his lower stomach and he almost came unglued. His erection was straining at the confines of his boxer briefs as she rubbed her fingers against the sensitive tip. Just as he was afraid he'd embarrass himself right there in his underwear, she gripped the top of his pants along with the briefs and started sliding them down. He lifted his hips to make it easier for her. His erection sprang free, almost level with her plump mouth. She left his pants around his thighs and took him into her hand, running her finger over the moist tip.

"Oh, God, baby," Gray moaned, "I need to be inside you." As he tried to shift to pull her up onto him, Suzy pushed his hands away.

"Not yet, just lie back and hang on, things are going to get a bit . . . bumpy from here on out," she purred.

With that warning, Suzy took him completely into her mouth. Gray almost came up off the chair at the sensation of her hot, wet warmth sucking his pulsing cock. Moaning so loud he was afraid the neighbors would hear him, Gray was helpless against the mind-numbing pleasure coursing through his body. One of her hands lightly rubbed his balls, while the other was gripped around the base of his shaft, pumping up and down in tempo with her hot mouth. He almost exploded as he felt his cock go down her throat as she took him deeper than anyone had ever dared. If he didn't slow her down now, he'd never be able to keep from coming.

He put his hands in her hair, pulling her head back from his erection. Her cheeks were flushed and her breathing ragged. She leaned down to kiss the top of his shaft one last time. He hissed as his body jerked, desperate to penetrate her sweet depths. He had just enough rational thought left to know he needed a condom. He started to sit up. "Baby, I have to get protection." He wanted to weep with gratitude when Suzy reached behind her and held up a condom like she'd just won the lottery.

With a wicked grin, she said, "You're lucky that I firmly believe in the BYOC policy."

"BYOC?"

With a laugh, she answered, "Bring your own condom."

Laughing along with her, Gray growled, "Thank God."

Suzy tore the wrapper and proceeded to torture him as she slid the condom onto his straining length. He gently hooked his hands under her arms and lifted her onto the chair. As she planted her knees on either side of his body, she was able to hang her cast off the front of the chair. She used her knees to lift herself over his cock, and then, with her eyes locked on his, she lowered herself inch by inch until he was buried to the hilt inside her tight sheath. She threw her head back in abandon as she used her knees to ride him. Gray cupped her breasts in his hands, using his thumbs to tweak her nipples, eliciting a low moan from her lips. He pulled Suzy closer to him so that he could take one stiff peak into his mouth. He felt her inner muscles contract around him as he nipped and sucked her nipple and then moved on to the other one.

He released her nipple and slid his hand down her body, lightly drawing circles on her stomach before reaching the curls where their bodies joined. Just seeing the intimate way that their bodies came together was erotic enough to make him lose control. As she slid up and down on his hard shaft, he ran a finger through her moist curls and lightly touched her swollen nub within. Suzy moaned, cupping her own breasts in a move that drove every thought from his head. He knew that he couldn't hold out much longer; especially when she flicked her finger against one hard peak mimicking his earlier action.

Gray increased the pressure against her clit and a scream started low in Suzy's throat as he felt her muscles start to contract. He surged his hips upward, driving even farther inside her and watched her eyes glaze as her orgasm started to ripple through her body. "Gray, ah . . . harder . . . please . . . don't . . . stop," she gasped out. He continued to pump into her as she rode the crest. Only when he felt her body go limp, did he allow himself to find his own release. With a shout, he felt his seed shoot out into the condom and for a moment he thought of how great it would be to have his seed inside her, possibly making a daughter that would look just like her.

Just that thought alone should have been enough to make him jump from the chair and run, but strangely it only filled him with joy to think of this woman with his child in her womb. With a chuckle he ran his hand down her smooth back and said, "Baby, if I died right now, I'd have no regrets. I lo. . . ." Suzy put her hand over his mouth before he could get the words out.

"Don't say it, Gray. I know you mean it, but it just seems wrong right now. I can't sit here and talk about love when we are going to meet your stalking ex-lover." She started to edge off the chair, needing to put some distance between them. Gray helped her to stand before she hurt her ankle in her struggle.

Her averted gaze broke his heart. If not for the lip she was chewing on, he'd have thought she was indifferent to the pain her words had caused. He pulled her back against his body. "It's gonna be all right baby, just hang in there with me please."

Suzy kissed him lightly on the cheek and took her crutches from the couch. She walked back to the bedroom, and as she was shutting the door, she saw Gray still standing in the same spot looking at her with pain-filled eyes.

As she shut the door, she slumped back against it. What had gotten into her? She'd gone to Gray, naked no less, and made love to him within an inch of their lives. Then when he wants to tell her that he loves her, she balks? She had mixed signals flying all over the place. Was it any wonder that he looked hurt and confused? He probably thought she was just using him to scratch an itch. In truth, she'd desperately needed to join her body with his before their meeting with Reva tonight. It was almost as if she was trying to imprint herself onto him. *What's next, raising your leg to pee on him so you can stake your claim? Maybe writing your name on his notebook?*

Ugh, she had to stop saying one thing and doing another. If she didn't want Gray to talk about love, then she needed to stop putting it out there. She knew how he felt about her so it was almost as if she was teasing him by running hot and cold. She couldn't help it if she was like a moth to the flame when he was near. She just wanted all of this to go away so that she could get past the overwhelming fear of losing him. She'd known when she met him that her life was never going to be the same again; that was why she'd run for so long. Surely they hadn't come this far only to fall apart.

Suzy gathered some clean clothing and headed for the bathroom. It was time to get on with this stalker meeting and then get back to their lives. Maybe they could even stop off on the way home for some Cool Whip. Her body tingled as she imagined licking it off Gray's body later. *Mmmm, now that's what I'm talking about!*

Chapter Seventeen

Gray was sweating bullets by the time he and Suzy parked at Sorin's Pub. The drive over had been quiet; both of them, it seemed, were nervous about this meeting. His gut feeling was that this was a mistake. He should never have brought Suzy; he knew how vicious Reva could be. What in the hell had he been thinking? *Oh, yeah, bring the woman you love to meet the woman you used as a replacement for her. Greeaat idea, buddy. Is this the best that a successful businessman can come up with?*

He stopped to brush a kiss across Suzy's lips before he opened the door for her. Sorin's Pub was an upscale bar in the Battery District that was popular with the locals. It wasn't so loud that you couldn't talk, but was loud enough to offer a certain amount of camouflage when you didn't want to be overheard. Gray quickly scanned the tables, looking for Reva. Just when he thought they must have made it before her, he spotted her sitting at a table in the corner anxiously scanning the crowd.

Reva hadn't seen him yet since Suzy was partially blocking his body. As they approached her table, she finally saw him. She looked at Suzy in annoyance, obviously thinking she was trying to pick up Gray. Her annoyance turned to confusion at the possessive arm that Gray placed around Suzy's shoulders as they stopped at her table.

"Reva, thanks for meeting us. This is Suzanna, my girlfriend." Shock crossed Reva's face, followed by a look that made him cringe.

Reva pushed her chair back from the table and Gray felt Suzy tense and the world tilt under his feet. Reva extended a hand toward Suzy and said, "Well, what a surprise. I'm Reva, the mother of his unborn child." All eyes dropped to the hand she laid against her swollen stomach.

How long they all stood there he'd no idea. "Reva, what in the hell is going on?" Gray realized they were all still standing and starting to get some curious looks. He pulled out a chair for Suzy and propped her crutches against the wall. Reva made a big production of settling back into her chair. He took Suzy's cold fingers under the table, trying to offer her the reassurance that he was far from feeling for himself.

With probably what Gray felt was one of her best performances to date, Reva promptly began to sniffle. "I . . . I'm sorry, Gray." With another sniffle, she continued, "I wanted to tell you sooner, but I couldn't get you to see me. I just didn't know what to do."

Gray felt like his tongue was lodged in his throat. He was surprised he wasn't choking on it. Beside him, Suzy sat unmoving, as if in shock. Hell, he was in shock, too. He cleared his throat, carefully choosing his words. "Reva, you have called and texted me daily for months. You have left letters and God knows what else behind for me, and you have also been calling Nick. Granted, I stopped reading most of the stuff, but I'm willing to bet there was no mention of a baby in them.

Now suddenly you're sitting here in front of me in full maternity glory? What gives?"

More tears followed his questions and he had a bad feeling that Suzy thought he was some type of insensitive bastard for badgering a pregnant woman. She'd no idea what he'd been subjected to since meeting Reva. He doubted there was a day in her life that she wasn't planning some sort of scheme.

With another sniffle, Reva said, "I didn't say anything because I didn't want you to feel like I was trying to trap you. I . . . I know you don't care anything about me. It was always her, wasn't it?" Reva finished miserably.

"Reva, we only had sex once and I used a condom, so there is no way your baby is mine."

Suzy suddenly pushed her chair back and stood. "Honey, where are you going?" Before she averted her eyes, Gray could see the tears shimmering in their depths. His gut clenched and his heart raced as he felt her slipping away from him.

Suzy said, "You both need time to talk and I don't need to be here for it. I'm going to catch a cab back." Suzy was already reaching for her crutches.

"No, you aren't. Give me just a minute and we will leave."

"Gray, let me go," Suzy pleaded. She had to get out of here before she exploded. At that moment, she couldn't stand the thought of being in the close confines of Gray's car with him. She knew if she were ever going to get out of here without him following her, she had to put his mind at ease. Forcing herself to give him a smile, she said, "Just stay and finish up, I'll be fine. I'll see you back at the condo. You know there are cabs out front so I won't have any problem getting one." She quickly fished the door key from the jacket pocket she'd saw him place it in earlier. She knew he was still torn so she reached up and brushed a quick kiss across his lips and took off as fast as her crutches would allow.

When she reached the door, she was relieved to see that although he was still standing there staring after her, he hadn't made a move to follow. She quickly walked out the door and hailed the next cab in line. She held it together on the short ride back to Gray's home. Her first inclination when she arrived was to throw herself across the bed and give way to all of the pain hammering to get out. Her second thought though was to just get out. Gray needed space to figure out his life and she couldn't be here with him while he was doing it.

Suzy pulled her phone from her purse and called the one person she knew she could count on. When her sister answered on the other end, Suzy simply said, "I need you to come get me, now."

Beth only asked one question: "Where are you?"

Suzy quickly gave her directions and Beth assured her that she was leaving within five minutes. After ending the call, Suzy went to the bedroom to gather her stuff. Luckily, she'd only unpacked a few things so within minutes her bags were sitting at the door and she was left with nothing but her worst enemy . . . time.

Reva was pregnant and, just like that, her life with Gray was over. Nothing would ever be the same again. Gray was going to be torn in two directions. She'd no doubt that he loved her; funny she could see that now. She loved him, as well, but things could never be like they were before. Gray's life would be tied with Reva's forever. Gray was an honorable man, so he might even feel that he needed to marry Reva because of the baby. Even if he didn't marry Reva, he'd still constantly worry about how Suzy was handling this. She had to let him go; she couldn't be another stress point in his life.

Suzy was startled to hear a knock at the door. She had Gray's key so it had to be him. She braced herself as she walked over and opened the door to find Beth and Nick standing there. "Wh-what're you doing here so soon? It's only been half an hour since I called you."

"Um, when Nick told me what you guys were planning, I decided to come down here for moral support or to you know . . . help you kick some ass if needed."

She pulled her sister into a tight hug. "You have no idea how glad I am to see you." When she pulled back, she saw the concern on Nick's and Beth's faces. She took a deep breath and said, "Guys, I don't want to go into this right now, but I need to get out of here."

Nick stepped forward and took her hand. "Suzy, are you all right? Where is my brother?"

Tears shimmered in her eyes as she looked into the face so similar to the man she loved. "Nick, please let me get out of here and we will talk, okay?"

Nick paused for another minute, clearly torn, but with Beth's urging, he grabbed Suzy's bags and they all made their way to the elevator. When they reached the parking garage, Suzy got the laugh that she needed when Nick and Beth walked over to the minivan. "Oh, God, you kept the van? Nick, it's just wrong somehow for a swinging bachelor to be driving this. What in the world do your dates say?"

Nick scowled at her, saying, "I'll have you know,

this baby has a lot of horsepower, tons of storage, and my chick digs it."

Still laughing, Suzy said, "Don't tell me you're dating a soccer mom now. That's about the only chick I could imagine digging this." Good grief, where had these two lost their sense of humor? Both of them stood there giving her a disgusted expression. This was one of the worst days of her life; if she wanted to make fun of Nick's damn minivan, then she would. Screw everyone; she had to do what she could to survive today.

Just as Nick walked around to help her into the van, Gray's BMW came roaring into the parking garage. Suzy had the desire to jump in the driver's seat and take off. She wasn't sure she'd have been able to control the urge if she hadn't been wearing the stupid cast. She stiffened her spine knowing it was going to destroy her to look into his eyes. She'd wanted to go home and regroup before she talked to him; she sure didn't want to have this conversation with his brother and her sister standing close by.

As Gray approached them, Suzy noted that he didn't seem surprised to see them all there. She'd a sneaking suspicion that Nick had called him. What had she really expected? Gray was his brother; of course, his loyalty was with him first and foremost. Her sister, though, could have given her a little warning. She idly wondered what her sister and Nick were doing together anyway. She knew they pretty much despised each other so why did they keep turning up together?

"Nick, Beth, can you give us a few minutes please?" Gray asked.

She knew it would be childish to object as her sister and Nick walked to the other side of the garage as Gray asked. He looked at her without touching her and Suzy noticed how tired he looked. There were lines of fatigue around his eyes that weren't usually there and his shoulders were bent as if he were carrying the weight of the world on them.

"Baby, what're you doing?"

Sometimes she hated being a girl because she was helpless to stop the moisture gathering in the corners of her eyes. "I don't know, Gray. I just need to get away for a few days. I need to go back home, where I can . . . breathe again."

He leaned his forehead against hers, closing his eyes as he searched for his next words. "I'm so sorry about this mess. I still don't believe that this baby is mine. I don't trust Reva to even give me her full name without lying about some part of it."

Suzy let her crutches fall back into the van as she put her arms around him and just held on. Her emotions were in complete turmoil, but she knew that he needed her right now as he never had before. Gray was a strong man, but he was floundering. Something like this was probably enough to knock the feet out from under even the strongest man.

"Gray, I love you." As his head jerked up to look at her with wonder, she continued. "It's because of that love that I have to leave now. If I stay here with you, you will be worried about me and unable to figure out what you need to do about Reva. I don't know if that's your baby she's carrying or not, but I know you need to decide what you're going to do."

"Suzanna, you have no idea how long I've waited to hear you say those three words. I promise you that we will be okay. When this baby is born there will be a paternity test and if it does turn out to be mine, then I'll support him or her financially, as well as be a father. I won't be marrying Reva nor will she be living with me. It would not be fair to a child to live in such an environment. I just have a gut feeling that something isn't right with this whole thing and I need to find out what it is."

Suzy had to wonder if it was a gut feeling he was really having or wishful thinking. The Reva that he'd described seemed very different from the emotional woman she'd met in the bar tonight.

Looking very vulnerable, he said, "I just need to know you will be here. I know that I'm asking a lot, but you're my life and I can't lose you now."

Suzy tenderly caressed the face of the man she loved so much and was helpless to deny him the reassurance that he so desperately needed at this moment. "I'm just going home, Gray. I'll be there when you finish here." She could feel the relief rolling off Gray in waves.

"Thank God. If you must go, please go to our house." As she started to protest, he silenced her with a finger on her lips. "I bought that house for us; it is your home. I'll be home in a few days and I don't want to worry about you trying to navigate any stairs while I'm away."

Suzy couldn't find the strength to argue over this request. Gray's lips took hers in a kiss so sweet and full of love that she felt her heart melt. At that moment, she didn't think it was possible to love another as much as she loved him. She only hoped her heart would survive the fallout if something happened.

Nick and Beth walked back up to them and Suzy was surprised when Gray told them what had happened with Reva. Nick swore violently, his face flushed with anger. "Gray, man, I know you aren't going to just take her word for it. The woman is a nut and if she's gotten herself pregnant, there is no way it's yours. For one, I know you wouldn't be that careless and she sure wouldn't have kept that a secret this whole time. She's ringing all of our damn phones off the hook daily for months and doesn't say a word? She'd have taken out a banner ad right after she found out if that were true."

Beth had moved close to her sister since recovering from the shock of Gray's words. While he and Nick continued to discuss what was going on, Beth looked at her with a mixture of anger and sympathy. "Sis, how are you holding up?"

Suzy gave her sister a weak smile. "It is what it is; there is nowhere else to go but forward."

"Is it very wrong of me to want to kick a pregnant woman's ass?" Beth asked.

Unable to control her laughter, Suzy looked at her sister and held her fingers apart. "A little bit, but thanks for the thought."

The men finally wrapped up their conversation and Gray pulled her close for one last bittersweet kiss. "I'll call you tonight. I love you, baby."

Suzy felt shy about saying the words in front of an audience, but she knew that Gray needed to hear them. "I love you, too. Try to get some rest tonight."

The breath left her body as he picked her up in his arms and deposited her into the seat. "I'm not taking the chance on you hurting yourself trying to get into my brother's minivan." With a smirk, he looked over at Nick. "Nice wheels, bro."

Nick simply replied, "Piss off," and had them all laughing.

Suzy's heart broke as they drove away and she looked back at Gray one last time and saw him standing in the parking garage looking like the last man on a sinking ship. Was leaving him the right thing to do? Like him she had to go with her gut and that told her that he needed to be alone right now even if being in his arms was what she needed more than anything.

What a big freaking mess. There goes the woman I love who actually loves me back and here I stand in complete hell. Was it even possible to make a bigger mess than I have? My father always told us that our dicks could lead us to our destruction if we didn't watch ourselves. Well, no shit, Dad, no shit.

Gray stepped off the elevator and into his home. He walked into the bedroom not really knowing what he was seeking until he looked down at the bed still rumpled from Suzy's earlier nap. As he collapsed onto it, her scent wrapped around him and he felt the first bit of peace that he'd felt since he'd held her in his arms earlier after they had made love.

He relived his conversation earlier with Reva. Gone was the conniving, confident Reva and in her place was a clingy, needy, emotional basket case. It had gotten to the point that he was actually starting to feel sorry for her before he'd left. Was this yet another act on her part or was it genuine? There was no denying she was pregnant, but was the child his? As he'd thought, and of course as Nick had pointed out, why would she have waited this long? He was the one who had contacted her to meet tonight, so was she ever planning to tell him? Sure, she still called constantly, but even she'd admitted that she hadn't left a message concerning the pregnancy. Why would someone stalk him for months and not use the one weapon guaranteed to get his attention?

Nothing about the whole thing made sense. He was very good at reading people and he was certain that her emotional distress earlier wasn't an act. He was going to check around with people he knew in her circle and find out if she'd been seeing anyone else. If the child turned out to be his, then of course it would want for nothing. Reva, however, would never be any closer to him than she was now. He'd be polite, but she'd never be the woman in his life. That spot was Suzy's alone.

Reva said that she hadn't told anyone who the father of her baby was. That also seemed strange to him. He was surprised that her parents hadn't already been on his doorstep demanding he do the right thing. From what he knew of them, he couldn't imagine that they were thrilled that their daughter was pregnant with no man in sight. Something was off, but damned if he had the energy to figure it out right now.

He smiled as he thought of Suzy finally admitting that she loved him. God, how long had he waited to hear those words from her? There had never been a time when he'd needed to hear them more. He missed her now, but he knew she was right. He was being torn to pieces trying to shelter her feelings while trying to figure this mess out here. As long as he knew she'd be there when he came home, he could handle anything.

Chapter Eighteen

Suzy walked in the door of Gray's beach home. Nick followed, carrying her bags through to the bedroom. Even though she'd argued with them, he and Beth were insistent on staying with her until Gray was back. Since she'd be returning to work tomorrow, she didn't really think it mattered either way. At least they had put their differences behind them and didn't argue as much. Nick still called Beth "princess," but she just shrugged it off.

They had stopped on the way home for dinner and she'd managed to eat enough of her food to keep the two mother hens off her back. "Guys, I'm beat so I think I'm going to go straight to bed."

Beth looked at her as if assessing her condition and asked, "Need any help, sis?"

Suzy gave her a smile, knowing that she was worried about her. "I'm good; I'll see you in the morning. You better get some sleep, too; I heard the bitch is going to be back at work tomorrow."

Nick's laughter boomed out, following her into the bedroom. She'd always loved her sister, but since her injury, they were closer than they had ever been. Nick had also wormed his way into her heart and he'd turned into the brother she'd always dreamed of borrowing leather from.

She sat on the edge of the bed, fatigue pulling heavily at her. Just as she was trying to find the energy to shower, her cell phone rang. She saw Gray's name on the caller ID and felt a thrill run through her body as she answered the call. "Hey, slick."

With a chuckle, Gray said, "Hey, baby. I miss you."

Suddenly the fatigue in her body was replaced by a rush of heat at the husky tone of his voice. She tried to keep the conversation light to take his mind off everything that had happened earlier. She said, "I miss you too and that hot body. Ohhhh the things I'd do to it if you were here."

"Oh, God, don't say that while I'm so far away. You can't imagine what I'd do right now to taste your sweetness and to feel you clench tightly around me as I drive into your beautiful body."

Suzy could feel her body catch fire as the erotic words flowed over her. Her nipples puckered and her body hummed, desperate for his possession. She tried to keep the need from her voice, protesting lightly, "Hey, no hitting out of bounds, slick. No one likes a tease."

"Ah, honey, you'll soon see that though I love to tease you, I always follow through on my promises."

For her own sanity, Suzy managed to keep the conversation away from sex, because if Gray mentioned anything remotely sexy again in that low voice, she'd probably come right there while holding the phone. They both carefully avoided any mention of Reva and her pregnancy, knowing neither of them could handle anything more tonight.

He said, "I love you, I'll call you tomorrow. Be careful going back to work. Make sure that either Beth or Nick drives you and helps you all the way to your office, okay?"

Rolling her eyes, Suzy said, "Yes, Mother." When Gray's laughter subsided, she quietly added, "I love you, too."

Suzy moaned as fingers caressed her sex, rubbing leisurely back and forth across the sensitive nub. Another moan was torn from her throat as a hand at her breast tweaked her nipple, then tugged the peak between insistent fingers. Dimly she was aware that it was still night outside and apparently she was in the throes of one hell of a dream. When she felt an erection push against the curve of her bottom, she started to stiffen; surely she wouldn't be lying here thinking she was dreaming if she actually was. My God, though, it seemed like hands were all over her body; she was burning with arousal and, suddenly, as a finger thrust into her heat, Suzy knew in a moment of panic that there was no way she was dreaming.

Just as she started to scream, Gray whispered in her ear, "I've got you, baby."

"Gray? What're you doing here?"

"Shhh, don't talk, just feel."

Suzy was powerless to resist as the heat continued to build in her body. Gray gently lowered her fully onto her back and came up on his knees, never removing his finger from inside her. He added another finger and she moaned, helpless to control the shudders rippling through her body. "Oh, God, Gray, that feels so good."

"Let go, baby, I want to feel you come."

Gray applied pressure to her clit with his thumb and increased the thrusts of his fingers. Suzy felt her body beginning to clench as her orgasm started to crest. He thrust harder, his fingers riding out the storm and wringing every last ounce of pleasure from her.

Suzy thought she'd black out. Stars exploded behind her lids as she tried to hold on. When Gray finally removed his fingers, she slumped back against the bed in delicious fatigue. She felt skin-on-skin contact as Gray lowered his body against hers, careful to keep his full weight off her. She felt light kisses teasing her eyelids and trailing down her neck as Gray whispered in her ear, "No sleep yet, baby. I came all this way to put my ball back in bounds."

Suzy rolled out a deliciously wicked laugh at his reference to her earlier comment. She saw the bedside clock glowing two in the morning and she knew that he must have gotten in the car right after they talked. She ran her fingers through his soft hair and pulled his head down to hers for a kiss that was pure sex. Gray's mouth took possession of hers, demanding that she hold nothing back. Heat slammed into her core as her body tightened in need.

Their tongues met and Gray nipped her bottom lip with his teeth, as if he wanted to devour her. He trailed kisses down her neck, finally reaching the puckered tips that were begging for the warmth of his mouth. As he sucked a stiff peak inside, Suzy took the hand that was resting on her neck and brought it to her lips. She ran her tongue over his palm, and as Gray groaned and flexed it, Suzy kissed each of his fingers. When she reached his thumb, she sucked it in her mouth simulating his suction of her breasts.

Gray stiffened, throwing back his head and groaning. "Oh my God, baby, you're killing me." She nipped his finger on the tip and he jerked back, freeing his thumb. "If you don't stop that, there is going to be a premature release of the ball, baby, and I don't think either of us wants that."

With one last pull on her nipple, he slid off the bed and grabbed his pants, pulling a foil pack out. Suzy moved to the side of the bed and set her feet onto the floor. She pulled the condom from his hand and gripped his length. Gray hissed as she caressed him and she marveled at his masculine beauty and impressive size. She was nowhere near an expert, but she'd bet that most men would kill to look like Gray. He was just as impressive naked as he was in his five-hundred-dollar suit. It wasn't fair for one man to have all of this going for him, but selfishly she was sure glad that he did.

A drop of moisture had gathered at the tip of his cock and she bent down to gently lick it away. Gray's hips jerked and his hands went into her hair, tugging her gently away. He took the condom from her fingers. "That mouth of yours is going to be my downfall tonight. I want to be inside you when I explode." He rolled the condom over his length with shaky hands. He sat on the bed beside her and pulled her onto his lap facing away from him. Her legs were hooked over his. "Is this okay for your ankle, baby?"

Suzy nodded and forgot to breathe as she felt his erection against her butt. Gray spread his legs, forcing hers to spread wider. He gently lifted her around the waist and positioned his tip at her entrance. He moved his tip back and forth and she could feel the moisture start to seep out as her body prepared for his possession. Just when she thought she'd go out of her mind from the torment, Gray suddenly plunged inside her to the hilt. Suzy gasped, feeling her body stretching to accommodate his size. "Ahhhh God, Gray, ohhh myyy."

Gray stilled for a moment, giving her time to adjust and then he spread their legs wider and started to lift her waist to meet the thrusts of his hips. His warm lips trailed fire down the nape of her neck and when he took her earlobe into his mouth, she almost came unglued. Never had she felt anything so erotic, so sexy. His tongue flicked against the shell of her ear before his mouth sucked the lower lobe. He repeated the same amazing action on the other ear and it was all she could do to hold back, she was already so close to coming.

Suzy reached down to where their bodies were joined and cupped Gray's balls as he pumped into her. She smiled as a growl erupted from his throat. She stroked his tight sack and trailed her nails lightly up his inner thigh before returning to his cock. She gripped the base and held it firmly as he plunged into her.

Whispering in her ear, Gray said, "You want to play, huh? Let's see how you like this then." With those teasing words, Gray's hand came around her and settled briefly over the hand that held his cock. He shifted above that until he was rubbing her nub. Suzy threw her head back and an explosion started building inside her. Holding Gray's erection in her hands as he slid in and out of her, coupled with Gray's hand stroking her clit, was just too much. She was having a sensory overload and her body was helpless to stop the orgasm that was starting to rip through her. Her inner muscles clenched and Gray pumped his hips harder against her, lifting her almost off his lap. Suzy screamed as her body seemed to crest one orgasm only to start another. Never had she felt anything like this. Gray's finger against her sensitive nub was now almost torture and Suzy put her hand over his, stilling his movement. When she reached down to cup his balls, he threw his head back and shouted her name as he found his own release.

When a knock sounded at the door, they both froze. "Um, Suzy, is everything all right?"

"Oh, shit." Suzy grabbed for the cover as she heard Nick's concerned voice from the other side of the door.

Gray chuckled. "Everything's fine, bro, thanks for checking."

Suzy heard laughter from the other side of the door, but thankfully Nick didn't ask any other questions. "I bet your brother thought I was having a hell of a dream in here." Leaning back in Gray's arms, she sighed. "Now I'll have to look at his smirking face over breakfast tomorrow. Great!"

Raising his eyebrow, Gray asked, "Are you complaining?"

Suzy wiggled her bottom against him. "No way, slick. I could get used to waking up to that."

Gray hugged her to his chest, suddenly serious. "Get used to it then, baby. I plan to do that for the rest of our lives. Just hang in there with me."

Suzy laid her arms over his and closed her eyes. Here in the circle of his arms, with his breath on her neck and the feel of his heart beating, she felt there was nothing that could ever tear them apart. Gray was home to her and she vowed to do her best to help him handle the situation with Reva. Even though it tore her apart to think of someone else giving Gray a child first, she knew that to have a future with him, she must also accept his past and fully embrace his child. Overcome with the love she had for this man, she whispered, "I love you."

Gray released the breath he'd been holding, and hugged Suzy closer. "I love you, too, baby, more than you will ever know."

"I can't believe you drove all this way. You must be so tired."

"Yeah, I am. I'm heading back to Charleston early in the morning. I told Jason since I planned to be there for a few days, that I'd handle a few issues we have at Mericom while I am there. I have a meeting at ten so I need to be on the road by seven or so."

It was almost four by that time, so they quickly showered and curled around each other in bed. Gray woke her up a few hours later with a long, drugging kiss. He was already dressed and looked so gorgeous and sexy that Suzy wanted to pull him back in the bed and devour him. After he was gone, she dozed for another half hour before rousing herself to dress for her first day back at work. There was something comforting and exciting about getting back into her normal routine.

Suzy dressed for comfort in a short black skirt with a white silk tank and a long silver necklace. She slid on a low-heeled flat shoe, and decided to leave her hair loose. God, she missed high heels. Ugh.

*   *   *

When Suzy walked into the kitchen, Nick and Beth were sitting at the table having pancakes and bacon. As she walked toward them, Nick snickered and said, "Look, princess, here comes your sister doing the walk of shame."

From the grin on Beth's face, she could tell that Nick had filled her in on her late-night visitor. Nick laughed when she flipped him a hand gesture as she settled into her seat. Beth poured her a cup of coffee and handed her a plate. Suzy's eyes rolled in bliss as she poured syrup over the pancakes. "This looks great, sis. I'm glad you were feeling ambitious this morning."

Nick chimed in, "That would be me, babe. Unlike some of us, I rolled myself out of bed at a reasonable hour this morning so I could fix breakfast for you lovely ladies."

With a chuckle, Suzy said, "Pouring it on there a little thick this morning, aren't ya? But hey, whatever the reason, I'm glad, this is great. I can't believe you and Gray can cook like this."

"I know my brother seemed to be cooking something up last night, too, say around two?"

Suzy choked on her coffee and Beth patted her on the back. "You're a pervert, Nick, has anyone ever told you that?"

"Ah, yes they have, but only in the most complimentary of terms."

Suzy had to give it to the man, he didn't lack for confidence. She could see how women would throw themselves at him on a regular basis. It was hard to believe that he'd been content to play house here for several weeks without as much as a date. Maybe he was having a lunchtime quickie or something.

When everyone had finished breakfast, Nick insisted on driving them to the office in his van. Suzy couldn't help it, she still had to chuckle every time he hit the button to open the sliding side door for her. Maybe Nick's inner soccer mom had been dying to get out for a while.

Chapter Nineteen

Suzy couldn't contain her sigh of contentment when she walked or hobbled back in the door at Danvers International. She hadn't realized how much she'd missed being here until she stepped out of the elevator and saw all of the familiar faces. Nick had continued to his floor while she and Beth were now walking toward the reception area and a smiling Ella. Suzy still couldn't get over the transformation there. Ella really was beautiful now and her personality seemed to have changed as well.

She'd frankly found Ella annoying and tried to avoid her. Now that people were finally seeing her, Ella seemed to have lost the need to constantly seek attention and approval. Her sister had done a good thing there. Suzy smiled warmly at her and said, "Good morning, Ella."

With a shy smile, Ella said, "Good morning, Ms. Denton. It's so good to have you back."

"Please, Ella, call me Suzy. I think we are past all of the formalities now. I'll even try to curb my four-letter words in front of you today."

"Th-that's okay, Ms. . . . . er, Suzy, I've gotten used to that here. This is a very colorful place to work."

"Colorful, huh? Yeah, I like that."

Beth followed her down the hall to her office and Suzy was surprised to see how organized everything was. Her desk was always rather like organized chaos. She assumed it was Beth who had neatly stacked messages on one corner, put her files in alphabetical order on the other corner, and set a status update on all of their current projects in the center.

"Wow, sis, did you do all of this?"

"Um, yes. I hope you don't mind that I decided to straighten your desk some. I thought it might be easier for you to find things." Then rolling her eyes, Beth said, "I know you're a little anal about your paperwork so if you want to put it back the way it was, I can do that."

Suzy couldn't contain her laughter. "Did you just call me anal? Beth Denton, I know you didn't use that dirty mouth when you were teaching."

"Like Ella says, this place rubs off on you. Now, Master, what do you want to start on today?"

Beth and Suzy worked steadily through the morning, returning calls and placing orders for an upcoming training conference. The first hour Suzy was in her office it seemed that everyone in the building had dropped by with their well wishes. Claire and Jason had stopped by and she and Claire had made plans for lunch. Claire looked even bigger than when Suzy had seen her last week. Suzy was afraid she was going to explode at any moment. Jason followed her around like a mother hen, obviously worried out of his mind about her. Suzy didn't know how the poor man would make it until the baby was born; he looked like he was close to a nervous breakdown now.

Gray called just before she was leaving for lunch and

her heart skipped a beat when she heard his sexy voice on the phone. "Hey, baby, how is your first day back?"

"Hi, yourself, you sexy man. My day has been great so far. Did you make it back in time for your meeting this morning without breaking too many laws?"

"I cut it a little close, but I made it." Then lowering his voice to that sexy rumble that she loved so well, he said, "Last night was mind-blowing. You blow me away, baby. Every time I take you, I just want you that much more. There seems to be no relief from wanting you, even after last night; I ache for you."

What girl could hold out against something like that? Suzy felt her body key up, nearly purring in pleasure at his words. "I know how you feel, slick. I can think of at least a dozen things I'd like to do on this desk right now and none of them involves work."

"Aghhh, God, don't even go there, baby. I really don't want to go to my lunch meeting with an erection; they frown on stuff like that. Sooo, what's the rest of your day like?"

"Just finishing up some things for a few events, how about you?"

"The lunch meeting that I mentioned and then this evening, well, um, I'm having dinner with Reva."

Suzy held the phone, but couldn't seem to force herself to say anything. *Dinner with Reva, really? You better get used to it. If this is his baby, Reva will always be there.*

"Suzy?"

"Uh-huh, I'm here."

With a sigh, Gray said, "You know this is just about the baby. I have to find out what's going on. There is nothing romantic here and never will be."

Suzy turned in her chair toward the window, trying

to will her voice to sound normal. "I know, Gray, it's okay." She was relieved when he changed the subject.

"Hey, a little birdie told me that someone is having a birthday Friday."

"Ugh, please don't say that out loud. I'm not acknowledging them anymore."

"Oh, yes, you are. I'll be back Friday evening early so I want you to have either your sister or my brother in his minivan to take you shopping for a new dress because we are going to do the town when I get home. I'm not opposed to something very sexy, Ms. Denton."

"Is that right, Mr. Merimon? Well, I'll see what I can do."

"I love you, baby. I'll call you tonight."

"I love you, too, Gray." As Suzy ended the call, she felt the unusual urge to put her head down on her desk and cry. Gray was having dinner with Reva? *Well what did you expect; she's going to have his baby. Did you think they would communicate via email or fax? Get used to it, sister; there's a new sheriff in town and it's not you.* She mentally flipped off the voice in her head and gathered her purse for lunch. Beth walked in with Ella and they all headed for the elevator to meet Claire.

Beth and Ella walked ahead of them to the restaurant down the street. Suzy and Claire walked at a slower speed due to her crutches and Claire's pregnancy waddle. She was surprised when Claire said, "I'm just going to throw this out there so you will know. Gray told Jason about the mess with Reva and you know Jason can't keep a secret from me to save his life."

"Geez, and they say that women are gossips. The men around here seem to keep nothing to themselves, do they?"

Claire looked relieved that she didn't seem upset about Gray telling them. "How are you feeling about everything, my friend? I have to admit, I'd probably be freaking out right now."

Giving Claire a smile of reassurance that she was far from feeling, Suzy said, "I'm either handling this really well or I'm still in shock and the freak-out will come soon. Actually, I think I was doing pretty well until Gray called. He's having dinner with Reva tonight."

"Oh, wow. Not what you wanted to hear, right?"

"No, not really. I think I'd managed to pretend it didn't exist for a while, and that just brought it all back home. Claire, you know besides my rather warped sense of humor I'm a good person, right?"

"Honey, of course you are, one of the best I know. Why would you even need to ask that?"

Suzy hated what she was going to say and she probably wouldn't have been able to admit it to anyone other than Claire. There wasn't a judgmental bone in her body and she loved that about her. "If I'm a good person, why do I feel the way I do about Reva and the baby? When I think about Reva I want to choke her. Did you hear me? I'm admitting to wanting to choke a pregnant woman. That's just wrong, isn't it?"

Claire put her arm around Suzy's waist and hugged her. "Oh, Suzy, I'd probably feel the same way. You and Gray have waited so long to be together and finally you're right on the verge of having it all and this comes along. I'm not going to kid you, I'd probably be freaking out."

"Oh, I'm freaking out inside. With Gray back in Charleston, I feel kind of removed from it all. It's almost like this happened to someone I know rather than to me." Suzy braced herself to admit something to Claire that she could hardly admit to herself. "I'm scared, Claire. I don't know if I can do this. When I think about our lives from this point forward if Gray is the father of her child, it terrifies me. We will never have a normal life together. I'll always be last, Claire, just as I have my whole life."

Claire noticed that Beth and Ella had stopped at the entrance to the restaurant waiting for them to catch up. She motioned them on inside and turned to her friend. "Suzy, God I wish I had the words of wisdom that you need. I know that you love each other, but only you can decide what you can or can't do. If going forward with it becomes more than you can handle, then you will have to know when to say when. Just take it day by day and hopefully you and Gray will be able to find something that works for everyone. That man has loved you since the moment he laid eyes on you and I know he's going to do everything in his power to make you happy."

With a sniff, Suzy said, "I really hate this. I feel like a crappy person for thinking of myself right now."

Giving her a light punch in the arm, Claire said, "Hey, that's my best friend you're trashing, you better lay off her."

"Okay, pregnant Rambo, calm down before you blow your plug over there."

Claire threw back her head and laughed. "Rambo, hey, I like that."

"Uh, okay, let's get you inside. All of that laughter is making your stomach twitch in a rather scary way. Just calm down, please."

Claire laughed even harder at the alarmed look on

her friend's face. Suzy really was priceless. Even though she knew that her friend was hurting, she never failed to make her laugh. She hoped and prayed that Gray knew what he was doing. She didn't know how Suzy would survive losing him, but the fear in her words had scared Claire. Maybe it was time to see if the pillow talk worked in reverse. Normally, when they were in bed at night talking about their day, Jason told her what was going on with Gray or Nicholas. Maybe she could let him know of her fears for Suzy and somehow try to communicate them to Gray without betraying her friend's confidence.

"Hey, Claire, Claaiiiire, come back."

"Whoops, sorry about that. When you're pregnant, you tend to zone out a lot." She grabbed her friend's hand and led her into the restaurant before Suzy could quiz her about what she'd been thinking.

Suzy was tired but satisfied when she hobbled behind Nick and Beth into the house. Of course, getting around at work had been more challenging with a cast, but it was good to be back in the office again. She and Beth worked well together, and Suzy secretly hoped that Beth would decide to stay for a while.

They decided to order a pizza since no one was in the mood to cook so Beth placed the order and Suzy went to the bedroom to change into something more comfortable. Having Nick and Beth here now seemed so natural. What would she do if she went back to being alone? People who knew her, even her closest friends, assumed she was a strong, independent woman who needed no one. She'd learned long ago that it was safer to keep that illusion going. It was all an elaborate act of smoke and mirrors. Even Jeff, whom she'd spent so many years with, had never known the real Suzy. She'd always held something back from him. Maybe she was afraid that if she gave him all of her he'd know that she wasn't good enough. Hadn't she learned that from her parents?

Through all of her childhood, Suzy put her heart on the line just as Beth had. She remembered how proud she'd been of a Christmas ornament that she'd made in school for her mother. She couldn't wait to get home with it. She just knew that this would make her mother happy and she pictured her picking her up to give her a hug and a kiss. The reality had been much different. When she'd handed her mother the ornament that she'd wrapped up in notebook paper, her mother had set it aside, scolding her for interrupting her work. When she'd asked her again to just please open it, her mother had huffed and finally pulled off the paper. She'd looked down at her with her usual frown and said, "Suzanna, I can see why your grades are so bad, you waste all of your time on such silliness. Now, go do your homework and have it finished before dinner."

Suzy had run to her room with her heart shattered and cried until there were no tears left. That was the last time that she tried to reach out to her mother. Her heart had frozen that day and it had never truly thawed until she met Gray. She'd loved Jeff in her own way. They had a comfortable relationship and he seemed fine with the part of her that she was able to give him. When he cheated on her and moved out, it shook her. A part of her said, "See there? You were right to hold back because he doesn't want your love, either."

Gray was different, though. He plowed through every line of defense that she had and refused to let her put her barriers back up. She'd managed fairly well while he had been based in Charleston, but she knew that it was all over the minute she found out he was moving to Myrtle Beach. She was helpless to hold back with him. He saw a part of her that no one other than Claire had. Her heart was his and she didn't know how she'd recover if he broke it.

"Yoooo-hoooo, Suzy, helloooo. I've been calling and calling you. You're not barbequing alone in there, are you?"

Suzy jumped at the sound of Nick's voice on the other side of the door. With a roll of her eyes, Suzy yelled back through the door, "What're you talking about, barbequing alone?"

"You know, the two-finger twirl, the solo mambo, the five-finger shuffle."

Suzy jerked the door open and clapped her hand over his mouth. "Oh, geez, please stop. You're such a pervert. If I was doing any of the above, which I wasn't, you would be the last one to know."

Nick threw an arm around her shoulders and said, "We're all family here, babe, no need to be embarrassed."

Just when Suzy was trying to figure out how to use her cast to trip him, Beth walked in from the deck asking, "What's taking you guys so long? The pizza is getting cold."

With a chuckle, Nick said, "Your sister was, um, exploring her feminine side and it took me a few minutes to tear her away."

At Beth's confused look, Suzy buried her elbow in his ribs and enjoyed his moan of pain as she walked away from him. Beth had opened a bottle of wine and set the table. When Suzy bit into her slice of pepperoni pizza, she closed her eyes in bliss as the vibrant flavors exploded in her mouth. This would be a perfect evening if Gray were here. She'd love to have him beside her looking out over the ocean and sipping a glass of wine. Instead, she was here with Nick and Beth and he was somewhere having dinner with Reva. Life had a cruel sense of humor and it truly sucked sometimes.

"Any word on when Gray will be back, sis?"

Suzy looked at Beth with a grimace. "He's supposed to be back Friday. He wants to take me out for my birthday. Of course, tonight he's taking Reva to dinner."

She didn't miss the quick exchange of looks between Nick and Beth at that piece of news. Nick cleared his throat, looking uncomfortable. "Suzy, don't give up on him. I know that most women would run for the hills with something like this going on, but my brother really loves you. I still don't believe that this is his baby."

"It is what it is, Nick, and I'm doing the best I can."

Suzy could tell that Nick wanted to say more, but changed the subject instead. "Hey, girls, let's watch a movie tonight. Whatever you two pick is fine with me."

Suzy couldn't resist teasing him a little. "I thought you were a ladies' man, yet here you're home again tonight. Are the ladies here immune to your charms, Nicky? Maybe we could sign you up on one of those dating sites tonight."

"Ha-ha, you're so funny. I'll have you know that there is nothing wrong with the Merimon charm. Just this morning Crystal in accounting asked me out for a drink."

Beth slammed her drink down on the table and

flushed when Suzy raised an eyebrow in question. "Oh, sorry, my glass slipped."

Both Beth and Nick seemed to be doing everything to avoid looking at each other. What in the hell was going on with these two? They had seemed to almost be friends the last few days; Suzy hoped the arguing wasn't about to start back again. Maybe she should encourage Nick to go out in the evenings more to give Beth a chance for some time away from him.

Chapter Twenty

Suzy and Beth picked the movie *Pretty Woman* to watch and Nick reluctantly agreed. She was pretty sure he was imagining himself as Richard Gere and debating trading his minivan in for a Lotus Esprit. That could only be a step up in her opinion. It was after ten when she finally settled into bed. Where was Gray? He should have called by now. Surely he wasn't still out with Reva? A stab of jealousy tore through her as she imagined the man she loved having dinner with the woman carrying his child. What had they talked about? What decisions had they made? With a tired sigh, she turned the light out and left the phone where she'd be able to hear it when Gray called.

When she woke up sometime later the clock showed five in the morning and a quick check of her phone showed no missed calls or messages. What the hell? Her gut clenched as a sick feeling came over her. He'd never missed calling when he said he was going to, and didn't he understand how she'd feel knowing he was going out with Reva? It wasn't like Gray to be this thoughtless. She knew that Nick and Beth would still be asleep so she turned on the television and watched *SportsCenter*. The news would probably have her crying.

After what seemed like hours, it was time to get up and get ready for work. She'd never been more grateful to have somewhere to go than this morning. Nick and Beth tried their best to cheer her up during breakfast and the ride to work, but finally they gave up and just shot her concerned looks when they thought she wasn't looking. Truthfully, she just wasn't in the mood to talk or joke this morning.

As soon as they arrived at work, Suzy gave Beth some paperwork to take care of and closed herself in her office. *Come on, shake it off. You can't keep moping around like a love-struck teenager every time Gray doesn't call. Since when have you made someone the center of your life? Remember, babe, smoke and mirrors.*

Around nine her cell phone rang and she saw Gray's name on the caller ID. She took a deep breath, trying to make sure her voice was upbeat, and answered the phone.

Chills went down her spine as she heard the sexy timbre of Gray's voice on the other end. "Hey, baby, how are you?"

"Um, hey there." Suzy rolled her eyes at the sound of her breathy voice on the phone. *Could you be more pathetic?*

"God, I miss you so much, baby."

Um, hello, I'm waiting to hear your reason for not calling me after your date last night? Can we cut the small talk and get on with the program, please? Maybe I should just throw it out there. I can't do another minute of love talk until I know what happened.

"So how was your dinner last night with Reva?"

Was she imagining it or was there a brief pause before he spoke? "It was fine, honey; things are very civil between us now. I'm sorry I didn't call you last night, but something came up." *That something that came up better not be attached to your body, slick.*

"Oh, nothing major I hope?"

"In the end, no, it wasn't. Reva wasn't feeling well when we finished dinner so I took her back to my place to make sure she was going to be okay. I live close to the hospital so it only made sense. It had gotten so late by that time that I let her use my guest room rather than going back across town."

For one of the few times in her life, Suzy could think of nothing to say. What did he expect her to say to that?

"Suzy, baby, are you still there?"

Suzy could hear the edge of what almost sounded like panic in his voice.

"Sure, I'm here. Where is Reva now?"

"I dropped her at home this morning on my way to the office." Then, releasing a deep breath, he asked, "Honey, are you upset over this? I certainly can't blame you. I want you to know, though, that there was nothing even remotely romantic that happened the entire evening. Reva never said or did anything out of line, nor did I. Hell, it's almost like ironing out a business deal with a customer."

"Except the customer isn't usually carrying your child, right?"

"Suzy—"

"Gray, don't. Please just don't. I can't continue this conversation without sounding like a total shit and I really don't want to do that. Are you still coming home Friday?"

"Ah, baby, you know I am. I wouldn't miss your birthday for anything."

"Here's what I want, Gray. Let's not talk on the phone for the rest of the week." Suzy continued on despite the protests that he was already making. "No, listen. I'm not trying to break up with you, I'm just giving you the time you need to handle your business there. Gray, I love you, but I can't hear about Reva right now. I don't want to know that you're taking her to dinner and that she's sleeping over, it's just too much for me at this point. I need time to adjust and so do you." She lowered her voice and said, "I'll miss you this week and I can't wait to see you."

"Suzy, this is killing me. I know I'm hurting you and I can't stand it. I'm trying to do what's right and I don't even know what that is anymore. I'll give you the time you need this week, but come Friday night, I want you in my arms again. I love you, baby."

Tears trickled down her cheeks as she ended the call. Was she making a mistake? Maybe it was better to know what was going on in Charleston than to sit here letting her imagination run wild. *Good grief, suck it up, Buttercup. You're sitting at your desk crying at work. Get over it. You can do this. Go do what you do best, shop. Buy something sexy for Friday and pretend that Gray is just away on business this week. Put your head up and your shoulders back. You're better than this drama.* Okay, I've got this.

Suzy picked up the phone and dialed Beth. "Hey, let's go shopping during lunch. I need a new dress for Friday. Invite Ella if you like and I'll ask Claire. It's time for some retail therapy." When she hung up the phone with Beth, she dialed Claire's extension. "Hey, girlfriend, how's it waddling?"

Claire chuckled. "My baby and I are just fine, Suz, thanks for asking."

One thing she loved about Claire, she had a sense of humor and she always got Suzy, no matter what. "Beth, Ella, and I are going shopping during lunch. I wondered if you felt like coming along. If we go to the mall, we can rent one of the scooters for you." Then as if the thought had suddenly struck her, Suzy snorted. "Hell, I'm gonna need a scooter, too. I'm so tired of this cast."

"If I can roll around with this bowling ball attached to me, surely you can work those crutches, Suz. Maybe we can have Beth drop us right at the front door so we won't have to walk as far. This is going to sound so wrong, but do you think Nick would let us borrow his minivan?"

"Yeah, that's a great idea. I know I make fun of him all of the time, but I'm going to have to give him credit; that thing rocks. I'd never be caught owning one but it's like riding in a blue-collar limousine or something."

Claire started laughing, gasping out, "God, please stop, if I laugh too hard I'll pee myself."

"Oh, yuck, why would you do that?"

"Oh, honey, you don't know how it is when you're pregnant. You have to pee all of the time. I barely get back in my chair before I have to go again. Ah, the boss just walked in. I better get off before I get in trouble." Claire laughed. "I'll come down to your office around noon."

After she finished her call to Claire, Suzy stood up and opened her office door. She refused to hide away and have a pity party all afternoon. She'd be cheerful and carefree even if it killed her.

As she was going to sit back down, she saw Beth standing in the doorway hesitantly. She gave her a warm smile and waved her in. "Is this a good time to go over the schedule for the rest of the week, sis?"

"Sure, fire away." She knew Beth was studying her for any sign of a chink in her armor, but she was determined that she wouldn't find one. She'd always hated people who brought their personal problems to the office. It's not that she was unfeeling, but she was really at a loss as to how best help someone who was crying all over their daily calendar. She generally asked them if they wanted to have a drink that evening and then prayed the rest of the day that they would recover before then.

Suzy was considered somewhat of a gypsy or free spirit at work, but it didn't take people long to realize that she was tough as nails when she had to be and sugary sweet when she needed a favor from a vendor. Until Gray, she'd always been very careful to keep her personal life disconnected from Danvers. Her job had been her escape when she'd broken up with Jeff. When she walked in the door at work, it was time to leave her problems at the door. She joked around with her co-workers and teased her friends but at the end of the day, she had a job to do.

Suzy was surprised to see that it was almost lunch-time by the time they had finished. "Did you ask Ella if she wanted to go to the mall with us?"

"Yeah, she's on board. I told her we would meet her at the elevators. Are you ready now?"

"Oh, crap, I forgot to ask Nick if we could borrow his van. Hang on while I call him." As Suzy started to pick up the telephone, Beth pulled a key ring from her pocket and dangled it in the air. "I've got it covered."

Suzy gave her a high five, asking, "When did you get it? I didn't see Nick come through."

"Oh, I just thought of it earlier and buzzed up to his floor to ask. I knew it would be easier for you and Claire to travel in."

"Well, that's good." *Why in the world is she blushing? Does she think I'm going to be pissed because she dared to leave her office and go to another floor without asking? Geez, I'm not that bad, am I?* "Let's see if we can head off Claire at the elevator so she won't have to walk all the way down here."

Suzy positioned her crutches and followed Beth down the hallway. Claire had just walked up to Ella's desk when they got there. Soon they were all settled in the van and on their way to the mall. Beth and Ella were indeed nice enough to drop them at the entrance and they walked inside the door to wait for them to park the van.

When they were all together again, they started browsing in the stores. Beth and Ella had picked out a few items, but Suzy had yet to find "the dress." By the fifth store she was starting to wonder if she ever would. Claire had split up to go into the Baby Gap, a store that gave Suzy cold chills. *Why couldn't they at least put heads on their mannequins? Seeing those little bodies without them kind of freaked her out.*

Surprisingly enough, she found exactly what she was looking for in the store next to the Gap. *Now, I see how it goes. You buy a sexy dress and a pair of "do-me" shoes and then in nine months you end up shopping in the Baby Gap. Note to self: buy a case of condoms and double bag that sucker!*

Beth and Ella stood outside the dressing room as she went inside to try it on. She hoped it looked as good as it did on the hanger. The dress looked simple from the front. It was an emerald green in a slinky jersey material with a boat neckline. It almost looked demure until you got a look at the back. The dress draped very low and exposed her back almost to the curve of her hips. It was both elegant and sexy, exactly the combination she'd been searching for.

Even though she knew it was crazy since she could only wear one, Suzy found a beautiful pair of sandals with mile-high heels in a tan color. The sandals were simple with thin leather straps over her toes and ankle. Surely she could wear one heel along with her cast. If it was too uncomfortable, she'd make do with a flat shoe. She couldn't wait until she finally got the cast removed in a few weeks.

Finally, everyone had their purchases and they grabbed a quick sandwich in the food court before heading back to work. There must be something to retail therapy because she did feel better when she got back to the office. Hopefully if she just stayed busy, the rest of the week would fly by.

Chapter Twenty-one

When Thursday evening rolled around, Suzy had to admit that she'd done pretty well during the week even though there were moments when she wanted to pick up the phone and call Gray. As she was lying in bed that night, her cell phone chimed with a new text message. She smiled when she saw that it was from Gray. *I know I'm not supposed to call or text, but I wanted to make sure that we were still on for tomorrow night. I'll pick you up at seven for your birthday extravaganza. I love you, baby. P.S., I guess asking what you're wearing is out of the question?*

Suzy threw back her head and laughed. He had no idea how much she needed this tonight. Just being able to go to sleep knowing that things were still okay between them was such a relief. She clicked on the reply to the text and typed, *Seven is fine, slick. Of course you can ask what I'm wearing. I'm already in bed so I have on my best granny panties, flannel pajamas, and knee socks. See ya Friday.*

Her phone almost immediately dinged back with another message from Gray saying, *You're a cruel woman, but I love you anyway. Sleep well.*

Suzy slept the best that she had in days and woke up tingling in anticipation of the evening ahead. She literally floated through the day at work. Even when an order was messed up from one of her suppliers, she simply told them, "These things happen." The poor guy had actually just stood looking at her in shock. Normally, she'd have ripped him a new one, but she just didn't have it in her to be pissed off.

Beth was going back to her apartment for the weekend and Nick had mentioned something about having plans. She certainly had plans of her own. She'd asked Beth to stop on their way home to pick up some whipped cream. Beth had literally thrown it at her when she got back into the car saying, "Ugh, I don't even want to know. FYI, though, you're washing your own sheets."

With an exaggerated wiggle of her eyebrows Suzy said, "Loosen up, sis, we can get you your own can of whipped cream and I'll let you borrow my handcuffs. I saw the way Greg was chatting you up at work earlier."

"Oh, please, he's like five feet tall, which means his eyes are right on level with my boobs. He stared at them the entire time while I was forced to look down at his shiny, bald head. I'm glad you have such high hopes for me, though."

"Hey, don't worry; we'll get you laid yet. It's next on my to-do list right after Gray and I . . ."

"Okay, stop! I don't want to hear what's on your list for Gray. I'd like to be able to look him in the eyes again without imagining where his mouth or your mouth has been."

Suzy laughed. They pulled in the driveway. Beth followed her into the beach house to pick up some clothing that she'd left, and within a few minutes Suzy had the house to herself. She flipped the television on in the bedroom and put on a music video channel. Soon she was dancing around the room. It wasn't exactly graceful since she had to work with her cast, but, hey, at least no one was around to witness the train wreck.

With fifteen minutes to spare, Suzy walked into the living room to wait for Gray. She had to admit that she looked and felt great. She was freshly washed, shaved, and groomed. She thought Gray would really get a kick out of the design she'd managed to make in her downstairs area with her bikini shaver. She'd applied her favorite lotion to every inch of her body, and the new green dress looked even better than it had in the store. She was wearing her one high heel, but had tucked a flat shoe in her purse in case she needed to change.

She could feel her nipples harden as the clock ticked seven. Gray should be here at any moment. Traffic was probably heavy on Friday between Charleston and Myrtle Beach. She got up to pour herself a glass of wine to take the edge off the hunger that was humming in her body. Would they even make it to a restaurant without making love first? She'd missed him so much this week and heat was pooling between her thighs just thinking of the last time he'd been inside her.

Suzy could easily picture Gray walking into the kitchen as he had the first time they'd made love. He'd mold his body to hers, pushing her against the counter. His big hands would come around her front to cup her breasts while his hot mouth would lick and nip down the curve of her neck. He'd then raise the back of her dress, lower her panties and part her legs. She'd hear his zipper lower and then the head of his cock would nudge against her sex. Still, without saying a word, he'd surge into her heat to the hilt. He'd pound into her over and over and she'd be helpless to resist.

Suzy's body was tight with desire; her fantasy had her so aroused that she was desperate to relieve the hunger that raged inside her. Surely she could make it until Gray arrived. A quick look at her watch showed he was already fifteen minutes late. *Oh, screw it. I can't even walk now, my clit is so sensitive.* Suzy pulled her dress up and slid her hand into her soaking wet panties. As she flicked her fingers against her swollen sex, she knew it would only take a few strokes to make her come. She worked her throbbing clit between two fingers. She could almost feel the heat of Gray's tongue sliding inside her as she increased the speed of her hand. Her body clenched, starting to crest as her orgasm washed over her. She continued to work her fingers, trying to relieve the exquisite pressure that still throbbed inside her. Just as she was slowing her hand, another orgasm took hold of her as the release that she so desperately needed washed over her.

Limp with relief, Suzy sagged against the counter surprised that she'd just pleasured herself in the kitchen. *Have I lost my mind? What was it that Nick had called it, "barbequing alone"? I think that was more like a four-alarm fire. Good grief, what if he or Beth had walked in? I'd never live it down.* Of course, imagining Gray walking in was enough to set her body humming again. She hurriedly grabbed another pair of panties from the bedroom and discarded the now damp ones. Another look at her watch showed it was almost eight. Where was Gray?

*   *   *

Suzy had roamed every inch of the house for hours it seemed. It was now after ten and Gray had still not shown up. She'd called him and left several messages, wanting to make sure he was okay. She'd even resorted to checking the Internet to make sure there were no accidents reported locally.

As midnight approached she had to look at an option that she'd tried to avoid. Maybe this was his way of telling her that it was over. One of the fastest ways to get rid of a woman that you no longer wanted was to stand her up on her birthday.

It was obvious that he was spending time with Reva and she was pregnant with his child. He was clearly torn between what he felt was his duty and Suzy. Maybe duty had finally won out. She couldn't believe that Gray would just not show up though. *You knew it was a mistake to show him how much you loved him. You gave him your heart and what if he doesn't want it either? How many more times are you going to let someone crush you before you learn?*

Suzy must have dozed off. She had no idea how long she'd been sitting in the chair in the living room when the light being turned on woke her. She blinked like an owl, trying to adjust to the sudden brightness of the room. She was able to focus just as Nick walked by her toward the back of the house.

Almost as if he knew someone was watching him, Nick suddenly stopped and looked around. When he saw her sitting in the chair, he had an almost comical look of disbelief on his face. My God, did she actually look that bad?

Turning, he smiled and walked back to where she

was sitting. As he drew closer, the smile slipped uncertainly from his lips to be replaced by a look of confusion and concern. "Suzy, what're you doing sitting out here by yourself?" Then looking around he asked, "Where's my brother?"

Bitter laughter spewed forth from her lips as she answered, "I don't know, Nick; your guess is as good as mine at this point."

Nick crouched down in front of her. "Did you two have a fight or something? I can't believe he'd just bail on you like that."

"No . . . he'd have to show up for us to fight. I haven't seen your brother tonight. I guess he had a change of plans. Nice of him to call, right?"

Alarm crossed Nick's face as the impact of her words sank in. "Suzy, that's not like Gray. Have you tried to call him?"

"Of course I have, Nick," Suzy snapped.

Suzy couldn't miss the hurt expression that crossed his face at her nasty tone. She took a deep breath, trying to remember that although they were brothers, Nick had never been anything but good to her. "Nick, I'm sorry. I did try to call him several times, and he didn't answer my calls or call me back. I also checked the traffic reports and there weren't any accidents reported." Running a hand along the back of her neck trying to relieve the tension there, she asked, "What time is it?"

"It's just after one. I'm supposed to fly out in the morning and needed to pick up some papers that I left here. I thought I could be in and out without bothering you guys. Suzy, let me make some calls. This just isn't Gray. Something must have happened."

Fatigue was bearing down on her fast. She wanted

nothing more than to slip under the covers and bury herself in the bed until she stopped hurting again. She gave Nick the best smile that she could manage and let him help her up from the chair. Her muscles were stiff from hours of sitting. He held on to her arm as she made her way to the bedroom and softly closed the door. She was safe in here. She didn't have to look into Nick's sympathy-filled eyes. Or were they filled with pity instead? She didn't even bother to undress; she simply pulled the covers back and curled up in a ball on the bed. Sweet oblivion reached out to claim her as she drifted off to sleep with a heart so heavy it was almost hard to breathe.

Nick paced the length of the living room as he reached his brother's voice mail yet again. What in the hell was going on? There was no way Gray would abandon Suzy on her birthday without a damn good reason or at least he hoped his brother better have one. He'd gotten pretty attached to Suzy since he'd moved in to help out. He'd never let anyone hurt her and that included his brother. Just as Suzy had said, Gray wasn't answering his phone or returning his messages or texts.

With a sigh of resignation, Nick knew it was time to bring out the big guns. He was going to be forced to call his parents and see if they knew what was going on. It was either that or take off to Charleston himself. Too bad he hadn't saved Reva's number all those times she'd called him looking for his brother. Surely he wasn't with her, though. Just the thought of it made him sick.

Nick walked outside onto the balcony to make the call to his parents. He didn't want Suzy to overhear the call in case something had happened. He was grateful to hear his dad's voice on the other end of the line. As he explained the situation, he could hear the concern in his father's voice as he fired off a series of questions. Nick answered everything he could, which wasn't much. His father promised to do some checking and call him back.

A bad feeling settled over him. He didn't think his brother was hurt, but he did think he was in trouble. There was no way his brother could love someone like Suzy and not call her to let her know what was happening. You just didn't leave someone you loved hanging like that. Man, where was Gray going with all of this? He was very close to losing Suzy, if he hadn't already.

Nick jumped when his cell phone rang. His father skipped all the small talk and got right to the point. "I called Reva's parents when I couldn't get any answers elsewhere. Apparently Reva was in a car accident earlier tonight and is in the hospital. Gray is there with her. Everything appears to be fine now. She just has some bruises and they're monitoring the baby's vitals. I guess they were all pretty worried earlier when it happened." Then releasing a weary breath, he said, "This is a damn fine mess, isn't it?"

"That's an understatement if I've ever heard one, Dad. Good lord, what is the world coming to when I'm starting to look like the considerate one in the family? I don't care what happened, he should've called Suzy. It's not like Gray to be such a prick."

"I know, son. Gray's lost, though. He's always been a stickler about doing the right thing." With a chuckle, he continued. "I have no idea where he gets that from." They both knew that Gray was a carbon copy of him and that Nick was more like his mother. "I know he loves Suzy, but I don't know if they can survive this mess. Gray will never walk away from Reva if that's his baby and if she throws any kind of guilt at him, then his sense of honor will demand he do what he thinks is right.

"I hear you snorting over there, son, but you're not so different. You may play hard, but you have as much honor as your brother. If you didn't, we wouldn't be having this conversation because you wouldn't have bothered to call looking for Gray. Just do me a favor, son, learn a lesson from this. If you have to keep sleeping around, buy some damn decent condoms."

"Dad! God, can we please not discuss this now? We had this conversation once before and I never, ever want to discuss it again, okay?"

Nick smiled at his father's first genuine laughter since their conversation had started. "You got it, but if you screw up, we will be having it again. I'll talk to you tomorrow. Love you, son."

He made another call because, unlike his brother, he'd no intention of leaving his woman to wonder what had happened to him. He briefly explained the situation and then decided to sleep on the couch for what was left of the night. He didn't want to bother Suzy if she was actually asleep, but he wanted to be close in case she woke up and wanted to know what he'd found out. He couldn't stand the thought of two Merimon brothers abandoning her tonight.

Chapter Twenty-two

Ugh, the one bad thing about living near the ocean was the bright sunlight so early in the morning. Suzy pulled the sheet over her head trying to hide her eyes from the glaring light pouring in the windows. Finally, she gave up the battle to return to sleep and slid her legs to the edge of the bed. She was surprised to see that she was still wearing her dress. *What the hell?* Then the night before came flooding back and Suzy dearly wished that she'd been able to block out the morning for just a bit longer. Where was Gray? Had he called? She reached for her cell phone on the nightstand. There were no missed calls or messages. *Don't jump to conclusions; there is a perfectly good reason, and it has nothing to do with Reva. Suck it up and find out what's going on. You can fall apart later.*

Suzy grabbed her crutches from where she had left them the previous night and hobbled toward the door. She could only imagine how bad she must look after sleeping in her clothes and makeup.

She found Nick asleep on the couch in his clothes, as well. Apparently neither of them had had enough ambition to change last night. She leaned down to tug on his foot, shaking him gently awake.

Nick suddenly jerked awake, looking around in confusion. "Wha-what the . . . Oh, Suzy, you scared the heck out of me." He slid his legs off the couch, making room for her to sit.

Even though she wasn't sure she wanted to know, Suzy decided to confront the elephant in the room. "Did you talk to Gray?"

"Um, no I didn't, but he's okay."

"Come on, Nick, it's obvious you know something so just spill it. I'm not going to lose it on you."

Nick shifted around uncomfortably on the couch, seeming to choose his words with care. "Suzy, he's at the hospital in Charleston with Reva. She had a car accident last night and I guess Gray found out about it. My dad said she was okay, but they were keeping her for observation. I . . . I'm sure there is a good reason why he didn't call to let you know," Nick finished quietly.

Well, there it was. The details might be different but the underlying cause was the same. It was Reva again that had kept her up long into the night wondering where Gray was. Suzy felt the life drain from her body as she sat there next to Nick. She could feel his concerned gaze on her bent head, but he wisely kept quiet.

When Suzy finally raised her head and looked at him, her expression was blank. Her eyes looked eerily vacant and her face was completely devoid of color. "Suzy—"

Shaking her head, she said, "Don't, Nick, leave it be. Weren't you supposed to fly out this morning?"

"Yeah, but Declan is going instead. I didn't want to leave you here alone."

"I don't need a babysitter, Nick. But since you're here, I could use some help this morning."

"You got it. Let me fix us some coffee. I think Beth is on her way over."

Suzy no longer questioned why Nick always seemed to know Beth's whereabouts. She was just glad that they had finally called a truce and appeared to be friends now. Even though she planned to see his brother as little as possible, she did still want to see Nick. He at least had never let her down when she needed him.

Without telling Nick what she needed him for, Suzy turned and went back in the bedroom. After a quick shower she changed into a comfortable jean skirt and top and started the task of packing. She was leaving the house that had been home for the last month. There was no reason to keep fooling herself; this would never be her home. It was time to accept that Reva was a game changer in her relationship with Gray, and there was nothing she could do about it. The only way she could stop herself from completely collapsing under the weight of the sorrow that threatened to drown her was to keep moving forward. If she stopped now, she'd fall apart and she wanted to be alone when that happened.

Just as she finished packing her suitcase, Beth walked in. One look at her sister's face had her wanting to curl up in a ball and sob her heart out. She sternly said, "Beth, stop please. I'm going home this morning, so please help me get packed and out of here. I don't want to talk about this now or probably ever, okay?"

Beth quietly accepted her wishes, reaching for the handle of her suitcase and rolling it to the living room. Nick was standing there wearing his heart on his sleeve. How had Suzy ever thought there was no depth there? He looked almost as crushed as she felt. Without a word he took the suitcase from Beth and asked, "Is this everything?"

No, my heart is lying here on the floor crushed into a million pieces. Is there any possible way you can glue it back together again before I leave? "That's all, thanks." With a laugh that was too brittle and loud even to her own ears, Suzy said, "One last ride for the three amigos in the minivan. I'll miss that sucker."

Suddenly Nick dropped the handle of the suitcase he was holding and strode over to her. Even though his actions were forceful, his words were gentle. "Suzy, just because you and Gray are having problems doesn't mean shit where you and I are concerned. I . . . um, think the world of you and unless you say no, I plan to still see you as much as we always have." With a chuckle, he said, "Well, except for the living together part." Then with the wicked expression she loved so well, he finished, "Unless you're into it, that is."

Beth playfully slapping him on the head saved her the trouble. "Thanks, Nick, and for the record I won't say no. You're kind of like a bad habit that I've grown quite fond of and have no intention of breaking. Now could you please take me home?" *Before I lose the cool façade and break down in front of you both. Please let me hang on to my pride; it's all I have right now.*

When she walked into her condo for the first time in weeks, it was almost like being in a stranger's home. It had been slow going up the steps, but she'd made it without too much difficulty. Nick had left her suitcase in the bedroom and now he and Beth stood studying her as if unsure of what to do.

"How about we come back this evening with dinner?"

Already shaking her head, Suzy said, "Thanks, Nick, but I'd just like some time to myself. I really appreciate your help and I'll see you both on Monday, okay?" Both Nick and Beth began protesting at the same time. It was time for some tough love. "Guys, I love you both, I really do, but you need to go now. I'm just hanging on over here so please do as I ask."

Beth was clearly torn as to what to do, but Nick put his hand on her back and pushed her forward. "Let's give Suzy what she needs, princess."

Suzy hugged them both and promised to call if she needed them. They all knew it was a call that she wouldn't be making. Finally, they were out the door and she was free to wallow in her grief.

As she sat on the couch with a box of Kleenex in her hands, she discovered something strange. No matter how much she wanted or needed to, she couldn't make one single tear fall. She was quite simply numb. She'd stared at the walls for hours when she heard her phone ringing. When she pulled it from the front of her purse she saw Gray's name on the caller ID. She dropped the phone as if it were a snake. My God, why now? Why couldn't he just quietly go away so she wouldn't have to hear the voice that she loved so much while she was this raw?

After the fifth phone call in about that many minutes, Suzy had finally had enough. What the hell? Was he trying to torture her now? Maybe it was time to go ahead and rip the Band-Aid off quickly and get it over with. With a deep breath, Suzy finally took his next call.

She answered the phone with a simple, "Gray?"

Some part of her was happy to hear his shaky breath on the other end of the line. At least she knew that he was suffering as much as she was. "Baby, I don't even know what to say. I missed your birthday and didn't even call to let you know why. I . . . I just feel like shit over it."

Suzy kept her voice steady and cool, refusing to let him know how much he'd hurt her. Smoke and mirrors; it was her only defense right now. "It's fine, Gray. Nick told me about the accident. I'm sure you had more pressing things to worry about than me."

"I was worried about Reva and the baby, yes. But it's no excuse. By the time things calmed down at the hospital and I knew everything was okay, it was already so late. I'm so sorry. I've been sitting here all morning trying to work up the nerve to call you. I let you down and that's something I swore I'd never do."

"Gray, just stop, please. You and I both know that we can't go on pretending that things are going to be fine between us because they aren't. This is just the first of many things that will come up. Maybe a better person could handle always coming last in your life, but I'm not that person."

"Suzy, I love you!"

She could feel the tears that she'd been unable to shed earlier start to clog her throat, fighting for release. "I love you, too, but it's not enough. I have to love you enough to let you go, Gray. If I stay with you, it will keep tearing both of us apart. I can't fault you for wanting to be part of your baby's life. You wouldn't be the man I love if you didn't."

Unable to hold back any longer, she sobbed, "Please love me enough to let me go, too, Gray."

She could hear the tears in Gray's voice as he said, "My God, Suzy, I don't know if I can. You're my heart, my life."

"Gray," she gasped out, "please. I can't hurt like this anymore. If you love me, don't call me again." She ended the call before he could reply and the sobs erupted from her throat with such intensity that it was hard to breathe. She curled up into a ball as her world crashed around her. She knew in her heart that she'd never love again. If and when she ever got involved, no part of her heart would ever belong to another. Gray owned it until the day she died, of that she was certain.

Chapter Twenty-three

Monday morning at work found everyone walking around her on eggshells. Claire had already been down to check on her, Ella had dropped by to bring her coffee and hovered like a mother hen, Beth had been eyeing her all morning looking for signs of a breakdown, and even Jason had been by for small talk. When Nick stuck his head in her office, she blew out a disgusted breath. "Oh, geez, do you all think I'm on suicide watch or something? Who's coming by next to make sure Suzy hasn't gone off the deep end?"

One thing you had to love about Nick, he wasn't easily offended. He threw back his head and laughed. "Sorry about that. Everyone is just worried about you. Don't be surprised if Beth hides your letter opener or if your scissors have disappeared. All kidding aside, how're you holding up, kid?"

Suzy had buried the hurt so far inside her that she was able to keep her expression blank at the obvious concern in Nick's voice. "I'm fine, really. It's nice of you all to worry about me, but there is no need. Gray and I were only together for a short time so it's not as if we were married or anything."

"Just so you know, I don't believe a word you're saying, but I'll let it be. Do you want to grab a bite to eat after work today or maybe a drink?"

"Thanks, Nick, but I've got some errands to run this evening. Rain check?"

"Sure, sounds good." Rising from the chair, Nick looked back at her one last time as if assessing her mood and left.

Just hold it together. Soon they will all tire of asking how you are and leave you alone. Until then, keep your happy face on and don't let any of them know how close to the edge you are.

If he didn't know the route by heart, Gray would probably have never made it. He hadn't slept in days and was barely hanging on. He parked his car and walked wearily to the front door, fumbling for his key. He was instantly soothed at the familiar sight of his childhood home. His mother walked out of the kitchen and handed him a whisk.

"I thought I'd be seeing you soon. I have everything set up waiting, so come on in."

Gray didn't need to ask her what she was talking about. Every major problem in his life had been solved with his mother in the kitchen. He had a feeling that baking a cake couldn't fix this problem but the routine was a balm to his soul.

True to her word, the kitchen island contained bowls, a mixer, and all of the ingredients to make something he could make in his sleep: red velvet cake. It had been a household favorite growing up and he'd grieved lost pets, lost loves, lost games, and almost every change of life standing at that very island with a whisk in his hand.

His mother seated herself on a bar stool on the other side, while he put on the apron she had left out. As he started measuring out his ingredients and then sifting them together, his mother said quietly, "I'm worried about you, baby boy."

Looking up at the first woman to claim his heart, he snorted. "I believe Nick is the baby boy in this family, Mom."

"Gray, you're my firstborn and Nicky might be younger, but you will both always be my babies. No matter how old you are, how big your job is, or how big your troubles are for that matter. None of it will ever change that. "

Their conversation was temporarily interrupted as he turned on the mixer to combine his dry and wet ingredients. All too soon he had his cake batter divided into his cake pans and was placing them in the oven. After he'd cleaned up the island and placed everything in the dishwasher, he came around and pulled out a stool next to his mother. Even though he knew it wouldn't solve anything, he needed this familiar routine as much as he needed to breathe.

Gray stared straight ahead as he said, "So I've really fucked this up, haven't I?"

"Gray! You know I'm far from a prude, but do we have to use the F-word before lunchtime?"

Gray snickered at his mother's expression. "Oh, come on, Mom, Dad said you rolled it at least five times when the dry cleaner ruined your leather jacket last month."

With her best innocent expression, she said, "Your father's getting senile, Gray, he doesn't know what he's talking about."

God, it felt good to laugh again. When the world seemed impossible, his mother always had a way to push the clouds away even if only for a moment. Reaching over to him, she ran her fingers through his hair just as she'd done countless times before. "Grayson, you were always my serious one. I never had to worry about you getting into too much trouble because you always had a very real sense of right and wrong. Nick could shrug off anything back then, but you wanted to right every injustice even in elementary school. It breaks my heart to see you like this and not be able to help you."

"No waving the mother-magic-wand and fixing everything for me, huh?"

"Oh, honey, if only I could. I know you love Suzy and I know you're tied in knots over Reva and the baby. The only piece of advice that I can give you is to be patient. When this baby is born, have a paternity test. Do not let Reva talk you out of it. If the baby is yours, then do what feels right to you."

Gray rubbed his face with his hand, exhaustion plain in every movement he made. "Suzy will be gone, though, Mom. Hell, she's gone now and I can't even blame her. I've been so shell-shocked that I've made a bad situation even worse. I can't ask her to stay, knowing that she needs to go. I don't want a life with Reva and she probably doesn't even want one with me. She's in panic mode right now and I've got a feeling that her parents are pushing all of her buttons. I can't ask Suzy to be stuck in the middle like that. She deserves so much better. In the end, I've turned out to be no better than the last guy who broke her heart."

"Son, you didn't go out and see Reva behind her

back. You and Suzy were not a couple when you slept with Reva. Sure, you both have to endure the fallout now, but you weren't unfaithful to Suzy. Give yourself a break and give Suzy some time. When you love someone that much, you often find a way back to each other, even if it takes time. I can't see you two being able to be apart forever. Even if this is your baby, things will settle down eventually and you'll be clearer. You're flying on pure emotion right now, which makes it hard to see the big picture. You've never been a quitter, Grayson, so don't start waving the white flag now, okay?"

Gray smiled at his mother and said, "Wow, you're pretty smart for a girl. I bet Dad doesn't know whether he's coming or going most of the time."

"Hey, you better watch that smart mouth." Then with a feline smile, she admitted, "Honey, your dad hasn't known whether to wind his butt or scratch his watch since the moment he met me and he wouldn't have it any other way. I have a feeling you and Suzy would be the same way."

Gray threw back his head and laughed. Oh, how he loved his mother, and she was right. Life with Suzy would never be boring. He'd never know what was coming with her, and like his father, he'd love it. Maybe his mother was right; he'd pull back and give Suzy some time and also try to find some workable solution between himself and Reva. He wasn't ready to give up yet and he never would be.

Chapter Twenty-four

Suzy had caved to pressure from her friends and she was sitting in a Mexican restaurant with Beth, Claire, Ella, and Nick. It had been two weeks since she'd last spoken to Gray and time hadn't dulled the grief she was suffering. She went to a great deal of trouble to put on a good front, but she was barely surviving most days. How could she let a man bring her to this? Jeff had been a walk in the park compared to the pain that coursed through her body when she thought of Gray.

Everyone was still worried about her and she knew that. The thought of food made her want to gag, and her clothes hung on her now. She pushed an enchilada around on her plate, trying to give the illusion that she was eating. Everyone said it would take time; well, how much exactly? When was it going to get easier to get up in the mornings? When would her heart stop physically hurting? When would she stop trembling on the street when she saw someone who looked like him?

Just looking across the table at Nick made her physically hurt. He looked so much like his brother. She knew it wasn't fair to him, but she avoided him as much as she could. He'd asked her to lunch and dinner several times, but she always found some excuse not to go. She cared so much about him, but right now he was just a painful reminder of the brother that she couldn't have.

She felt a hand on her shoulder and looked over into Claire's sympathetic eyes. "Hey, girlfriend, you zoned out on me there for a minute."

Suzy put on her best carefree smile and joked, "Just appreciating that fine specimen of a man at the bar."

Claire looked to where she was pointing at a cute blond surfer type. "Oh, Suz, please, he probably begins every sentence with 'dude.'"

"Dude, what's wrong with that?"

Claire's entire stomach jiggled as she laughed. Suzy asked, "Hey, how much longer before that oven timer goes off?"

Laying her hand on her stomach affectionately, Claire said, "A little over a month if I make it that long."

Nick, apparently hearing her comment, raised his hand, saying, "Please, no talk of your hemorrhoids again."

"Oh, come on, Nick," Claire teased, "just think about how far ahead of the game you will be when you finally marry and your wife gets pregnant. You won't even need to buy *What to Expect When You're Expecting*; you'll already know it all."

Nick visibly shuddered. "God, woman, can you please not jinx me over there? I have no desire for a kid or to know about all you girls' weird bodily functions. Now, onto something I do know something about: who wants another margarita?"

Suzy was relieved to get home and away from the scrutiny of her friends. They meant well and she loved them for worrying about her, but she just preferred her own company right now. At least when she was home, she didn't have to pretend that everything was great. Only the walls of her apartment knew that she cried herself to sleep more often than not. She'd turned into one of those pathetic creatures that she'd always pitied, brought to her knees by a man and not in a good way.

At least she wasn't walking around the office with a box of tissues, sobbing on everyone who would listen. Work was her refuge, the one place that she could focus on something else. Gray had remained in Charleston, and even though it was torture not knowing what was going on, at least she didn't have to see him every day.

According to what she'd read in her lower moments, this grieving process was normal. Why, then, did it feel like she was losing her mind? Maybe she should start dating. If you can't be with the one you love, lust the one you're with or something. Just the thought of it, though, held zero appeal.

Apparently, Beth had even said something to their mother, which was horrifying. When she called last week, she'd gone into a twenty-minute speech on the pitfalls of romantic silliness and how a woman should only rely on a solid education and a challenging career. When the moment was right, you should align yourself with someone of similar intellect and ambition to co-habit with. *Ugh, how did my parents ever have children? She could only imagine the long debate that resulted in her conception. It was probably for additional tax deductions and to possibly birth the next Einstein. Boy, that must be a real kick in the ass now.*

Tomorrow, after her cast removal, she vowed to go to the mall and get a pedicure. She'd force herself to take that small step toward normalcy. Maybe next week she'd even ask everyone to lunch without them, forcing her to go. Baby steps surely were the first step to recovery.

Nick was surprised to get a text from Gray on his cell phone when he was leaving the restaurant, asking him to come to the beach house. He'd no idea that his brother was going to be in town. It gave him an uneasy feeling when he thought of Suzy. No matter how much she tried to joke everything off, she was fragile. Hell, it had only been a couple of weeks since things ended with Gray and she didn't even look healthy anymore. She still had a snappy comeback for most everything, but the light was gone from her eyes.

Suzy was a gorgeous woman, but the thing he'd always found the most eye-catching about her was the way that energy just seemed to shimmer off her. She pulled you into her force field and it was damn near impossible to leave her orbit once you were there. That energy was gone now. She had dark circles under her eyes that her careful makeup couldn't conceal, and even though she'd always been tiny, she was close to frail now. If she kept this up, where would she be in another month? He knew that Beth was worried sick about her but, like all of her friends, she had no idea what to do.

When he opened the door to his brother's home, he was surprised at how much he'd missed the place. He'd always enjoyed living alone, but they had been somewhat of a family here for a while. Gray strolled in from the bedroom and Nick grimaced when he took a good look at his brother. "Bro, you look like hell."

A smile lifted the corners of Gray's fatigue-lined face. "Yeah, hello to you, too, Nicky."

"Man, when's the last time you slept or had a Big Mac? It looks like you could use a big supply of both."

"Thanks for the kind words, bro. I've just been busy lately. I'm only here for tonight before I fly out to Seattle tomorrow."

"Please tell me you didn't stop over here to see Suzy?"

With a snort, Gray said, "If I did it wouldn't be any of your concern. I'm actually just here first to pick up the new contract for Lawson from Jason. He dropped it by a few minutes ago."

As if unable to stop himself, Gray asked, "Since you brought her up, how is she?"

Nick could see the desperation behind the casual question. "She looks like a stiff wind could blow her over, pretty much the same as you. Since we're on the subject, are you any closer to digging yourself out of that mess with Reva? I'm not saying walk off and leave her, but don't go out and start buying china together before you know for sure that you're the father. It might not be an ideal situation, but if you are the father, then be the kid's father without marrying the mother."

"Trust me, Nick; I've been through all of this a million times. I'm not marrying Reva regardless of the outcome. I don't love her and it wouldn't be fair to her. I'll be a very active father and I will of course support them both financially."

"I'm confused then. If you have all of this figured out, then why aren't you over there begging Suzy to give you another chance? Why are you letting this drag on when it's making you both so damned miserable?"

"I don't want to hurt her anymore. I'm trying to give her time to come to terms with everything. If I push her now, she'll only resent it later. Look how long it took me to get her to agree to a date. It's killing me, but she asked me to love her enough to let her go. I can't give her that, but I can love her enough to give her time."

Nick uttered the question that terrified Gray the most about his plan, "What if it's too late then? What if you're just giving her enough time to move on instead?"

Chapter Twenty-five

Suzy found the old saying to be true, life does go on. No matter how much you seem to be running in place, the world moves on and you learn to move with it. It had been a month since she ended things with Gray, and she was slowly picking up the pieces again. It was still so damned hard to get out of bed each day, but she managed. She was even trying to put back on some of the weight she'd lost. There was a big difference in slim and skinny, and right now she'd lost a lot of her curves and looked more like a stick figure.

Her cast had been removed a few weeks back and although her ankle was still weak, she was enjoying not having to lug crutches everywhere she went. Her friends had slowly backed off and were no longer giving her those nervous looks that she'd received for so long. Claire looked like she was going to go into labor at any moment and was no longer working at Danvers, per her doctor's orders. Beth and Ella had gotten even closer and, Suzy had to admit, she was pretty fond of Ella, too. It was hard to believe she was the same person that used to annoy her daily. Nick was, well, just Nick. Her heart still hurt when she talked to him, but she managed to hide it. She cared a lot about him and it wasn't his fault that things hadn't worked out with Gray.

It was Saturday and Suzy was lazing on the couch flipping channels before she met Beth for lunch. When the doorbell rang a few minutes later, she looked at her watch. Apparently, Beth had been running early and decided to come here instead of meeting her around the corner. Flipping off the television, Suzy swung the door open and then stood frozen in the doorway.

Standing on the doorstep with her cheeks flushed a brilliant shade of pink and looking very uncomfortable was Reva, clutching the hand of a man that Suzy had never seen before. The man cleared his throat. "Ms. Denton, we're sorry to drop in unexpectedly, but I hope that you can give us a few minutes of your time. Reva would really like to speak with you."

Suzy stepped aside and motioned them in because she simply couldn't think of anything else to do. What in the world would bring Reva to her doorstep, and who was the man with her? He was too young to be her father so maybe her brother?

The couple was now standing in her living room looking around uncertainly. "Please, have a seat," Suzy said, pointing to the couch. Then sitting in the chair across from them, she decided to just get right to the point. "So this is a little weird to me. What exactly can I do for you and how did you find me?"

Reva was nervously working the strap of her pocketbook with her fingers, looking completely miserable. The man beside her spoke up again. "Ms. Denton, I'm Mark Wyatt and I believe you have met Reva before. We owe you an apology and an explanation."

Suddenly, Reva's head came up and she turned to

the man beside her. "No, Mark, I did this and I need to be the one to explain." He reached over and gripped her hand, love evident in his eyes as he looked at her.

Okay, so obviously not a brother with the vibes flowing between them, so what now? Does she want to ask me about being the live-in nanny or something?

Then taking a deep breath and getting another squeeze of encouragement from the man beside her, Reva began. "Suzy, I don't really know where to start so I'll just go from the beginning. Mark and I have been in love for several years. He works for my father as a security guard. You would have to know my parents to understand why this would be a problem. I love them, I really do, but they're obsessed with climbing the social ladder and I've always been one of their ways to do that. When they found out that I was involved with Mark, they hit the ceiling. No way was their daughter going to end up with some blue-collar worker, especially one who worked for them. Th-they fired Mark and threatened to cut me off completely if I ever saw him again."

Suzy had a feeling that she knew where this was headed. Even though this woman had turned her life into a living hell, she still felt sympathy for the obvious pain that she was going through as well. "Reva, can I get you some water?"

Reva and Mark turned grateful expressions to Suzy at the offer. When she returned with two bottles of water, Reva took a long drink of hers before continuing her story.

"Even though I wanted to keep seeing Mark behind their backs, he wouldn't do it. He said that I either stood up to my parents or we were finished. I . . . I just couldn't do it. I wasn't strong enough to stand up to them so I let Mark go. I figured I could either make him jealous enough to take me on my terms or distract myself from my misery with someone new." With a rueful expression, Reva said, "That's where Gray comes in. I found out via a home pregnancy test that I was pregnant right before I met Gray."

"You panicked," Suzy said softly.

With tears running down her face, Reva said, "Yes, I did and thus started months of the most horrible behavior that anyone could ever fathom. Gray is a nice guy and I pursued him heavily, even though I could tell that he really didn't want to get involved with me. I think he only slept with me the one time out of pure pity. He'd probably never met a woman so desperate." Looking over at Mark, Reva said, "I'm sorry, honey, I know this is hard for you, too."

"Yes, it is, love, but if I'd stood up to your parents, this probably wouldn't have happened. Go ahead and finish your story and don't worry about me."

Reva kissed their hands where they were joined and turned back to Suzy. "Gray broke it off with me almost immediately and I took advantage of his guilt to literally stalk him for months. I was desperate to get him back. I don't know why I didn't just tell him I was pregnant after a few months, but something held me back. It would have probably been less painful for him than my constant stalking. In my defense, I think I really just lost it there for a while. When I finally couldn't hide my pregnancy from my parents any longer, I told them that Gray was the father instead of the truth. Instead of looking upset, they both looked thrilled. I strung them along for a few months, telling them that Gray was traveling a lot and that we would all get together when he was back home. Gray didn't even know at that point."

"My God, Reva, you must have been about to collapse under the pressure." Suzy gave a rueful laugh. "I can't even be that pissed off at you when I know how much you have suffered."

A smile lit Reva's face as she looked at her in relief. "Suzy, it kills me that I've caused two such good people so much pain. When I met you for the first time in the bar that night, I could see how much you and Gray loved each other and I had probably my first attack of conscience. I had a feeling that Gray had another woman in his life, but I had no idea how serious it was. Gray stepped up after that and really tried to take care of me. He even suffered through dinner with my parents, where they almost drooled with delight over me trapping such an eligible man. I still managed to go ahead with the deception. The night of my car accident was a turning point for me, though. Gray was by my side the entire time and then the next day I found out he'd missed your birthday. He was so sad after that. It took that for me to finally see all of the lives I was ruining."

Suzy was wondering why it had taken her a month to come forward after that revelation, but kept her silence, letting Reva finish without interruption.

"I'm not proud to say that I was still hesitant to do what I knew I had to. I'd never stood up to my parents before and the thought of doing it terrified me, but I knew that if I were ever going to be with Mark, that I couldn't rely on him to fight my battles. Last night I told my parents the truth." Then, on a whisper, Reva admitted, "They don't want to have anything else to do with me. I . . . I left there and went to Mark, where I poured out the whole story. I'm going to start seeing a therapist because I know that a normal person would never have done all of the things I've done to Gray. I stalked him and tortured him because I was so terrified of what would happen when my parents found out about the baby. I was desperate for them to think it was Gray's."

"Holy crap, that's a lot to take in. Reva, I'll be frank and say you have put me through hell this last month and probably Gray, as well. Somehow, though, I think you have been kicked enough. It took a lot of guts to come here today and face me. How did you do that, by the way?"

With a shy smile, Reva admitted, "Google Maps. Scary right?"

With a laugh, Suzy said, "You got that right. I'm sorry that your parents are being such boneheads, but it looks like Mark has your back."

With a look of relief and gratitude, Reva reached out and took her hand. "Thank you, Suzy, for being so good about this. I can see why Gray loves you. I'm going to talk to him as soon as he gets home today."

As Reva and Mark stood to leave, Suzy impulsively pulled her in for a quick hug. After a moment of hesitation, Reva returned the embrace. After she'd shut the door behind them, she fell down onto the couch and tried to process it all.

What if this made no difference? Had too much happened with Gray to start over now? *Oh, blah, find your backbone. That's your man and it's about time you stopped whining and went after him, or do you need another disaster to realize how much you love him?*

One fist pump in the air and Suzy had her game face on. She had a user conference tonight that she had to attend. It was the entertainment portion of the conference and consisted of drinks, dinner, and live entertainment. She was going to pack a bag and when it was over, she was heading to Charleston and to the man she loved. She was hitching up her big-girl panties and going after what she wanted.

Chapter Twenty-six

Suzy found Beth going over the dinner menu with the caterers in the kitchen. "Is everything on schedule for tonight, sis? I don't want any delays so let's stay on top of things. Has the band arrived yet?"

Beth stopped to study her in surprise. This was the most animated she'd seen Suzy since her breakup with Gray. "Um, have you been drinking?"

"What? Of course not, why?"

"Well, you look kind of high or something. Are you feeling okay? Your face is all flushed, and your eyes are glassy."

With a dramatic sigh, Suzy snickered. "I'm high on love, sis, nothing else."

"Oh God," Beth groaned. "You're drunk. Couldn't you have at least waited until we hit the dinner phase of the evening?"

"Beth, chill, I'm not drunk, geez. I'm a little more professional than that." Then, with a little dance, she said, "Gray isn't the father of Reva's baby, and I'm going to Charleston tonight for some long overdue makeup sex."

"What, how, who?"

"Close your mouth, Beth, before something flies in it. We'll talk later. How about checking to make sure the band is ready to go on in about an hour, and I'll finish here and check with the bartender next."

Beth took off to find the band, shooting confused looks over her shoulder. She was probably still questioning her sobriety, but didn't know what to do about it.

When she finished in the kitchen, she saw Nick standing at the bar talking to Jason. They were both due to give a brief speech tonight before the band went on. "Hey, guys, how's tricks?"

"Suzy, everything looks great. I've gotten a lot of compliments on the setup for the conference this year. I don't know how you do it, but you constantly come up with something new every year."

"Thanks, Jason, it's pretty easy when you have the world's best job. Where is Claire this evening?"

Jason grimaced, worry evident on his face. "She wanted to come tonight, and I argued all the way to the door, but finally managed to reason with her. Her feet are the size of footballs, but getting her to stay put for any length of time is almost impossible." With an exasperated shake of his head, he continued. "This pregnancy may yet be the end of me. I spend all my time trying to get her to take it easy, and she spends all her time trying to prove to me why it's not necessary. If I have to hear, 'back in the old days, women had babies in the fields while they continued with their work,' one more time, I'll explode."

"You think that's bad," Nick piped in, "you should go to a meal with all the women and let them describe their female issues in full detail. I'll never be right again after that. A man needs to stay ignorant to a certain point."

With a nod of agreement, Jason bumped his fist

against Nick's shoulder and said, "I feel your pain man, for sure."

Turning back to Suzy, Jason asked, "So, who's the band playing tonight?"

"Oh, it's a local rock band that does a lot of eighties music, along with some current Top Forty stuff. I think you'll like them. I've used them before and had nothing but compliments."

When she looked at Nick again he was studying her in a way that had her raising a brow in question. He quickly turned away, saying that he needed to hit the men's room before his speech. She shrugged it off as she sent Jason toward the stage for the opening speech and met Beth at the back for a final status check.

Nick met up with Jason and Gray backstage. "Do you think she suspects anything?"

"Nope, nothing, bro. Hell, I don't think she could guess this in a million years. Hey, you never told me what happened with the girl in accounts payable who was giving your new numbers to Reva. How did she even have access to that information?"

With a grim look, Gray said, "Apparently there is online access to our cell phone accounts to make changes and dispute charges. It also lists all of our phone numbers. She was fired by her supervisor this afternoon. Reva really didn't want to tell me who her mole was, but I insisted. We can't have people like that on our staff. She was actually Reva's cousin."

"Damn, I guess family loyalty will get you so far, and then it'll get your ass fired."

Jason shook his head. "This whole mess is like something from a bad soap opera. I'm glad Reva finally came forward, though, and hopefully soon you and Suzy will be able to look back on it and laugh."

Nick chuckled. "She should at least be able to laugh about this evening, if nothing else."

Jason walked onto the stage for his speech and Nick clapped a hand on Gray's shoulder as he prepared to make a complete and utter fool out of himself. If it worked, though, it would be well worth it.

As she settled in beside her sister, she could tell Beth was dying to know what was going on but, with the speeches starting, it was impossible to carry on a conversation without disturbing a nearby table. Jason and Nick were both very good public speakers and used the right amount of humor and sincerity to captivate their audience.

Finally, the entertainment portion of the evening arrived and Nick introduced the band at the end of his speech. Soon, light rock filled the room as the band eased into the opening set. After a short break, the lead singer took the microphone and joked around with the audience.

"Our next number goes out to a special lady in the house, your very own Suzy Denton. I'm going to step aside and sing backup on this one."

As the lead singer stepped back to make room for the guest singer, Beth looked at Suzy. "What's going on?"

Suzy shrugged her shoulders. "I have no idea. It's probably some joke at my expense."

When the spotlight hit the figure striding toward the lead microphone, Suzy almost dropped the drink she was holding. There, standing at center stage in an old pair of faded jeans and a Bon Jovi shirt from their Crush Tour, stood Gray.

Beth grabbed her arm, pulling frantically. "Did you know about this?"

"OH MY GOD! Of course not! What is he doing?"

Suzy's eyes were riveted to him as he started to speak. "Hey everyone, sorry to interrupt this fabulous band, but they have been nice enough to humor me. I'll warn you now I have very little singing talent so this might be a good time for a bathroom break."

As laughter rang out in the room, Gray continued on. "There's a special lady here tonight who has no idea how much she means to me or the lengths I'd go to in order to show her that she's now and will always be first in my life." Then squatting down to eye level with the audience, as if they were old friends, he said, "The woman I love is a free spirit. She was always accusing me of being something of a stuffed shirt, and maybe she was right."

Gray smiled at the choruses of "no" that rang out in the audience. "Ah, thanks, guys. One of the things that Suzy said about me early on was that I was probably too uptight to own a Bon Jovi tour shirt, but as you can see, in the name of love, I now have one."

Suzy couldn't help but laugh at the way the audience was hanging on his every word. As he looked toward where she was standing in the back of the room, she could have sworn he could see her even though she knew it was impossible. My God, what was he doing? If he tried to drag her on the stage, she'd kill him.

"Well, guys, since I now own the tour shirt, I thought

it was only right that I also do something to show Suzy how much I love her. Anyone who knows me knows that I'd normally never do anything like this. There is only one person in this world that I'd do or be anything for and that's Suzy Denton."

Suzy was glued in place when the opening strains of Bon Jovi's "Born to Be My Baby" suddenly filled the room. Oh, shit, he's not going to sing that. No way would her uptight man be up there in front of an audience preparing to belt out a rock song for her.

Beth grabbed her arm, squeezing it tight. "Oh, Suzy, I can't believe what he's doing for you. He's crazy, but oh, man, how romantic."

When Gray started singing the first part of the song, there was absolute silence in the audience. "Holy moly, he's actually good, sis, I mean *really* good and that hip action, wow!"

"Hey, keep your eyes off my man's hips," Suzy growled. Oh, brother, Beth was right. Gray was good. He wasn't Jon Bon Jovi, but he brought his own brand of sexy to the song. She wanted to march up to that stage and rip his shirt right off his back. When he got to the part of the song that said, "I know you'll live in my heart until the day that I die," Suzy felt tears well up in her eyes. He was doing something that he knew would take him completely outside of his comfort zone. He was trying to show her with actions rather than words how much he loved her. She could never doubt the love of someone who would do something like this for her.

Suzy started making her way to the front of the room before Gray finished the song. Gray's eyes tracked her progress as she drew closer to the stage. When he finished the last line of the song, the audience started chanting, "Suzy! Suzy! Suzy!" Oh, God, they wanted her to go up on the stage. Well hell, try to stop her. If Gray could belt out a song in the name of love, she could at least kiss the man.

Nick stood at the top of the stairway to the stage as she made it up the last step. "Wipe that shit-eating grin off your face," Suzy joked as she ran by him. His laughter followed her as she was suddenly under the bright lights with Gray. She didn't bother to act coy, she literally launched herself into his arms and he caught her in midair. "Oh, my God, you're crazy, but I love you!" Suzy shouted as her lips locked on his.

The cheer from the audience was deafening as Gray's mouth devoured hers. How long they stood locked in each other's embrace she had no idea. When Gray settled her back on her feet, he immediately went down on one knee. Suzy froze, hardly able to believe what her eyes were telling her. The audience had likewise stilled, completely captivated by the events unfolding on the stage.

When Gray drew a box from his pocket and looked up into her eyes, Suzy could feel the tears starting to flow. "Suzy, I hardly remember a time when I haven't loved you. Before we met, my life was mostly in shades of black, white, and gray. When I first met you, color exploded in my world, making everything in it exquisite and vibrant. You're my love, my life, my heart, and every color under the rainbow all rolled up into one. Please marry me and keep me outside of my comfort zone every day of my life."

With tears running down her cheeks, Suzy shouted, "Yes! You've completely lost your mind, but I love you with all my heart." Holding a trembling hand out to him, Suzy watched as Gray slid a beautiful blue sapphire ring set in platinum and surrounded by pavé-set diamonds onto her finger. My God, he did know her. A normal engagement ring after this evening would have seemed just wrong. This ring suited her completely; it was fiery, sassy, and unique.

The applause continued as they made their way from the stage. When she saw Jason and Nick standing near the steps, she walked up to hug them both. "Sorry about this, Jason. I'm sure you would rather we took our profession of love elsewhere."

Jason laughed and said, "Are you kidding me? We already have people scrambling to sign up for the conference next year. You can't buy this type of advertising. I'm happy for you both, you guys deserve it. I'm pretty impressed with the singing, my brother. It took some balls to do that."

Gray clapped Jason on the shoulder and pulled Nick in for a quick hug. "Thanks for the help. Now if you don't mind, I'd like some time alone with my fiancée."

Suzy snuggled against him as they made their way through the crowd. Gray had apparently picked up something of a fan club and Suzy figured someone would be throwing her panties at him if she didn't get him away soon. They finally made their way to the back, and she spotted Beth waving frantically as she made her way to them.

Beth squealed and threw herself at Gray. "You totally rock, future brother-in-law! Welcome to the family."

She then turned to her sister and grabbed her ring finger. Tears were swimming in her eyes as she pulled her close. "I told you that someday you would find your prince. Our parents might believe that fairy tales are silly, but you and I know the truth, don't we?" Beth whispered.

Suzy gave her sister one last hug and allowed Gray to pull her back into his arms. Finally, she was where she'd always belonged, in the arms of the man who completely understood every crazy part of her and loved her anyway.

Gray looked down at her, "Ready to go, baby?"

Locking her gaze with his, Suzy replied, "I'm all yours, lead the way."

Epilogue

Gray led her quickly out the door of the house that they shared on the beach. When they were both settled in the car, he took off at a fast clip. He reached over and took her hand, giving her a squeeze of encouragement. "You okay, baby?"

Suzy's face was flushed and her heart raced in excitement. "Yes, but please hurry! At the rate we are going, the baby will be born before we even make it to the hospital."

"Honey, calm down before you have a stroke. What good is it going to do us if we have an accident on the way? I can't risk your life by driving too fast. If the baby is born while we are in the car, then it will just have to be."

Suzy turned toward the man who filled her days and nights with such love that she literally had to pinch herself often to make sure she wasn't dreaming. True to her word, she kept him on his toes and he kept her grounded. She couldn't imagine how she ever thought of him as a stuffed shirt because the man definitely had a bit of freak in him.

When they finally made it to the hospital, Gray pulled up to the valet stand, grateful that the hospital offered that amenity. As he handed the keys over, he asked the valet, "Where can we find the maternity floor?"

"It's on the third floor, sir. Go left when you get off the elevator."

Gray muttered a thanks and quickly led Suzy toward the elevator. Once inside, he rubbed her back, trying to calm her. "It's okay, baby, just breathe."

As they exited the elevator, they ran into Beth, Nick, and Ella. "Hey, guys, any news yet?"

Beth walked up and quickly gave them a hug. "Nothing yet and it's making me nervous. Maybe we should ask someone at the desk."

As Suzy approached the nurse's station, a tired but beaming Jason walked toward her. She squealed and threw her arms around him. "How's Claire? Where's the baby?"

"Claire and the baby are both doing great. They're checking her out now and then I'll bring her out for a minute for you guys to meet."

"She? It's a girl!"

"Yeah, I got my two girls now. We are naming her Christina Louise."

"After her sister and her second mom," Suzy said softly.

"Claire was planning to name her Christina Evelyn, but her mother asked that she use Louise. She felt like she deserved the honor of having our first child named after her. Speaking of them, they're all in the room with Claire."

Suzy put her hand on Jason's arm. "I'm so happy for you both. I know you'll be wonderful parents."

Squeezing her hand, Jason said, "Thanks, Suzy, that

means a lot to me. I'll see if they're ready for me to bring the baby out, stay right here."

"Great, let me grab the others and we'll be waiting." Suzy ran back to the waiting room and motioned for everyone to follow her. When they got back, Jason was standing proudly where she'd left him with his new daughter in his arms.

There were tears of joy and laughter as everyone welcomed little Christina into the world. Suzy's heart was full to bursting. She was standing in the circle of Gray's arms surrounded by family and friends while she gazed into the eyes of her new goddaughter. Even a cynical person like her couldn't help but feel blessed. She'd waited a long time for her happily-ever-after and here in this hospital, in the hallway, she was surrounded by it. Happily-ever-after was neither one person nor one place; it was a collection of things that brought you peace, love, and contentment, and, if you were lucky, a little magic.

Acknowledgments

I also want to give sincere thanks to all of the people who loved *Weekends Required* and have emailed and friended me on Facebook, Twitter, and Pinterest. Your support has truly touched me and I'm so grateful for your friendship.

A special thanks to the Fifty Shades of Grey Chat Group as well. It's truly an honor to have such a great group lending their support to my books. Thank you!

Author's Note

Thank you for purchasing *Not Planning on You*. I hope you enjoyed reading it as much as I enjoyed writing it. I'd love to hear your comments. Please feel free to e-mail me at Sydney@sydneylandon.com or visit my Web site sydneylandon.com for updates on future books.

About the Author

Sydney Landon is a *New York Times* and *USA Today* bestselling author. When she isn't writing, Sydney enjoys reading, swimming, and being a minivan-driving soccer mom. She lives in Greenville, South Carolina, with her family.

Please continue reading for a special preview of the next Danvers book,

FALL FOR ME,

which is Beth's story.

Find it wherever books are sold in March 2013!

"You're what?" Beth cringed as her sister's voice rang out in the sandwich shop. So much for thinking she wouldn't make a scene if she told her somewhere public.

"Will you please keep it down, sis? I don't want everyone in here knowing my business."

Suzy flicked her hand as if she didn't care, but lowered her voice as she asked, "How can you be pregnant? You actually have to have sex to get pregnant and you aren't. Oh, God, you didn't get frozen sperm, did you?"

If she wasn't so mortified by this conversation, Beth would have laughed at the question. "No, I wasn't artificially inseminated so obviously I had sex. I know this is somewhat of a shock to you, but I had sex!"

Now it was Suzy looking around as Beth's last sentence seemed to echo off the walls of the restaurant. "Okay, let's talk about this rationally. Who is the bastard and where can I find him? He took advantage of you, and now he'll suffer the consequences. Has he even offered to step up and take responsibility?"

Beth rolled her eyes and wondered if her sister was going to challenge the father of her baby to a duel next. For such a modern woman, her sister was freaking out much more than she'd have thought. Clearing her throat, Beth admitted, "He doesn't know yet. I . . . haven't told him."

"Well, when are you planning on telling the man? When the kid is in college?"

"I just found out, sis, so I haven't had time to make a lot of plans. I'm trying to come to grips with it myself. I took a home pregnancy test last week and then had a blood test with my doctor. I got those results this morning. I'm pregnant. I've got my first appointment in two weeks."

Suzy felt like she'd landed in the twilight zone. How could she not know her sister was seeing someone? Hell, not just seeing him, *sleeping* with him. Maybe she'd been so wrapped up in Gray that she hadn't noticed things that she normally would.

Suzy took a deep, calming breath and studied her sister. She didn't look freaked out; she actually kind of glowed. "Sis, how long has this been going on? Why didn't you tell me that you were involved? I never see you with anyone but Ella or Nick. Crap, they probably already know, don't they? Am I always the last one to know everything?"

Beth had been working for Danvers International for about six months now as her sister's assistant. Suzy supervised event planning at Danvers and had recently become engaged to Grayson Merimon, whom she'd met when Danvers International had merged with his company, Mericom, over a year ago. Suzy had fought her love for Grayson and had almost lost him when a woman from Gray's past had come forward to say that she was pregnant with his child. That had truly been a dark time for the couple until Reva, the woman in question, admitted that someone else was the father.

Her sister was now the happiest she'd ever seen her. Grayson had moved from Charleston, South Carolina, to Myrtle Beach, South Carolina, where Danvers was headquartered. His brother, Nick, or Nicholas, had moved as well and was a vice president of Danvers. The CEO, Jason Danvers, was married to Suzy's best friend, Claire. They recently had a baby, whom everyone doted on.

Beth had been an elementary school teacher until budget cuts had caused the district to lay her off. She'd only been filling in temporarily to help Suzy out until she hired a new assistant. They were both happy with the arrangement right now, and neither of them was ready to make a change.

Now her beautiful sister sat before her with fire flashing in her eyes. Her red hair was pulled back in a French knot, and as usual she was on the cutting edge, style-wise. Beth always felt frumpy around her. As a former fatty, she never felt comfortable in her new, smaller clothes. She'd lost over a hundred pounds several years ago and even though the mirror showed her one thing, she always saw her old self staring back at her. Suzy had taken her red hair after their mother, and Beth had gotten stuck with their father's unremarkable brown hair. Suzy was on the tall side and she was on the petite side. Geez, she'd missed out on the best family genes for sure. Realizing that her sister was staring bullets at her, she took a breath and dove back into the fray.

"Geez, you would think I'd told you I only had a month to live or something. Freak out much there?"

"Don't mess with me, girl, I have the parents on speed dial. I can only imagine the horror of having that talk."

"You wouldn't dare," Beth whispered.

Suzy pretended to study her fingernails. "Ordinarily I wouldn't, but I'm gonna need something to work with here. So you either start talking, or I'm going to pull our brilliant parents from whatever laboratory they're in and tell them all about their wayward child. Oh, God, the shame, the disappointment, the heartache," Suzy finished dramatically.

"You suck," Beth grumbled. "All right, I'll tell you, but you have to promise me you won't overreact; I mean it, Suzy."

"Who, me? I never overreact."

With a snort, Beth took a deep breath and prepared herself for the sheer hell that her sister was fixing to unleash. Maybe Ella was right; this might have been a very, very bad idea, but there was no turning back now.

Addison Fox

Come Fly With Me
An Alaskan Nights Novel

A story of risking it all for love—the sky's the limit...

When Grier Thompson is called to Indigo, Alaska, to deal with the estate of her late, estranged father, she meets pilot Mick O'Shaughnessy, a rugged dream guy. But then an unexpected visitor from Grier's past unsettles the entire town. By the time Mick comes out of the clouds to realize he's fallen head over heels in love, it might be just too late to win Grier's heart.

"I cannot wait to return to the wonderful town of Indigo, Alaska."
—Romance Junkies

S0431

LOVE
ROMANCE NOVELS?

For news on all your favorite romance authors, sneak peeks into the newest releases, book giveaways, and much more—

"Like" Love Always on Facebook!
LoveAlwaysBooks